THE
MEDITERRANEAN
WALL

THE MEDITERRANEAN WALL

Louis-Philippe Dalembert

TRANSLATED FROM THE FRENCH
BY MARJOLIJN DE JAGER

PUSHKIN PRESS

Pushkin Press
71–75 Shelton Street
London WC2H 9JQ

Original text © Sabine Wespieser Editeur 2019
English translation © Marjolijn de Jager 2021

The Mediterranean Wall was first published as *Mur Méditerranée*
by Sabine Wespieser Editeur in Paris, 2019

License to reprint granted by:
The French Publishers' Agency
30 Vandam Street, Suite 5A
New York, NY 10013
Telephone: 212-254-4540

First English language edition published in the USA by Schaffner Press in 2021
First published with revisions by Pushkin Press in 2022

This work received the French Voices Award for excellence in publication and
translation. French Voices is a program created and funded by the French Embassy
in the United States and FACE Foundation (French American Cultural Exchange).

French Voices Logo design: Serge Bloch

1 3 5 7 9 8 6 4 2

ISBN 13: 978-1-78227-709-5

Typeset by Tetragon, London
Printed and bound by CPI Group (UK) Ltd, Croydon, CR0 4YY

www.pushkinpress.com

To the friends of Lampedusa,
who fight to give dignity back to
the living as well as the dead.

I do not know what world exists on the other side of
this sea, but each sea has another shore, and I will get there.

CESARE PAVESE,
The Business of Living

Yo vann tout sa yo genyen lakay
Pou yo vin chache on mèyè vi
Lè yo rive se nan prizon yo mete yo.
[...]
Gen nan yo k pa menm rive
Reken manje yo depi nan wout
Move tan bare yo sou dlo.

They sold everything they had
To come to find a new life.
Upon arrival they were thrown in prison.
[...]
And some never did arrive.
Sharks devoured them on their way.
And storms at sea took them by surprise.

FROM THE SONG *LIBERTÉ* BY MAGNUM BAND

CONTENTS

ON BOARD THE TRAWLER

PART THREE: DIMA

ON BOARD THE TRAWLER

THE
MEDITERRANEAN
WALL

CAST OFF!

NIGHT HAD JUST FALLEN on Sabratha when one of the jailers entered the warehouse. The sun had suddenly retreated, giving way to an ink-black sky in which a rather pale crescent moon and the first stars of the bordering desert were beginning to appear. The man was holding a flashlight, which he directed at the pile of bodies tangled in a heartrending mess right on the rough concrete floor or, for the luckiest among them, on some mattresses that lay scattered around. At the first sound of the key in the lock the girls had moved very close to each other, the scorching heat inside the building notwithstanding. As if to protect themselves from a danger that could only come from outside. The nauseating smell of the supervisor's cologne came rushing in to mix with the musty odors inside. He inspected the faces contorted from daily bullying and deprivations before focusing the light on one of them, immobilizing it with terror. The building resonated with a '*You. Out!*' accompanied by a commanding motion of his index finger. The girl he'd pointed to hurried to comply, gathering herself and the bag with her measly belongings together, as she'd been told to, at the risk of being forced to rise by boots kicking at her sides.

Normally the jailer, the same or a different one, would choose three or four, bringing them back a few hours later, or sometimes at the end of the day, shoving them like bags of shit amid the others lying huddled on the floor. Most of them would find refuge in a corner of the room, enclosed inside their pain or nestled in the arms of someone who still had a little compassion left to give. Some let out a stifled sob but not for long. Out of modesty or dignity. They all knew the hell the 'returnees' had been through from the moment they'd been dragged from the warehouse until they came back to the group. Even the most recent arrivals knew, since the older ones had clued them in. If need be, the state of their companions in misfortune, holding their underbelly with one hand, their buttocks with the other, their face sometimes swollen, was enough to give them a sense of what was awaiting them the next time the key turned in the lock.

That night, the prison guard pointed at many more than usual, shouting at them, manhandling them to get them up and out faster. '*Move! Move!* Bring your stuff. Go on, move your ass.' God only knows what criteria they had for their selection, the evacuation happened in such a rush. As luck would have it Semhar and Shoshana were part of the group. The two had become inseparable except to go to the toilet, or on the day the captor decided to take away one and not the other. Were it not for the difference in physical appearance and origin—Semhar was a small sharp Eritrean while Shoshana was a stoutly built Nigerian—one would have said they were like a baby koala attached to its mother. They slept glued to each other, shared what little they were given to eat, exchanged words of solace and hope in English, in which Semhar was quite fluent although it wasn't her mother tongue. They each prayed in a language unfamiliar to the other. And would hum songs the other didn't know. 'Whatever happens,' Semhar thought, 'at least we'll be together.'

All in all, there were almost sixty of them, now outside, clustered together in the dark waiting for the Cerberus's orders. They knew, whether from experience or from hearsay, that trying to flee would be of no use. And even if they'd manage to escape the vigilance of their tormentors, where would they go? The depot in which they were held was at some distance from the nearest town; a long walk on a clay road where it seemed only the prison guards' 4 x 4's and the pick-up trucks that had transported them to this wreckage of a building ventured, forgotten by heaven and men. These were the only engine sounds they'd heard until then. No chance of running into a charitable soul that might take the risk of helping them.

The most intrepid ones had paid a high price, perhaps even with their lives. No one had any further news of those daredevils. Unless they'd reached their goal at last. Who knows! God is great. *Elohim HaGadol.* Or maybe they'd reached their final destination and found a land where milk and honey flowed. After wandering for months, no years, on the roads of the continent. Braving wind and high water, forests, deserts, and a whole range of calamities. All of it to end up in this bloody land they hadn't chosen, held hostage in this nameless penal colony subjected to all kinds of hard labor. Despite their own compliance in the ransom from their loved ones who'd stayed behind. As they waited for a crossing that depended solely on the whim of the smugglers.

The women remained quiet, grouped together, barely daring to breathe until other flashlights cut through the darkness, showing three armed men surrounding them. A few more minutes of waiting and then from the mouth of the overseer came the order to advance:

'Move!' Still in that English as sharp as a cudgel on the back of a slave, followed by a command shouted in Arabic: 'Yallah! Yallah!' A hundred yards further on they were ordered to get into the back of one of two pick-up trucks. The rear panel already open to expedite boarding. Despite the mad scramble, Shoshana and Semhar managed to get into the same vehicle. They hadn't even settled down when a loud explosion paralyzed the group, making them think an escapee had been fired on. Actually, one of the smugglers had only shut the tailgate behind them with a loud crash. Once the women were loaded onto the truck, crammed so tightly they could barely move a muscle, the jailer sat down in front next to the turbaned driver and an armed man, while the other two traffickers slipped into the second pick-up. Signaling departure, he moved his hand across the window and hit the side of the truck. Flooring it, headlights off, they

drove for half an hour before reaching the sea, whose presence Semhar and Shoshana guessed at first from the smell,
then from the rolling sound of the surf. They had no concept
of time or day.

★

Earlier that day, in the old Italian quarter of Tripoli about
sixty kilometers away, air-conditioned minibuses, with about
twenty seats each, were waiting in front of the entrance to a
three-star hotel, watched over by a charming porter in uniform. Loud voices preceded the arrival of a group of whirling children mocking each other in an Arabic dialect quite
unlike that of Libya. Elegantly dressed adults followed closely
behind them. They were pulling suitcases on wheels that they
left close to the vehicle to which they were assigned so the
porter could put them in the trunk. The men led the way,
iPhones stuck to their ear. The women flaunted brand-name
handbags, taking out a small mirror to replace a lock of hair
or a lipstick, unless they were busy on their phones, tapping
them with carefully manicured hands. Every now and then
they'd take out a piece of candy or a cookie, handing it to a
child who'd rushed over for a snack, before they were called
to board one of the tinted-window minibuses.

Dima, her husband Hakim, and their two daughters were
among the first to get settled in the bus. Their contact had
alerted them the previous evening that the grand departure
would happen the next day. 'Are you sure this time? Not
another lie?' Dima had asked. 'On the Koran of Mecca,' the
guy had answered confidently. It was 16 July 2014. They'd

been waiting for a month. The girls wouldn't stop asking her when they were leaving for Europe, but Dima was no longer able to give them a convincing response. She'd used up every credible answer to the point of returning to basic formulas like: 'In two days, *Inshallah, rouhi,*' in the hope that they'd forget by then. One day her older one, a furious Hana, told her that Allah obviously wanted the family to stay confined to the hotel, all four sleeping in the same room; she, without any of her friends, having to share a bed with her younger sister Shayma while at home they each had their own room. 'Stop blaspheming!' Dima had yelled. 'Don't let me hear you like that again, or else watch your backside.' And added: 'The ways of Allah are unfathomable. Only He knows what it is He wants for us mortals.' She was aware that she'd masked her own helplessness with anger. What choice did she have? Besides, when the guy had come to tell them they should be ready because they were leaving the next day, she was unable to hide her joy or to hold back her tears when he left.

She couldn't bear hiding any longer in this single room, just eighteen square meters. After the first week she was fed up playing at being a tourist in Tripoli and its surroundings. It was not the reason for her presence in the Libyan capital. Sick of the Saint-Gilles Citadel, the Clock Tower, the Al-Harajb souk, the Ezzedine Hammam, the city's thousand and one mosques (may Allah forgive her). She was sick of forcing pretend smiles, of spending time with people whom she wouldn't even have greeted in Aleppo, of having tea or dinner with them. 'We're all in the same boat, aren't we?' Hakim would say to ease the pain. 'And besides, they are our compatriots.'

'So what?' Sick of embraces on the sly while the children slept, she who loved getting laid the right way. This phase was supposed to last three days, a week at the very most. But it was a month now that they were moldering in this seedy room. Before long they'd be turning into mushrooms. She was within an inch of falling apart, of throwing in the towel and going home to Syria. Come what may! And then came the word of their departure. Finally.

That night Dima had trouble falling asleep. She couldn't stop thinking about everything she'd left behind: her family, her friends, her country, a solid job. By leaving Tripoli, the second phase of their journey, she'd be putting even more distance between herself and her native land. It was as if there'd be no going back. All of it to pursue the most complete unknown. Without knowing whether they'd be welcome over there, whether they'd get the refugee status that would enable them to start a new life. She'd have to learn a new language, other lifestyles, other systems. Adapt to other landscapes, get her palate used to other foods that would never, she already knew that, never live up to Syrian gastronomy. If, after all these twists and turns, they'd manage to get to England, the potion would seem less bitter. It would also be a good opportunity for their daughters: 'English is useful everywhere.'

For now the only thing they were certain of was that the boat would take them to Lampedusa. That bit of deserted sand three hundred kilometers away, in the middle of the Mediterranean Sea, which apparently was already Italy. Dima had checked Google Maps, saw that the island was located at the level of Tunisia, farther south than many North African towns. According to the reference, the crossing wouldn't take more than a night and part of the next day. Perhaps less if the weather forecast kept its promise. In one month she'd learned not to trust the words of their contact; she could only hope the Mediterranean would be more trustworthy than this con artist. She was born far from the sea, and had never been on a boat in her life. For their tenth wedding anniversary Hakim had promised her a week's vacation at the golden sandy beaches of Latakia with a dinner-cruise every night.

But the war had broken out three months before and they had other priorities, among them the arduous education in daily survival. Then had come the decision to take refuge at her brother's home in Damascus. And then, unimaginable until just recently, deciding to leave with her family for Europe, as illegal immigrants… She'd mulled it over for nights on end. Just in case, she'd slipped some seasickness pills into her handbag since she didn't know how she or her girls would react. Then came the seemingly endless day, each hour feeling like a week. Until the long-awaited phone call asking them to come down and not to forget settling their accounts at the front desk: buses were waiting in front of the hotel.

★

Once they emerged from the unnerving ride and put their feet on the ground, Semhar and Shoshana actually understood. At first, they thought it was a change of location, it had happened before. Some of the women had stayed in

Tripoli, Zuwara, or some other Libyan town before eventually landing at the warehouse. Nor was it a bad joke of their tormentors. They were leaving for real. The big day had arrived, the day for which they'd paid so dearly, both literally and figuratively, endured so many atrocities, deprivations, gone through so many horrible experiences. They barely had any time to appreciate it before they were pushed into jampacked dinghies that were waiting for the passengers who'd arrived on the minibuses to board and head for the open sea. Thirty to forty minutes later, the dinghy with the two friends pulled up against the side of another boat. In the darkness it seemed gigantic to them, and therefore safe. That was Shoshana's first thought. Semhar's was different: the smell of the Mediterranean seemed less pungent, more ethereal to her than that of the Red Sea.

When it was their turn to board, they were kept hanging on the rope ladder, blocked by an Arab lady who was unconcerned with the passenger flow behind her. Shoshana's patience had its limits, but the fortuitous arrival of a smuggler put an end to the start of a clash that was threatening to develop. On the bridge, barely lit up by the glow from the sky, three big guys directed the two friends to the hold where they took a ladder down. Many people were already there, judging by the difficulty they had clearing a path and creating a small space for themselves amid the throng. 'Welcome to the "bottleneck",' a voice in the dark joked in French. Throughout the entire operation Semhar and Shoshana hadn't let go of each other's hand, gripping it like shipwreck survivors clinging to a life vest. After a few minutes they heard other dinghies stop near the hull, followed by the sound of steps on the bridge above their head.

★

Hana and Shayma were thrilled to finally embark on their adventure. The wait had seemed interminable to them. All excited they followed their parents who were looking for a place to settle down among the pile of passengers on the bridge. Hakim opened the way, Dima closed it. Their father found a not very comfortable space where they sat down on the deck near the guardrail. This would make it easier in case one of them felt like vomiting. It was anything but the cruise Dima had dreamed of. But it was the price to be paid to escape the war and its nightmares. And besides, the crossing wouldn't take long. In any case, less long than the weeks they'd spent under the bombardments, stuck in the crossfire of opposing factions. Beneath her arms two suitcases containing their entire life. In the half-dark Dima had trouble seeing the faces of the other passengers. Provided they weren't seated next to any weird people, like the two *zenjiyat*, those brazen Negresses with whom she'd run into trouble while boarding.

There was the sound of the engine, the strong smell of diesel, and then a deafening rumble ripping through the night that now enveloped everything around. A few minutes went by before they could feel the trawler actually moving. Down in the hold Shoshana and Semhar felt it, too. 'Thank you, God', *'Baruch Hashem'*, they echoed deep inside their heart. They squeezed each other's hands until it hurt. Like children looking for reassurance. Semhar made a quick, inconspicuous sign of the cross. As if anyone could see her in the dense obscurity of the hold.

On the bridge, wedged between her family, other travelers, and the railing, Dima muttered: *'Shukran ya Rabbi'*. A slight breeze came at her. Misting her eyes with tears of both solace and hope.

PART ONE

SHOSHANA

Where a terrible drought struck Shoshana's native village, like the ten plagues Hashem inflicted on Egypt that forced the Pharaoh to set the children of Israel free. It dried up the river, rendered the earth barren, decimated the herds before flinging the young onto every road to the Mediterranean.

In all thy ways acknowledge him,
and he shall direct thy paths.

PROVERBS III–6

DEPARTURE

SHOSHANA WOULD remember it for as long as she lived. It was a Saturday evening after the Sabbath. She'd prepared everything the night before. In a manner of speaking, that is. 'Everything' referred to a backpack, holding only the most urgent necessities: a pair of pants, two tops, three panties. Food for three days, a liter-and-a-half bottle of water that she would certainly be able to refill on the road, if needed. Some money, which she'd hidden in every nook and cranny of her backpack, the heels of her shoes, in the pockets and the inside of her jeans belt. 'Don't put all your eggs in one basket, a five-year old could tell you that.' In case a robber should catch her on the road. And then her fetish, the *hamsa* with the Star of David in its center, to keep the evil eye at bay and bring her good luck on difficult days. Displaying it as a pendant around her neck, as she did in the village, would surely get her killed were she to fall into the hands of the raging madmen of Boko Haram. She'd put it away in her backpack beneath some tiny objects at the bottom of a double pocket that had a zipper. She felt reassured knowing it was there within easy reach wherever she'd go. She had refused to slip a copy of the Torah in the bag, as her mother suggested. Basically her mom was right: two precautions are better than one. But that was just too much.

That's what Shoshana had prepared the night before her departure. She'd already planned the rest for months, if not for years, down to the smallest detail. Ever since she'd accepted the idea that her native land offered no future for the youth of her age, and that she had to give up her law studies, which had been her father's dream for her. He could already see her as a star lawyer, taking the loudmouths in Lagos and Abuja down a peg or two. Eventually she'd begun to believe it as well. Until the drought hit their village. Interminable and cruel, like an eleventh plague on Egypt. She wasn't the kind of person who made decisions on a whim. She'd taken her time checking things out, absorbing the experience of others, their successes as well as their failures. Listening to the elders of the community whose words were worth their weight in gold as a code of conduct. In their opinion, times had changed and portended nothing good. Quite the contrary, in fact.

'You have to expect many more disastrous times,' one of them had predicted, hiding behind his bushy white patriarch's beard.

There was a time before this dark era when you'd put a seed in the ground, and it would grow all by itself. You didn't have to do anything else. Sometimes, you'd throw out wastewater with some tomato seeds in it and a few weeks later there'd be beautiful tomato plants all around the house. The rain came down copiously, like the manna Hashem sent from heaven to feed the Jews when they wandered in the desert for forty years. Crops were abundant and would feed the families for an entire season, with surplus for export to the big cities. Often it rained more than profusely, and the water collected enhanced the reserves meant for the fields and animals. When harvest time arrived, all you had to do was bend down and reap what the earth supplied. There were never enough hands in one family. Friends and the friends of friends had to be called to the rescue or else the crops would rot away. For days on end, for weeks actually, everyone worked as hard as they could. Men and women shared the tasks, some in the field, some in the kitchen, depending on their abilities and their good will. Children, too, gave it their all with their clumsy little hands. At the same time they were learning for tomorrow. It was one grand party. When the work was done, the conversations, the singing and dancing would go on until deep into the night despite their weary bones, until every star was shining while some had already vanished. And at the break of dawn all these good people would get up and start all over again. The harvesting would go on for days on end, except for families like Shoshana's who observed the Sabbath, stopping from Friday before sunset until Saturday evening or Sunday morning.

According to the elders, they wanted for nothing, and Shoshana was quite willing to believe them. Her family had owned more animals than they could count. Truly as far as the eye could see, she'd tell Semhar many years later. Sheep, goats, even a few cows, whose milking she liked to watch. When she was a child she'd even tried it herself a few times, with that delicious feeling of the creamy, tepid liquid trickling between her fingers. One day her father surprised her as she was squatting on her heels, her hand on the goat's udder. He'd scolded her, quite gently, for her daddy adored her, had had her quite late in life with a younger woman. Hence this exaggerated love that her mother never stopped criticizing.

'It verges on idolatry, Hiram. Idolatry.' That was the day her father added that this was no work for his daughter, his Compass Rose. His plans for her were more ambitious.

Sometimes at night, jackals or hyenas managed to elude the guard dogs, approach the herds, and carry off some inexperienced young animals that hadn't caught the predators' scent nor heard the muffled sound of their steps. The shepherds didn't realize it until weeks later, when they'd discover a torn-up carcass, its teeth yellowed by the sun. In any event, the elders would say, it was just part of the natural food chain. There had to be enough for everyone. It served no purpose to stand in their way unless you wanted some species to completely disappear. But it wasn't up to us humans to make that decision. Everyone played their part, everyone got something out of it, and life went on. As long as the results weren't too harmful to humankind, of course.

Then the town grew larger, because of the high birthrate and the mass arrival of people from other parts of the country who were fleeing bad weather, natural disasters, and plagues that humanity itself had caused. This influx led to slapdash makeshift building, stripped of any refinement. Suddenly the village changed. At her bat mitzvah Shoshana ran into people she didn't know from Adam. In addition to having lost its charm, the place had lost its soul. Then the rain began to come more infrequently, the earth began to dry up, and the animals began to languish without anyone knowing why. Some said it was because of the arrival of the 'outsiders'. The earth might well be bountiful, but it couldn't feed all those mouths. Others said that the newcomers, whose ancestors hadn't watered the soil with their own sweat and blood, were practicing animist rituals, invoking violent spirits like Shango or Ogun-the-dog-eater. And this displeased God. The One and Only. The True God.

One morning they got up and found six, seven rigid animals with swollen bellies, as if they'd been grazing poisonous plants. Flies were busy rummaging about inside the cadavers before the arrival of the scavengers, all of which ended up as part of the landscape. From then on, they stayed around; they knew they'd find easy feasting. They were everywhere, on the ground and in the sky. Shoshana could watch them whirl above her head for hours on end, before they folded in their interminable wings and sank their hooked beaks into the prey that was rotting in place, motionless, already stiff or in the process of getting there. It wasn't unusual to see jackals, hyenas, and vultures fight among themselves for the choice pieces, under the helpless gaze of people who no longer even tried to chase them away. At least it spared them the trouble of having to dig a pit in which to bury the bodies and avoid the spread of some epidemic. Wings flapping, a pack of scavengers would swoop down and clean up.

The earth itself seemed cursed, had become as sterile as the womb of Sarah, Abraham's wife, before in His immense compassion, Hashem decided to bless her and grant her to procreate. The soil was as hard as stale bread, crisscrossed with striations as wide as two adult hands. It scorched the heels of the shoeless crowds. Water reserves had run dry at the same time the rain stopped, contrasting with the tears that filled the people's eyes. Just like other children her age, Shoshana would cover several kilometers to carry one bucket of potable water on her head back to the house. The wells dug in the surrounding area were unable to meet everyone's needs. Nobody knew how to explain the why and wherefore of these calamities, which might have helped in fighting the evil and starting anew, as in those hallowed times the elders would talk about. The agronomists dispatched by Abuja and Lagos, those from the NGO's who came rushing in from the far corners of the world, they all blamed global warming. But no one had a solution for managing the climate, for helping parents fulfill the dreams they'd nurtured for their children, for preventing the latter from seeing their fathers complain and weep like oversensitive old women and thinking they were just rambling, that the hallowed times of which they spoke were coming straight from their half-crazed brain.

Shoshana couldn't pinpoint the exact moment, but it seemed to her that was when people had begun to leave the village.

Even the newcomers were heading elsewhere. More than one tried their luck in Lagos before returning, having lost all hope, paralyzed by disillusionment. With its twenty-one million inhabitants, Lagos was a hellhole. Endless promises at first, endless nothing in the end. Besides, all that was most unwholesome was fermenting there. In comparison, Sodom and Gomorrah were nothing. The villagers told each other that perhaps they should push on farther and so they went abroad. Anywhere they might find some semblance of life. In the Gulf countries, so rumor had it, they were treated like slaves, where men were beasts of burden and women were made to do anything and everything. But submissive, they clenched their teeth, they were not where they belonged. In Libya construction was in full swing, manual labor was needed, hard workers who, ideally, were compliant. At first the men went there by the thousands, while the women would follow later.

Europe was the most sought-after destination. The United States, so far away, was a pipe dream. Unless one were to win in the annual immigration lottery, whose entry ticket cost several hundred dollars. Too unpredictable, Shoshana told herself when she, too, began to think seriously about leaving. After the years of suffering, neighbors and childhood friends of hers had managed to gain a foothold in Italy and Germany. And in England as well, that former metropolitan area where a significant diaspora now lived. She'd stayed in touch with two of them. According to them, Europe was a fortress, as impregnable as the wall of ice in Game of Thrones, a series to which she was madly addicted. Getting there would take years, getting in even longer. As if that continent was located on a different planet, lightyears away from the Earth. Perhaps it was out of egotism, Shoshana wondered, that those in the diaspora spread such rumors. The type that thought there wasn't enough for everyone. The last one in shuts the door, it's as old as the hills, she told herself.

As time went by, some of the streets in the village had become deserted, like a ghost town from a Western, and been turned into a playground by the ingenuity of the kids, one of whom was Ariel, Shoshana's little brother.

Although they'd been spared until then, the misfortune ended up touching the families in the community as well. One Saturday night after Sabbath, the elders, Shoshana's father among them, held a meeting in the synagogue, which went on long into the night. When, after endless, *ad nauseam* deliberations they finally emerged at dawn, it was to consult the members of the community who might want to do *Aliyah*, in short, to emigrate to Israel rather than take untold risks on the world's uncertain routes. Cross seas that all too often turned into graves, instead of opening before them as the Red Sea had opened before the Israelites when they were fleeing from the Pharaoh. As *Igbo B'nei Israel*—Igbo Children of Israel—the Law of Return gave them that right. There in the Holy Land, they would be welcomed among people of the same faith. Decades before, the Operations Moses and Solomon had united the Falasha of Ethiopia with the Land of Israel. Now it was their turn.

They sent an emissary to Abuja, the capital city, to speak with a diplomat at the Israeli Embassy and apprise him of the situation. The latter explained that there was, indeed, a Committee for Immigration, Absorption, and Diaspora Affairs. However, it would have to refer any request to the Chief Rabbinate of Jerusalem, which alone had the authority to approve, or refute, the Jewishness of an individual. Even more so since it concerned an entire community. If they were recognized as Jews then, of course, they would be eligible under the Law of Return. From that point on, they would be able to take the steps that led to the Land of Israel. They could rest assured that he would take their steps very much to heart. As would the government. Consequently, the interview, which the messenger reported in great detail, filled their hearts with hope. For the elders it was a matter of time. They'd been Children of Israel forever.

After a long year of waiting, the emissary was summoned to the Israeli Embassy. 'Better to discuss it face to face', mistrustful to the point of paranoia of the new technologies, 'one cannot control everything, you understand?' the civil servant said. Once there, the special envoy was told that the investigation of the Chief Rabbinate would take more time than expected. For now, they hadn't yet found any tangible proof of their Jewishness, nor of their being descendants from one of the ten lost tribes of the Kingdom of Israel. But they should feel confident that their case was under serious deliberation in a high place. When the messenger returned, the elders told themselves that it must be yet another Talmudic story. And, as with all Talmudic stories, it could go on for centuries. With one question leading to another, each time there was something over which hairs would be split.

While waiting, they suggested that the young who could afford it should go and find refuge elsewhere. The oldest ones would stay where they were, it was too late for them.

'"To everything there is a season, and a time to every purpose under heaven," as Ecclesiastes already wrote,' old Hiram pronounced. In any event, eyes were certainly needed to watch over the synagogue. In these troubled times with Boko Haram, this was not the moment to leave and receive a message while abroad announcing the destruction of the synagogue, like Solomon's First Temple. Furthermore, in case the response from Jerusalem would not take forever to get to them, there would be someone present to receive it and alert the others. What was of utmost importance was for the community to stay connected, no matter where in the world they landed. And to remain who they were.

'We are what we are and have been for centuries, Black and Jewish, and we will continue to be so. May it please Jerusalem,' Shoshana's father railed, as he desisted cursing all the bearded ones in the holy city.

ON THE ROAD

THE DAY SHOSHANA decided it was time to leave, after analyzing the ins and outs of the situation, weighing the pros and cons, going over every possible, imaginable circumstance, she received the joint blessing of the elders and of her parents. Although with some reluctance on her mother's part, the latter had agreed that she take Ariel, her seventeen-year old younger sibling, along with her on the journey. 'He has no future here at all,' Shoshana had pleaded. She listed the arguments accumulated during the long time that her decision had been developing, arousing the admiration of her old father, who had abandoned his dream of her becoming an attorney. In any event, the two siblings were inseparable. Even as a little boy, Ariel would stick to her like a leech. He followed her everywhere, until he'd collapse with exhaustion and force his big sister to carry him on her back. And she'd groan: 'I'm not your donkey. You'll find out, I'll stop doing this when you're big.'

But it didn't change with time. Under duress but amused, Shoshana kept on dragging him in her wake. Just to kid around, she'd often accuse her brother of preventing her from finding a fiancé because he was hanging on to her coattails from morning to night. And with his quick wit, he'd respond: 'You don't get it do you, sis. Your sweetie is me.'

Then he'd run off, chased by Shoshana threatening, 'as God is my witness,' to spank him if she hadn't found a fiancé worthy of the name by the time she was twenty-five. And Shulamite, her mother, whose ears were always picking up things, would play devil's advocate by reminding her daughter of the second commandment: thou shalt not take the name of the Lord, thy God in vain. 'Besides, you're setting a bad example for your little brother.' Already well-informed, Shoshana warned Ariel that it wasn't going to be a picnic, or one of those adventure movies her younger sibling was so crazy about.

Before making her final decision, Shoshana had conferred with Rachel, her best friend since kindergarten, who jumped at the opportunity. It had been forever since she'd been fretting over getting out of this godforsaken hole, she was fed up, so fed up you can't imagine, with running after jobs and guys who refused to commit themselves under the pretext they couldn't support a family. 'They want to get laid for free, without getting involved, you follow me?' Shoshana declared they'd need one or two other men. 'Real ones, you mean? In addition to "Shoshana's brat", as Rachel had labeled him. Shoshana had to admit that her brother was a little green behind the ears and too much of a mama's boy. Nevertheless, there was no discussing it, he was part of the journey. As for the others, they'd be there to watch their backs, the risks were too great for women traveling alone. 'Guys aren't just made for that. It's freezing in the desert at night, if you see what I mean,' Rachel said laughing loudly. The question remained: whom should they bring along?

'Don't worry, I'll take care of it. Guys are my department,' Rachel added.

'You'll tell me who they are before you have any contact with them. Literally and figuratively,' Shoshana replied. In the end they were five, including Ezekiel and Nathan whom Shoshana had known off and on, and to whom she now gave carte blanche after checking their background, their character references, and their family tree. Except for Ariel, they were all the same age and members of the same community. They'd known each other forever. They knew that if things got rough, they could count on each other.

It took Shoshana almost a year to make the right contacts, to make sure she wasn't dealing with any crooks, of which there were plenty in Nigeria. Everybody was looking for a way to survive, which included finding an easy mark.

'We've waited this long, we can wait a little longer. We're not going to rush into anything only to get fleeced,' Shoshana said, meticulous as usual, facing the others who were impatient to put some distance between their birthland and their hope for a better tomorrow. Thanks to the grapevine and to information gleaned on the Internet, she managed to avoid the most conspicuous crooks. The first traffickers she contacted—those peddlers for networks of smugglers—tried in vain to direct her to a ring in Benin City. Shoshana flatly refused the offer.

Located at three hours' driving from the port city of Onitsha, Benin City was reputed to be at the heart of a prostitution network that preyed on naïve Nigerian girls wanting to leave for Europe. First, they put you in touch with a 'mama', a mother madam, herself a former prostitute, who promises you a job in a beauty salon in Italy or France. 'The only thing you have to do once you're there is work in the salon until you've repaid the money you owe for the crossing.' Before leaving, the mama hauls the girl off to a ceremony, the *juju*, allegedly to bring her luck. In reality, it concerns a submission ritual where, after swearing on the goddess Ayelala, the girl is brainwashed to obey the orders. Then she is linked for life to the mama who controls her, even from a distance. 'If you break the bond,' the officiant who's in cahoots with the mama tells her, you'll have to deal with Ayelala's wrath. One after another the members of your family will die like locusts. Then it will be your turn, and it will come with atrocious suffering.' Thereafter, it's a tall order for the girl to break the spell.

Having evaded this trap, Shoshana managed to track down a contact who, for a pretty penny, offered to get the five of them to Agadez in Niger, then to Libya, from where they would embark for Europe. It would simply require paying cash before each leg. 'I guarantee you,' the trafficker told her, 'you'll be in Europe in at most three weeks.' He also gave her his word of honor that, from Abuja, the trip to Niger would be made via the western route in order to avoid the lawless gang of Boko Haram whose tentacles were spreading more and more to the north-eastern part of the country. Even the devil would stay away from those guys, the man said, who himself was a Muslim.

'You see, we're serious people. We're concerned with your safety. I challenge you to find anyone better,' he added, straight-faced.

At first, the talks hit a snag over the fee: one thousand two hundred dollars to Agadez. A tough businesswoman, Shoshana managed to bring him down to a thousand dollars. But that wasn't the end of it. Having achieved this reduction, she launched into a new negotiation. It was her idea to reach the town of Sokoto on their own, located about a hundred kilometers from the Nigerian border. The caravan would pick them up on the way, at a meeting point to be decided upon together. Hence, six hundred dollars a person seemed a correct price to her. It would be a nice saving for them, she thought to herself. She argued as much as she could, but the guy defended his bit of meat like a starving jackal. However he didn't know Shoshana, who refused to let go of her piece, too. She knew the guy was already hooked, it would be a pity not to take advantage of that.

'That's not how it works,' the trafficker said, beginning to get annoyed. 'Number one: we have our own transportation network. Otherwise we'd have no margin left at all. Number two: it's much simpler for everyone. Once the departure has been set, there's to be no stalling, right? It's like a target window. If you miss it, you'll have to wait for ages more. So we're not going to play games here looking for people left and right.'

After an endless exchange of words, Shoshana and the trafficker came to an agreement on the fee of seven hundred dollars. It would be their responsibility to get to Abuja by the appropriate day. If not, it was simple—everything was simple with the trafficker—they would leave without them. Thereafter they shouldn't count on the organization reimbursing them the installment paid. It was a matter of give and take. Somebody, whose references he would give her when the time came, would pick them up at the bus station. They were to give the remainder of the agreed-upon money to this individual before getting into the 4 x 4.

In the interim, the five of them entered a race against the clock to gather the needed sum, which mounted with each stage. Thus the Nigeria/Niger leg cost less than the Niger/Libya one, which in turn was less expensive than the crossing to Europe. The last one was set at one thousand five hundred dollars per person; non-negotiable, the contact had announced. 'We must also prepare for the unforeseen,' Shoshana told the others. The five of them accepted every small job they could find. Ariel got it into his head to do a bit of fishing for the last fish in the river, which had now shrunk to a ridiculous trickle of water in the center of an immense bed of stones. He was convinced he could catch some tilapia, which he would sell at the village market. They called upon people close to them, family and friends of good will settled abroad, who advised Shoshana not to travel with large sums of money and suggested that, if needed, they would serve as intermediaries.

Shoshana and her brother were able to count on their parents as well, who had put aside a small nest egg for when they could become active again, even if it had shrunk considerably because of the difficulties the family had recently been forced to confront. Once they arrived in Agadez, Niger, they would pay the second installment via Hawala, an informal payment system the smugglers preferred, as it left no trace. Before their departure, the young Nigerian bought sunglasses and balaclavas to brave the dust of the Sahel and the sand of the Sahara. One of the synagogue's elders gave each of them a warm jacket in anticipation of the desert's chilly nights. It was one thing less to pay for and wouldn't land in the purse of those vultures.

To spare them any tears, the goodbyes, one Saturday after Sabbath, were brief. Shulamite might well accuse her husband of too much sentimentality regarding his daughter, but she didn't show any less of it toward her son, flesh of her flesh, the apple of her eye. Shoshana felt a twinge in her heart, which she hastened to hide behind a bit of banter. 'Don't worry,' she told her mother, 'I'll take care of your baby.'

'*Mazeltov*,' the father said as he clutched them both to his chest. "I'm sure you will arrive safe and sound, *B'ezras Hashem*—with God's help.' Then, flanked by her younger sibling, she left to join the other three at the meeting place she herself had suggested.

THE LEADER

BEFORE THEIR DEPARTURE, Shoshana insisted on setting things straight with the others. This had been her idea from the start. Besides, she'd studied the matter from every angle, more than any of them had. So, no two ways about it: she was the leader and they were to follow her instructions.

'This is not some damn Talmudic meeting,' she'd let go when her mother wasn't around. 'Democracy is all very good and well, but if we start discussing every decision, we'll never make a go of it. Also, the ones we'll have to contend with are no joke. I'm saying this especially for you, Rachel. Is that clear?'

'Crystal clear, boss,' Rachel said.

'Clear as can be,' Ezekiel and Nathan, the other traveling companions answered.

'Yes, *sir*,' Ariel added.

'You, you stop your nonsense right now. In case you hadn't noticed, I'm not a guy. Boss is fine with me, but *sir*, no.' And then added, while she was at it: 'Come on, let's get out of here.'

The self-appointed leader guided her group in the direction of the bus station to take a bush taxi to Abuja. These minibuses with about a dozen seats rarely left with fewer than sixteen passengers, one extra per row. Sometimes they'd add one or two more on the steps, and one up front next to the drivers, a more expensive seat. It would certainly have been more comfortable to make the trip by train, but the five of them couldn't count on arriving by Sunday evening. In addition to moving at a snail's pace, the train might stop in the open countryside without giving the passengers any explanation. This way, with the minibus and two drivers who relieved each other along the way, with time for a pitstop, they were at the Abuja bus station around ten-thirty the next morning.

Coming from all over Nigeria, people were milling about beneath the burning sun, bound for the four corners of the country and the continent. The countless pickpockets among them started their workday very early. Then there were the stranded cripples, holding out their begging bowls to the rest, having failed to find even a bit of sympathy elsewhere. In addition to being the administrative capital of the country, Abuja's central location made it an obligatory crossing point. A constant coming-and-going of men, women, and children, colliding, loudly calling out at each other in pidgin English, Yoruba, Hausa, Igbo, and other minority dialects. The five of them, who must have only set foot once or twice in Onitsha, the town closest to their village, seemed lost. Rachel grabbed the opportunity to proclaim once again: 'Don't worry. I'll take care of it.' The result was that they were obliged to ask repeatedly for directions. Shoshana took advantage of her childhood friend's failed efforts to reestablish her authority over the group. She knew that if she allowed her pal to take the reins, Rachel would do whatever came into her head.

'Don't forget what we agreed on, Rachel. I'm the one who decides. I'll ask for your opinion if necessary...'

'Crystal clear,' Rachel said, anticipating Shoshana's question.

Their contact, around thirty, with dreadlocks and a Rasta bracelet around his wrist, was waiting for them at the pre-arranged spot. He shook everyone's hand, appealed to his interlocutor with his enthusiasm before putting his free arm around her for a hug that almost made them forget they were doing business. Then he brought his right fist to his chest, on the side of his heart and said: '*Jah Rastafari.*' Once the ritual ended, he told them point-blank that the departure had been moved back until some time later. Two of the 4 x 4's were at the service station, which was late in returning them.

'A complete overhaul is needed before a trip of this kind, you know. We're looking at three days on the road if all goes well. The cars had better be in good shape,' the guy said.

'And you didn't know that beforehand?' Shoshana snapped back.

'Don't worry, sister,' the guy answered.

'When do we actually leave in the end?' Shoshana wanted to know.

'In three days, *Inshallah*,' the man said and, laughing, began to sing Bob Marley's:

Don't worry about a thing
'Cause every little thing's gonna be alright

Broadly speaking, Shoshana needn't worry. Everything would go well, notwithstanding the delay. 'These things happen.' Having said that, her friends and she could still back out, the trafficker said ironically, looking Shoshana straight in the eyes. She seemed to be the brains of the group. It was she he'd have to convince. He used every trick he knew. 'The choice is yours,' he said raising his hands to the level of his shoulders, palms out toward his listeners. If they were still game, they could either go to a hotel or agree with his suggestion to find lodging in a *connection house* on the edge of town. The second option offered a double advantage. 'One: it costs less. Two: it's the spot from where the convoy will depart.' The reason for this approach? Avoiding the indiscreet looks and the checkpoints where the uniformed Babylon took pleasure in taxing passengers and driver, which could go as far as seizing the car. And then everything would be postponed indefinitely. 'Goodbye Niger, goodbye Libya. Goodbye Europe.' Shoshana called her little group together for a quick consultation, foreheads together, while the smuggler looked on, amused, before telling him that they would take the second option.

The Rasta had them get into a half-dilapidated old jalopy, similar to many of the other cars on the road. Throughout the drive he did nothing but hum 'Everything's Gonna Be Alright'. After three-quarters of an hour of a bumpy ride, of honking horns and sudden braking to get away from the heavy traffic in the center of town, the friends were brought to a house that lacked any comfort. In fact, nothing more than four walls covered by a roof of corrugated iron, open to the four winds; the smugglers didn't think it necessary to add any doors. People waiting to depart were already there, chatting in a corner in the shade. Others were serenely asleep, despite the humid heat.

The five friends spent three days in the connection house, Shoshana refusing Rachel's proposal to visit the city of Abuja. 'That's not what we're here for. And just think, what if their damned 4 x 4's are fixed sooner than expected and we don't get back in time, you think they'd wait for us, these guys? They'd be all too happy to sell our seats to other folks and keep our money, too. So, the answer is *nyet*.' They slept right on the floor, their backpacks serving as pillows, which simultaneously allowed them to protect their meager possessions as well as the money for the second payment that the three others had brought with them. That strategy had caused them to be duly told off by the leader, out of earshot of the other occupants of the hideout.

'I mean, really. Do you have mush for brains inside your head or what?' To avoid getting robbed, she asked the boys to take turns being on guard duty while the others slept.

There was a hole dug in the ground, surrounded by cinder blocks to stabilize the edges, for their bodily needs. The house was enclosed by two-meter high walls, the only privacy they enjoyed during their time there. They used newspaper to wipe themselves or, for want of that, stones. When they reached the point of having to do without, Rachel chose to hold it in until they could stock up again.

'Be as prissy as you want,' Shoshana told her. 'Just don't come moaning later on when your belly hurts. We're tough when the going gets rough. Right, boys?'

'Yes, boss, yes,' the others said in unison.

The three days went by rather quickly. Tuesday evening, as the Rasta had promised, the five of them with Shoshana in the lead took their seats in the back of a pick-up, with about twenty other travelers. Metal rods were attached throughout the truck to hold onto and prevent being ejected during the transport, which was happening at top speed. Only once did they run into a patrol that had emerged from nowhere. Three police officers were waiting for them, weapons and flashlights in hand, as if they'd caught wind of their route in advance. 'Routine check,' the officers said, distributing the vehicles between them.

'We don't flinch,' Shoshana warned between her teeth. 'We do what they say.' They got the message, all five of them. They each put their hands in their pockets and the cops went back to wherever they came from, while the convoy of three continued on its way.

The vehicles traveled throughout the night and reached the outskirts of Sokoto at the crack of dawn. Unsettled by the journey, Shoshana, her friends, and the other passengers were left at another connection house where the day dragged on as they waited for the following night. When evening came, the convoy got back on track in the direction of Niger, at the same cruising speed. Shoshana knew they'd crossed the border when the 4 x 4's made a pitstop. In spite of the darkness, she realized they were in the Sahel, that broad strip of land marking the passage to the desert. In the morning she noticed its ochre color when the caravan stopped at a roadblock where the gendarmes, under the guise of carrying out routine checks, extorted money from them with the same lack of compassion as their colleagues on the other side of the border. A final stop in a ghetto, the Niger equivalent of the connection house and, the next night, the convoy went back on the road, swallowing the miles, as well as the dust for the passengers piled up in the cargo bed, in contrast to the smugglers who were behind glass inside the air-conditioned cab.

Having planned everything in advance, Shoshana's group suffered less. 'Who's the boss here?' she reminded them when they put on their balaclavas and sunglasses. The rest of the time the five exchanged very little, except for the food they brought, which was visibly diminishing. When it began to disappear, they settled for the meagre fare for which they paid in local currency in the ghettos. Shoshana didn't have to be asked to share her portions with Ariel who had always had a big appetite. 'I have enough extra,' she explained as she patted her well-rounded bottom with the palm of her hand. In reality, she didn't want to make her sibling feel guilty. Shoshana hadn't expected the trip to be this long and exhausting. And they were only just beginning. She was looking deep inside herself for the strength the group would need to make it to the end. Without really knowing where the limits were. What she was sure of was that she would lead them to the realization of their collective dream. She was the one who'd gotten them into this. It was her duty.

At dawn the next day they reached the periphery of Agadez—the gateway to the desert.

THE GHETTO

IN THE OUTSKIRTS of Agadez, since the traffickers avoided the very busy center of town, the travelers were parked in another ghetto, even more run-down than the one before. It stood in the middle of nowhere. The slightest breath of air transformed the ochre soil surrounding them into lethal dust, which penetrated every possible orifice: eyes, nostrils, ears. A few scrawny shrubs were waging a centuries-old battle against the combined Sahel and Sahara. There was absolutely nothing other than a large sand-covered courtyard behind the clay walls of the enclosure. Some imbedded posts were covered by tattered tarpaulins so filthy they would make you retch. At this stage of the journey no one paid attention anymore to such details. Except for Shoshana's childhood friend, her airs of grande dame having earned her the nickname

Lady Rachel from the young men. In fact, she played up to the name, as good a way as any to attract attention and ease the atmosphere.

Following the example of everyone else seeking shelter beneath these strange tents, Shoshana and her group spent their days performing a ballet of incessant moves to the rhythm of the sun's progression through the sky. No other way to find any refuge. Unless it meant digging a tomb and burying yourself there. As Cain did, in a useless attempt to flee the ire of Hashem after he'd assassinated his twin brother Abel, Shoshana said, lessening the tension. There was no respite until evening fell, in that crevice of transition separating the end of day and the dark night's beginning, when the temperature would drop sharply, and they would brace themselves to resist Mother Nature's merciless attacks. Then the club of five would huddle as closely together as they could, in the hope that it would shield them from the wicked cold coming out of the desert. There was plenty of self mockery, thanks in part to Ariel and Lady Rachel. Despite their jackets, all five had to press so closely against one another that Shoshana's little brother said to her one evening:

'See, sis, I told you we'd end up being engaged.'

'You, you're just lucky I'm too wiped out to beat you up,' his sister replied.

Rachel, in turn, let Ezekiel have it when he lay a little too close for her taste.

'Zee, what's going on, that hard thing against my bottom? You didn't bring a weapon with you, I hope? If you did, you'd better put it somewhere else. I don't want to piss them off, those angry dogs.'

They all had a good laugh. Except for Shoshana who went after her friend, having promised her mother she'd watch over her sibling:

'Stop your nonsense, you. You forgetting we have a child with us?'

'Hey, sister! I'm not a kid anymore. I'm seventeen, I'll have you know. Besides, I've already done things you can't even imagine.'

'I'd rather not.'

Such rare moments of banter notwithstanding, Shoshana was under the cautious impression of having moved toward her destination just a little—they'd been on the road for an eternity—and heading for the worst with every step. Since she'd boarded the bush taxi for Abuja, the situation had only gone downhill. Here she was, she who so loved to be in control, stuck in this hole, awaiting the goodwill of smugglers to enter Libya. Only God knew what awaited them there on the other side of this new frontier. In the meantime, she'd spoken briefly with her parents to ask them to deposit the second installment via Hawala at the relay point the network had specified. She reassured them, told them everything was fine. No point in letting them know, even between the lines, about the doubts that colonized her mind once night came. Neither one of them had ever gone beyond Onitsha. How could they possibly imagine their children on these unfamiliar roads toward an elsewhere about which they didn't have a clue? 'Ariel is in good shape, he's gained some weight,' she lied to her mother to calm her fears. Soon they'd be crossing over into Libya. 'Baruch Hashem,' her mother said.

Once the money was collected, the smugglers showed an entirely different face. The travelers were reorganized by nationality or ethnicity, so as to prevent discord and create a more manageable herd. The trip was already spawning tensions enough. A caravan of nomads might be concealing highway robbers, racketeers or worse, paid by ISIS. All they needed now was for those bastards to come bust their balls. It wasn't what they were getting paid for. Each group was placed under the iron rule of a boss who spoke its presumed language. Messages could get across more quickly that way. No need to repeat them at the risk of being forced to keep order by harsher means. It was grueling work beating up on these assholes in this heat.

Sudanese, Ghanaians, and Nigerians were added to Shoshana's group, English being their common language. The whole little unit answered to the commands of a Hausa, a particularly brutal man from the north of Nigeria. Always chewing on a stick of licorice, he'd only take it out of his mouth to spit a blackish glob at the feet of whomever he was talking to. As a gesture of defiance. The least one could say was that he didn't pull any punches when addressing them. Shoshana suspected him of pilfering some of the already meager amount of water and food they were given once a day and exchanging it for dollars or small favors from some of the girls after sundown. He had a weak spot for girls from

Ethiopia and Eritrea, who were more exotic in his eyes. It explained why Shoshana and Rachel escaped his clutches.

Those with whom he couldn't do any business were treated like pieces of shit. 'No one asked you, slave,' he shouted at Ariel the day he dared to question him about the date of their departure for Libya. They'd been stuck in the ghetto for more than a week, boredom their only distraction, excreting what little they had in their belly under dozens of pairs of eyes, unless they could manage to wait for the night to relieve themselves in the dark. Despite his efforts not to disappoint his sister, Ariel was beginning to find that time was dragging. Hence the question that brought him the Kapo's wrath. As for those girls who resisted his advances, the Hausa took a sadistic pleasure in tormenting them:

'You'll see, in Libya you'll really be in for it. The Arabs will discipline you. They won't do you any favors. They'll screw you in every hole. Might as well get ready. By the way, I have condoms for sale, if you're interested.'

He carried on all day long, the stick of licorice between his teeth, terrorizing his little realm. His djellaba, gray with filth, could barely hide the fact that he was obese, to put it mildly. 'He's expecting quadruplets, at the very least,' Nathan joked. The hem came down just to his sandals, showing feet with grimy nails curved like talons that couldn't have been near any nail clippers in ages. Shoshana felt trapped under the thumb of this despot. The mere sight of the layer of whitish foam accumulated in the corners of his mouth, which he spent his time clearing out with the back of his thick tongue, like a cow, made her want to puke.

What if she were to go back? Perhaps she'd find something to do in her native land to scrape a living together? Without being forced to seek sustenance from others and risk being treated like less than nothing. A sub-woman. Perhaps with her people she could fight nature's collapse? When united by good will and determination one can do many things. 'Didn't Joshua show us how, because of his tenacity, he made the walls of Jericho come down?' she mused in her corner.

That being said, if she went home now wouldn't she be admitting failure? The neighbors who'd seen them leave. Most of them envious, not having the means to go away as well, wishing them a good journey. May the Eternal One go with you. The shame if she were to come back with her head down, not daring to look people in the eyes, a true Ibo Bat Israel. Furthermore, her parents had spent all their savings so that she and her brother could undertake this trip of survival. They trusted her. She had to go through with it. For them, for herself. And for Ariel, too. So many questions racing through her mind when sleep kept getting away from her. In spite of the beauty of the night sky at the border of the Sahel and the Sahara. Then, to suppress her doubts, she'd wrap herself around her younger brother who was muttering in carefree sleep. As if all of this, all these ups and downs, had been a mere adventure from which he was sure to escape unharmed.

And then one evening three pick-ups and two trucks appeared in front of the ghetto. Night had just begun to fall, still warm from the day's temperature. The smugglers burst into the courtyard, slamming the large sheet metal and wrought iron barrier behind them, making a huge racket. They barked orders left and right. 'Let's go, get a move on. It's not the only thing we've gotta do. Move your ass if you want to get away from here.' Shoshana managed to grab her backpack on the move before being shoved by one of the men directing the flow of people toward the vehicles. Their distribution seemed to be random rather than based on some specific logic. Just as they were about to climb into the bed of the pick-up, a couple with a child of about five, with whom Shoshana had exchanged a few smiles during the long days of waiting, was pushed back with kicks and sticks behind the four walls of the enclosure, under the watchful eye of the Hausa.

'You, you're not paid up yet. Get lost,' the Nigerian Cerberus said and then, when everything was settled, got into the cab of the pick-up at the front.

Shoshana was in the same truck as her little crew. Once again they were leaving, on a new leg toward their objective. She was propped up lopsided, like a bale of merchandise tossed loosely into the hold of a ship, one hand clutching onto one of the wooden parallel bars between the two sides of the bed; the other gripping the rail. Impossible to move, much less to sit down. She was going to travel this way, standing, jerked back and forth between bodies and asphyxiating discharges from sphincters, which their owners struggled to hold back.

They covered two thousand five hundred kilometers, seven days and seven nights in the Sahara, under conditions that even camels would have had a hard time coping with. Only one stop a day was allowed. The rest of the time they'd have to restrain themselves. Too weak to continue, some of them were abandoned in the desert. Without a drop of water or a crust of bread. They didn't have the energy to get up and run after the truck. Not even enough fire in their eyes to provoke an uprising of solidarity from the rest of them.

'You, be quiet, say nothing.' Shoshana whispered to Lady Rachel, the one most likely to rebel. Others died of dehydration or hunger. Their bodies were chucked out of the truck by other passengers, on the orders of the traffickers. And then, as the hours and the days went by, on their own initiative, acting out of fear of being beaten by their guards, or of a possible contagion resulting from prolonged contact with a cadaver that would have rapidly decomposed in the sun.

Shoshana and her little group managed to hang in there, undoubtedly thanks to their rugged youth. To the 'reserves' of the young Nigerian woman and her childhood friend, equally endowed with well-placed curves. 'A generous body and a generous heart,' as Rachel described herself. But on the third day Ezekiel became delirious and started hallucinating. He wanted to jump over the edge of the truck and get to the Promised Land.

'It's there. Let's go. I can see it now,' he said, his index pointing to the horizon where dunes formed the only obstacle to the visual expanse. Shoshana felt a sudden panic when he began to chant in sacred Hebrew. She was afraid that devils from ISIS or Boko Haram may have imbedded themselves among them. It was one of the main arguments of European countries for not receiving those they referred to as migrants. And she was afraid of that for other reasons.

THE MEDITERRANEAN WALL

Nevertheless, she managed to keep her composure and take things in hand.

When she asked him, Ariel put his hand over Ezekiel's mouth as if to calm him down. He'd grasped the seriousness of the situation. Since leaving their village—about a month ago, maybe more, maybe less—he'd matured at an incredible pace. As if he'd been waiting to get away from his mama's apron strings to spread his wings, to the point that his big sister would sometimes treat him as 'silly little patriarch'. While the others tried to control their companion, Shoshana succeeded in getting one of the passengers to give her a few drops of water that he had left. She sprinkled them in their friend's face while Rachel slapped him, fanned him with a piece of cardboard she'd found heaven knows where, alternately kissing and cursing at him. She kept on shouting at him:

'You're not gonna do that to us, guy. You're not gonna drop us now. Hey, you're not gonna do that. Fuck! Pull yourself together, shit. Are you a man, yes or no?'

And then she'd kiss him again: 'Zee, honey.' Finally, Ezekiel regained a semblance of consciousness under the combined force of Rachel's kisses and the *Tefilat HaDerech*, the Traveler's Prayer, Shoshana was murmuring between her teeth so she wouldn't be heard by inquisitive ears: 'May it be Your will, Eternal One, our God and God of our fathers, to lead us in peace and direct our steps in peace, and guide us in peace, and support us in peace, and cause us to reach our destination in life.' Still muttering, she ended: 'Baruch atah Adonai shomea tefillah.' Zee, still dazed, was back on track.

WELCOME TO LIBYA

ALL THESE VAGARIES were nothing compared to what awaited Shoshana and her friends on the other side of the border. Far from it. Dead with exhaustion, she wasn't thinking when, as soon as they'd gone through the checkpoint, supposedly closed at night, she heard her Hausa compatriot say loudly and clearly to his Libyan counterpart: 'That's it, they're all yours.' As if he were delivering common cattle, or worse, slaves, and they'd been sold as such. At the time these words seemed strange. But between the lack of sleep, the concern about the days to come, and the questions she couldn't stop asking herself, the phrase had left her mind. However, from this new border onward their situation would radically change. Not only were the conditions of the rest of the trip as dreadful as before, four days and four nights on roads where they had to get out more than once to dig the truck out of the sand, but the treatment of the passengers would be even more brutal, more perverse, more inhuman.

As soon as they changed vehicles, a few dozen meters from the roadblock right under the nose of the customs officers, Shoshana picked up on the altered atmosphere. Armed with Kalashnikovs and clubs, the traffickers didn't take well to them dragging their feet.

'From here on in, you'll do what you're told, *Niggers*. We won't say it twice,' one of them shouted angrily, sunglasses on in the middle of the night. With them, everything was done on the double, day and night, in the scorching heat or not. The tone was set with blows of rifle butts or clubs, of a gun shoved in their side, in concert with their '*Yallah! Yallah!*'

It was the first time Shoshana heard the expression. Without knowing any Arabic, she got the gist of it at once. Some words, especially accompanied by violent gestures, need no translation. Others, like *qird*, monkey, enforce their meaning simply by being flung in one's face. Before Shoshana could react, the guy with the sunglasses grabbed one of her buttocks as if she were a piece of merchandise picked up from a market stall. She felt his breath, reeking of tobacco, on her neck as he whispered in her ear: 'Move it, *habiba*. Move it.' The guy seemed to have a soft spot for her or else he would have snarled at her or beat her as he was doing with the others. Not that, out of a combined rage and sense of help-lessness, it made Shoshana cringe any less. Not react to his provocation above all. Perhaps that was all he was waiting for, the bastard. Then he would have been happy to punch her, to make an example of her for the unruly. She clenched her jaws and picked up the pace.

Ariel, Zee, and Nathan were each eligible for a pistol-whipping on their shoulder blades. One way of wishing them 'welcome to the land of chaos' where each clan, each vigilante group made its own laws. And the presumed authorities closed their eyes, either out of powerlessness or through corruption. It was how the smugglers made their point as well. Reeling from the shock, Ariel collapsed to the ground, face down. He recovered almost immediately and without bothering to dust off his clothes he rejoined the flow of passengers. His big sister who wasn't far off rushed over to him murmuring under her breath: *'Everything's gonna be alright, babe. Everything's gonna be alright.'* In the presence of his sibling and the others, the young boy didn't want to show any sign of weakness. He refused to become the millstone they'd have to drag around to the end. He had his pride. Brother and sister walked as one, then hoisted themselves as best they could into the bed of the truck, with the help of a rope tightened across its back. More supple, Ariel clambered up first, then held out his hand to help his sister get in. Shoshana used the opportunity to say: 'Whatever happens with Rachel or me, do not move. You hear? Look at me: you hear?' she insisted. Ariel was unable to verbalize his agreement. All he did was nod yes.

The rest of the trip to Sabratha didn't offer any great change. Other than the blows the travelers, like it or not, were getting used to, which the smugglers delivered at every stop as a distraction, to pass the time, and unwind from the stress of the drive. At one point the caravan was pursued by two pick-up trucks with bearded, turbaned men on board; they couldn't tell whether these were ISIS, desert outlaws, or a rival militia gang trying to seize the windfall of hopefuls on their way to Europe. They were received with Kalashnikov rounds and didn't persist, almost like dogs chasing a car, barking loudly and then, for no apparent reason, suddenly stopping in their tracks. No one in Shoshana's group was hurt. Still, she had the fright of her life, although she'd done her utmost not to show any signs of it. She was taking her role as their leader too much to heart for that.

In Sabratha, a coastal town seventy kilometers from Tripoli, Shoshana landed in a nightmare, pure and simple. Upon arrival, telephones were immediately confiscated. Accompanied by thorough physical frisking to make sure no one was hiding any. One can never be too careful. The traffickers were deathly afraid of being surreptitiously filmed or taped and having the video end up on the Internet. It had happened before. Shoshana received preferential treatment: a hand slipped into her bra—'apparently, you *kahlouchettes*, you hide your little secrets between your breasts'—, into her panties after being forced to lower her jeans in front of everyone else. Rachel couldn't keep from uttering a pathetic attempt at protest: 'Oh, you're tickling me.' It didn't make the guy laugh, if he even understood the English word 'tickle'. Men and women were duly separated. Without exception. Although they were traveling with their mother, two boys of about eight or ten landed in the men's hangar.

Shoshana and Rachel were in a shabby warehouse, covered with a corrugated metal roof whose sole function seemed to be that of intensifying the heat of the day and the cold of the night. No questions were permitted. No information was provided about the length of the stay before making the crossing to Europe. 'As for latrines and showers, make do with what's already there,' barked a guard whom Shoshana would get to know. In another era, the man would have been a perfect foreman of slave quarters on the plantations. The two friends lay down on the cement floor of the humid, filthy, stifling shelter. Among countless numbers of young and adolescent women from all over sub-Saharan Africa. Shoshana noticed that some had a mat or a square piece of fabric, undoubtedly acquired in exchange for banknotes or a sexual favor. In view of how things were going, it wouldn't be a bad idea to get one herself to share with Rachel.

Since they'd been dropped in the warehouse, Shoshana had lost not only any count of time but also all physical trace of Ariel and the other two youths. Repeated questions for the smugglers got her nothing but guffaws or a slap from the back of a hand, the way one swipes at an annoying insect. One morning, a gloriously bald big-bellied guard, with a flat skull and bulging eyes, more amphibian—a bullfrog to be exact—than human, suggested to her point blank he'd give her information in exchange for a blow job. As if it were simply a common barter.

'I can just help myself, of course. But I'd rather have a minimum of consent. Always better, no?' he said with a snort.

Horrified, the young Nigerian resisted for a week. She avoided the guard's eyes for fear he'd come back to it later. She didn't mention it to Rachel either. Her childhood friend would start laughing: 'Maybe he's uncircumcised, this guy. Imagine shoving his cowled thing in your mouth, still with the scum of several days in its folds.' Then she would advise her to settle on something else, 'a handjob or just holding your breath.' Lady Rachel would say this to make light of it, without really thinking it, or maybe only halfway. Her way of helping her friend. For days on end, Shoshana mulled over the brutal proposition by herself. Her sense of responsibility and the need to know soon got the upper hand. That evening she threw up everything she had in her stomach. Beforehand and afterward. She felt befouled. Until the end of her days there wouldn't be enough water to cleanse her. No disinfectant could take away the stench from her soul. All of it to learn, in the end, that her brother was in the next warehouse, some thirty meters away, which she somehow doubted. Other than the guard's word she was given no tangible proof.

A few days after the exchange of friendly services, as the guy called the act he'd forced upon her, the trafficker with the sunglasses appeared in the hangar. Standing with legs spread wide above two pairs of legs outstretched on the floor, he explained to the girls that they were going to phone their relatives to ask for money for the crossing, the price of which had doubled since the last verbal agreement. The information was bellowed in English, French, and Arabic. 'There we go, trapped like rats,' Shoshana whispered quietly to Rachel.

'We're fucked,' her friend replied. 'Unless some of you already have the dough tucked away somewhere,' the man sneered, showing chewed wads saturated with nicotine. The conversation was to be limited to total sum, date, and manner in which the money would be paid. He expected full cooperation from them. So he wouldn't have to punch them in the mouth, he added.

When it was her turn, Rachel tried to play it smart and slipped in some words in Igbo different from what they'd been told to say in English. The Cerberus swung a blow at her that made her head and the telephone spin in opposite directions. A little Eritrean girl, whose words were too hesitant, because her family at home didn't have the means to pay—'it's a lot of money for them, you understand?'—was subjected to a veritable torture session during the conversation. Hearing her shriek with pain, her relatives promised even what they didn't have.

Shoshana also spoke with her parents that day. During the quick chat—'I don't have many minutes,' the young woman lied—they tried to reassure her, told her not to worry, they would pay for her and her brother. They'd find a way. As their parents that's the least they could do for them. Shoshana hung up before her father could add a *B'ezrat Hashem* or something else in that vein. She concluded from the conversation that her contact hadn't told her any lies: Ariel was alive.

But her troubles weren't over yet. A week later—maybe less, the days went by so slowly—her referent let it be known that the sum her parents had sent wasn't enough. Unless she wanted to call them again to have them pay in full, the organization was offering her the possibility of doing so herself by working as a maid in the affluent homes of Sabratha and surrounding areas. 'Calling my parents again is out of the question,' Shoshana heard herself say. 'They've given more than enough already.' What she really wanted to avoid was for them to worry whether she and her brother had ended up in some mysterious wasps' nest. Still, she tried to find out if the job would pay enough to meet the cost of her brother's crossing as well. The man laughed in her face, his only response:

'Here it's each for himself. Allah for all.'

'Whatever,' Shoshana said to herself. It would allow her to get out of the warehouse, breathe some less foul air. Appease her hunger a little thanks to the food on the tables where she'd be working—too bad if it weren't kosher. She was entitled to half a liter of brackish water once a day, and another one every other day, and an insipid broth that could hardly be called a meal. However, in the beginning, overpowered by violent attacks of diarrhea and vomiting, she spent her time going to the toilet. Then, except for a few passing stomach aches she learned to live with, her body grew accustomed to it.

She saw that working outside was also an opportunity to escape from being a distraction for the traffickers wanting to relieve their boredom and the long wait. As on the day when, before their lecherous gaze, she was forced to take off her clothes for the so-called shower she'd been anticipating for two weeks. She knew she had no choice. On the demand of the traffickers, she lay down on the ground without giving it much thought. Armed with a rubber hose, the youngest one spurted jets of water across her body. She shut her eyes to keep herself from thinking about the situation, instead making the most of this small pleasure, a luxury for her. Then she felt the shock. Paralyzing! Rigidifying her body before it slackened and violently hit the ground again. For a timeless moment, her naked body reared up, as in an epileptic fit, watched by a pack of hyenas laughing uproariously. Her howling in pain didn't compel them to lift the exposed electric cable one of them had put on the wet ground.

On the outside news traveled faster. Shoshana learned that the organization holding them prisoner was under the control of a mysterious Al-Ammu, the true coordinator of the district. The Uncle, as he was called, was the head of a militia known as the Brigade of Martyrs Al-Dabbashi that ruled the roost in Sabratha. Apparently, his reputation extended well beyond the borders of Libya. The man was so powerful that the Italian oil company, ENI, was supposed to have had recourse to his services to guarantee the protection of one of its gas plants, located about thirty kilometers from Sabratha.

Shoshana worked ten, twelve hours a day, going from one opulent home to another, earning a pittance, which her jailers confiscated as an instalment on the total amount due. Some, in a surge of kindness, occasionally allowed her to keep a few dinars. Throughout this entire period, which lasted she had no idea how long anymore, Shoshana never touched the tiny reserve of money hidden in her seams. The experiences of the past days and months had taught her that the worst is bottomless. These sons of bitches, a term she'd picked up from

Rachel, would be capable of taking it from her without giving her anything in return. In any case, the amount was far from enough to pay for her and her brother's crossing.

To avoid feeling sorry for herself, she relied on the One who shall not be named, or the banter of her childhood friend. Lady Rachel was one of those people who could find a reason to laugh even standing on the edge of a precipice with an executioner behind their back ready to push them into the void. When they'd relate their misery to each other, her friend's upbeat chatter let her shrug off some of the suffering lodged in the hollows of her flesh and her soul in a mirthless chuckle. Then she'd regain her courage, feeling once more like a leader, ready to guide her little group toward a more luminous future. The widest sea in the world, the Mediterranean or a different one, was bound to have a shore somewhere. She was determined to get there.

THE BIG DAY

IN THE WAREHOUSE forsaken by Allah and the State, where no law existed except for that of the traffickers, the opportunities to get to know one another were as rare as rain in the desert. Their troubles, obstacles, and hopes were the same and so specific. Curled up in the secrecy of the night, each licked her own wounds. When, overwhelmed by exhaustion and unanswered questions, the other bodies had sunk into a fitful sleep filled with nightmares carried over from the day, the preceding weeks, even from an entire life; from being born in a place where you suffered so much from the day you were born that you wound up regarding it as the wrong place to start life and, even more, to continue living.

Hearing words fall uncontrolled from the lips of others at night, Shoshana wondered upon waking in the morning whether, during this daily apprenticeship of death that was sleep, her own hadn't betrayed her thoughts. Whether, in spite of herself, they hadn't revealed her most acerbic judgments about the masters of the place. Even if they weren't naïve enough to think their victims might hold any feelings of affection for them. Nevertheless, other than Rachel, she distrusted the unknown bodies lying next to her. Perhaps, she caught herself imagining in a fit of paranoia, the girl next to her who sometimes smiled her way would be capable of selling out her neighbor for some small favors—a bit of meat in her food, a piece of soap...

All of sub-Saharan Africa was represented in the hangar. In its desolation and its humanity. In its diversity and its youth. The oldest ones among these wandering girls were barely over thirty, Shoshana noted on days that she didn't go to work outside, when the hours crawled by in humidity and hopeless reflections. Quite a few of them would rub at their offensive adolescent acned skin. Some were hauling around a pregnancy picked up in the course of their restless roaming. If Rachel and she were fleeing an increasingly less nurturing land, a nature whose bosom had withered like the hand of Jeroboam, others were trying to escape from war, and still others from dictatorships that denied its youth any dreams of a future.

That was Semhar's case, a young Eritrean girl, so frail you wouldn't dare touch her for fear she might break. She was always together with one of her compatriots. Alone in their corner, glued to each other, like Shoshana and Rachel. Retreating into their words and woes. When one of them went to the toilet, the other would go with her and mount a vain guard, which the first passing trafficker could put an end to if he saw fit. Then one day, Meaza, Semhar's companion, didn't come back to the warehouse. Except for imagining the worst, nobody had an answer nor got one from the traffickers whom, in any case, they'd do better to avoid unless it was to respond to their questions. Shoshana saw how lost Semhar was and took her under her wing, protecting her from the others who'd mistreat her without a moment's hesitation for a mouthful of food or some trinkets brought back from the outside. They exploited her aloneness in this jungle where survival justified any form of malice. She was the wounded animal discarded by the rest of the herd. So, the jackals came rushing over.

With her military training, Semhar could have defended herself on her own if she'd wanted. But after her friend disappeared it was as if she'd lost her fire, lost the courage to keep on going, to continue believing in a possible future on the other side of the Mediterranean. Insults and acclaim, blows and caresses, none of it seemed to make any difference to her one way or the other. Shoshana understood and intervened to put an end to the assaults. She stood up for her, together with Lady Rachel whose words and voice managed to keep even the most reckless at a distance. As the days went by, the two Nigerians and the Eritrean became a close-knit trio, each one looking out for the others.

Despite the favors the prison guard demanded ever more frequently, Shoshana had some concrete news of Ariel only once. The rest of the time the toad would put her off until tomorrow, until the following week, *Inshallah*. However, he never forgot to claim his one-way exchange of courtesies, to which Shoshana yielded without too much grumbling, without encouraging them either. It was her way of protecting herself from the other predators since she was the bullfrog's favorite. The girls' heartrending moaning during the night reminded her constantly of this. She prayed daily that she wouldn't get pregnant, for the man didn't bother taking any precaution at all when he threw himself on her like a starving dog on a bone, a jackal's smile on his lips, unceremoniously pushing himself into her flesh, tearing her private parts. He also insisted that she keep her eyes open, move her groin, feigning pleasure. If she didn't, she'd end up with one punch after another. Until she agreed to wiggle under the bullfrog's weight, but not too fast or he'd accuse her of wanting to bring it to an end, of not giving him enough in exchange for his information. Then he'd spew: 'You like it, don't you, bitch! You like it, bitch!' He'd impale her up to the hilt, until he could go no further, and she'd start squealing like a pig, while he stayed above her, unperturbed, the usual ferocious smile making his ugly *shaitan* face even uglier.

One evening, back at the warehouse after a day of cleaning other people's houses, the guy brought her a hurriedly scribbled note from her brother. *Everything's alright, sister*, was essentially what Ariel had written. He was working in construction on the outside to meet the cost of the crossing. She recognized his spidery scrawl, riddled with spelling errors. He never did have a gift for language, her Ariel. Not very motivated. Despite some flashes that could lead one to believe he had a sharp brain. He just didn't have that kind of patience. In fact, he didn't give a damn about school. It was a stopgap measure, on his way to becoming a world-renowned singer, like his idols Tiwa Savage, Wizkid, or Yemi Alade who was Igbo as well.

Reading the three lines scrawled on a bit of greasy newspaper, Shoshana knew that he wasn't telling her everything there was to be told. That he was withholding the main thing, namely the harsh treatments he must be suffering, like everyone else. Sometimes cries would reach her ears, coming from the men's hangar, ripping through the thick silence around. Each string of screams was followed by an even heavier silence that made the girls hold their breath, on the alert. Awaiting the imminent passage of the angel of death across their own hangar. Thank God, among the voices hoarse with pain Shoshana had not yet recognized her brother's. Unless the agony had altered it.

The night Shoshana read Ariel's note she had trouble falling asleep. Even more than usual. Not from thinking he might have kept the truth from her, but from imagining him experiencing such dreadful things that he couldn't bring himself to tell her about it. To protect her, his older sibling. She'd heard stories about men whom the traffickers sold at auction, like slaves, or forced to sodomize other men to punish them or amuse themselves. How could she even think about her Ariel in such a situation? Maybe he also knew his note would be read by the one who brought it to her and so didn't want to add anything more. Finally, toward dawn,

Shoshana allowed herself to read her brother's silence as proof of his having grown up. That all these calamities were making him into a man. She thanked Hashem before she fell asleep.

A week later, they didn't call her to go to work when she woke up. She'd been paid the day before. So to speak, anyway, for as usual one of the traffickers had taken the money instead. Only this time he hadn't left anything for her. Not a single dinar. Back at the warehouse, she had collapsed next to Rachel on the square piece of fabric they'd found after a month. She had barely even heard her friend say goodnight.

The day, during which she was served the everlasting foul broth she ate without appetite just to keep her body going, passed with unreasonable slowness. Rachel had gone to work very early. Shoshana and Semhar, who'd also stayed behind, told each other their respective stories for the nth time, adding episodes they forgot on previous occasions. The early moments of wariness now behind them, the two had grown comfortable with each other, and now opened their hearts. With a great gift for languages, the Eritrean spoke English almost like a native. Shoshana confided to her new girlfriend how envious she was of her being born on the shore of the Red Sea, a place so symbolic for her. The heat's humidity would make them drowsy one at a time, but when they woke up, they'd pick up the thread of their conversation wherever they'd dropped it. At the very end of the afternoon, when the sun was beginning its retreat behind the horizon and Rachel had just come back to the warehouse, one of the traffickers showed up and began to point at some of the girls, one at a time.

'Get your things. *Yallah! Yallah!* Move your ass.'

They didn't know what to think. Had the big day finally arrived? Were they being transferred to another place? In that case, what were the criteria for selection? They gathered up their things, a bundle here, a backpack there, the two or three knickknacks they owned inside, before forming a line at the entrance to the hangar. They were all staring at the trafficker's eyes and index finger. They'd been here six months, a year, or even longer. They'd watched others leave. Their turn was bound to come someday, they wanted to believe that. No matter where they'd be taken, it couldn't be worse than the warehouse. You could see lips muttering prayers, fingers frantically counting the beads of a worn rosary. The three women took each other's hands, as in a prayer chain, but didn't utter a word. Seconds passed while the '*You! You!*' dropped from the trafficker's mouth, assisted by an underling who eagerly directed the girls to the exit. Shoshana and Semhar were pointed to, first one, then the other. Not Rachel.

Shoshana hesitated an instant, she had a bad feeling. Loosening Semhar's grip, she grasped both hands of her childhood friend and held them. In a split second, a thousand thoughts raced through her mind. Would Rachel be pointed to as well? Would she be one of the lucky ones chosen? If not, could she, Shoshana leave her, abandon her in this warehouse where day and night her humanity and womanhood were sullied? She wasn't prepared for this. What would become of her friend? Would Ariel be part of the contingent? Her hesitation unleashed the trafficker's wrath. He shouted:

'Hey, you, black girl. Wanna move it along, yes or no? I don't give a damn. If you don't, there are plenty ready to take your place here. Starting with your friend. And while you're at it, tell her to finish paying up so she can join you wherever you'll be.'

That was it: her lifelong friend would not be leaving with them. Rachel was the first to pull out of the embrace, not wanting to make things worse. She stroked Shoshana's face before pushing her in the back, after whispering in her ear:

'Go on, sister. Go for it. It's the will of Hashem. Look ahead. I'm big enough to fight with these sons of bitches. We'll meet again over there. On the other side of the Mediterranean. Go!'

Rachel's words gave Shoshana the burst of energy she needed to tear herself away from the place where they'd come to know what hell was but that, ultimately, had helped to bring them closer to each other. She stepped over bodies anxiously waiting for a word, a sign, from the man standing in their midst. As she passed, an underling with a bucket of paint and a brush in his hand, put a green mark on her face to show she was paid up and could leave. Semhar followed her like a shadow. They joined the line of girls standing at the entrance. Some fifteen minutes later, the huge door of rolled steel slammed shut with a bang. The girls were ordered to get into the beds of two 4 x 4 trucks waiting on the side. There must have been more than thirty in each vehicle. Shoshana and Semhar hadn't let go of each other for a second. The young Nigerian was still thinking about Rachel, and Ariel, too, whom she hoped to see on the boat. Perhaps he would be part of the group. Semhar was thinking of her friend Meaza, while the pick-up trucks drove through the night that had now fallen, taking them toward a shadowy unknown.

ON BOARD
THE TRAWLER

there's still another sea to cross
oh still another sea to cross

AIMÉ CÉSAIRE

IF I FORGET YOU,

JERUSALEM...

AFTER A GOOD HOUR on the road, the convoy stopped on a half-deserted beach where inflatable dinghies were waiting, lazily rocked by the backwash. All told, Shoshana counted seven of them. The motors, already running, were spluttering like consumptive cats, one after another ready to give up the ghost, before suddenly resettling and going back to a more regular purr, causing the water to spew white foam. Standing at the helm, the pilots glanced indifferently at the arrival of the pick-ups. One of them was finishing a cigarette, taking a final drag so powerful it seemed like the last smoke of a condemned man. As he inhaled his cheeks grew hollow while his chest swelled. About thirty, his face deeply lined from exposure to sun and salt water, he exhaled the smoke in small puffs, inspected the butt carefully to make sure nothing was left, then flicked it into the sea.

Vehicles crammed with men were already waiting on-site, coming from who knows where. Perhaps from Tripoli or Zuwara, where migrants were also held; perhaps from the hangar where Ariel was being held. Once she had her feet on the ground, Shoshana scanned each face by the pale meager light of the distant crescent moon. With a little luck, her baby brother would be among them. Thinner. Bearded. Changed, almost like a stranger to her. But very much there. She would have recognized him by his smile, that eternal adolescent smile of his. For he would have recognized her first and smiled at her. The face of an already completed woman, no longer changing very much. Beaten maybe from the ordeals of the preceding months but not to the point of being unrecognizable. Her brother's on the other hand, would be. He must have grown into a real little man. Or a tall one, she wouldn't know. How many months had it been since they last saw each other? Kissed each other? Since she'd scolded him for yet another inanity before he tried to hug her, so she'd forgive him. 'Come on, big sis. After all, I'm your precious brother.' She'd try to escape from his embrace, but he was faster, would quickly catch her again. And she'd be his prisoner. Prisoner of her younger sibling's overwhelming affection. And her own affection for him.

'You said so yourself: I'm your sister, not your mother, not your girlfriend. You won't bamboozle me,' she'd respond in a vain attempt to hide what she called her Achilles heel, her inability to refuse her brother anything. Shoshana had to defer to the evidence: not one of these faces, ashen from the long wait, the exhaustion, and the mistreatment, smiled at her. Her heart knotted up in disappointment. But just in time she held back the tears that were welling up in her eyes. To avoid making a spectacle of her weakness. It would make her appear too fragile.

The embarkation took place under the tense gaze of armed men in uniform. Policemen or soldiers, Semhar thought, unable to explain their presence to herself. At this stage, no one would think of fleeing. Instead, they were all in a hurry to be at sea, to vanish from under the eyes of their tormentors. Indeed, it wasn't unusual for a rival group to take advantage of the moment that they weren't at sea yet, to seize the merchandise. For the Uncle, whom Semhar would never see, it was simultaneously a matter of honor and credibility. If he let it happen, he would lose a juicy deal in the end. And for those who were about to leave, everything would start all over again. For they'd have to pay again by working for other masters.

Semhar embarked, incited by the 'Yallah! Yallah!' of the smugglers. Her chest felt a wandering hand by way of a farewell. There were about fifty in her group. The inflatable dinghy sank to its brim under the passengers' weight. All of them black. Some had found refuge in the back of the dinghy; others on the edge where, shifting their bottom, they'd managed to put down one cheek. They were so closely wedged in that there was no risk of falling overboard during the trip unless they capsized during the embarkation. Still,

Semhar tried to steady herself more by placing a firm hand on Shoshana's thigh, right beside her.

The two friends were almost settled when some minibuses showed up. After they stopped, a cluster of men, women, and bawling kids, mostly Arabs, came out. Dressed as if for a cruise, suitcases in hand, they were directed to three still-empty dinghies. In the interim, two armed men sat down on board of the already filled ones, one up front, the other in the back. When everyone was in place, the one who seemed to be the leader gave the departure signal. In a barrage of noise and foam the dinghies pulled away toward the open sea. Only the drivers of the vehicles who'd helped with the boarding of the recent arrivals, remained behind. The boats followed each other at a safe distance, forming a single, long wake in the water, the three with the Arabs heading the procession. Semhar and Shoshana's dinghy were sixth in line. In just a few minutes the convoy had moved away from the coast.

No one said a word. Faces showed a mixture of apprehension and tension, rather than relief in finally getting away from the place where they'd been sequestered for weeks, or even months. Semhar and Shoshana didn't speak either. Their minds were already turning toward that elsewhere, where they hoped their dreams would take root. A light breeze blew in their faces, but was unable to chase away the questions they'd been asking themselves since they noticed the outboard motors, which neither one dared ask the other out loud. Would the crossing be made on these flimsy boats? What if the motor broke down? Would there be enough gasoline to make it all the way to Europe? What if they were to run into a storm? On the Mediterranean the wind could rise without any warning, swelling the waves in a lightning flash. A girl who learned this by bitter experience had told Semhar her story. After three days of being adrift, clutching onto the wreck of their boat, she'd been rescued on the high seas by Italian coastguard ships who'd passed her back to their Libyan colleagues. Back to square one.

A sudden sense of emptiness overcame Shoshana. Seeing the dinghy widen the distance to the African continent filled her with sorrow. Yet, her decision to leave had ripened over a long period of time. It had taken a while for her to accept the idea that her motherland could not nurture her. That there was no future for her there. She had dreamed so much of this departure. She'd struggled, overcome a thousand torments, confronted hell and high water. Now that she was on her way to fulfill her dream, she felt like weeping. It had overtaken her suddenly. And not only because she was leaving her younger brother behind without knowing what would become of him. Rather than going toward the unknown, she felt as if she were going into exile. As if she'd been banished. Without any possibility of going back. She knew that once she was on the other side she'd have to learn to hide in the shadows, live clandestinely for years on end before she'd be settled and able to return home. 'How shall we sing the Lord's song in a foreign land?' she recited in silence. And if one of her people were to die in that period of time, she wouldn't be able to go home to lay him in the ground; recite the Kaddish of the mourners for his soul to rest. Hence the need to weep, as she did when she was a child and would go sit by herself on the bank of the river, before it died. There, she'd let the flow of the water carry her grief of the moment. She made a huge effort to get control of herself. She watched the dinghy, nose in the air, cut its path across the gentle waves that were hurrying to meet it.

The driver was whistling. Standing at the bow, surrounded by seated passengers, he was the only one whose face was, if not serene, at least neutral. Dressed in a green padded K-Way the color of goose-droppings, the wind in his hair, both hands on the helm, his eyes didn't leave the dinghy in front of him. Very soon, Semhar could no longer see the shore on the horizon. Although she'd grown up on the coast, it still impressed her. Truth be known, she'd only once in her life set foot on her father's fishing boat. She'd been forced to insist, beg, sulk, and resort to every kind of pressure typical of her tender age. Her father knew her cantankerous side and had given in. But he swore it would be the first and last time. Whatever happened. His daughter was not going to be a fisherwoman. And in spite of Semhar's sly attempts, he'd kept his word. The trip they took that day felt like a dream to her, even if the shore remained in sight throughout. She'd felt like the princess of the waters. The queen of the Red Sea. She was ten years old.

The immensity of the Mediterranean was all around, occasionally obstructed by the backs of the passengers in the boat ahead of them. The noise of the motor alternated with the navigator's whistling. Sometimes it would take over, sometimes it faded, letting the high pitch drift through the air, carrying unfamiliar notes to the ears of the two young women.

Suddenly, a robust young man, a good six foot two, pulled away from the crowd of bodies and stood up, causing the dinghy to sway. He seemed possessed, his eyes rolled upward. He was shouting in a mix of English and some other language that Semhar tried to catch. It was the first time he'd seen the sea and the Mediterranean seemed like a dangerous universe. Its span terrified him. He wanted to be taken back to solid ground. His panic spread to other passengers who stood up to clamor. They, too, wanted to go back to shore. The dinghy began to pitch in every direction. The others tried to calm them, but it was no use. The driver intensified his moves to try to keep the boat afloat before deciding to cut the motor. Then he turned to the man in uniform next to him at the bow, and yelled:

'Do something. Make that *kahlouch* shut his mouth, damn it!'

The latter finally got up, made his way through the jungle of legs and bodies stuck in the back of the dinghy. Reaching the man who'd started the rebellion, he drew his pistol and pointed it at his temple:

'Hey, you, Negro. You gonna calm down, yes or no?'

The man stopped short in his delirium and fell back onto sympathetic legs. The overseer at the stern quickly imitated his colleague, pointing the barrel of his gun toward the others who, petrified, sat right back down again. The young man himself seemed shattered. Like a featherweight who'd presumed to get into the ring and face Iron Mike. Despite the drop in adrenaline, it felt as if at any moment they could start all over again, so great was their terror. Making the most of the thick silence that followed, the driver spoke in a voice that finally managed to put them back in their place:

'You're gonna stop your nonsense, all right? I'm telling you once and for all: there's no going back. Nobody asked you to come. If one of you wants to go back to land, you'll have to swim. A bigger boat is waiting on the open sea. The crossing will take only six hours. Now, shut up. I don't want to be late.'

And he started the motor again, followed by the pilot of the dinghy behind them who'd stopped alongside to find out what was happening. They were running the engine at full power to catch up with those ahead of them who, not having noticed the incident, had continued on their way. The rest of the passengers remained silent, torn between wanting to go after the smugglers and the desire to lambast the mutineers who'd almost wrecked their dream. The two armed men kept their eyes riveted on the rebels and their guns drawn until they reached the ship.

Semhar and Shoshana stayed quiet, too, communicating only through the pressure of their intertwined hands. The dinghies had picked up their earlier speed and made up for the lost time, now back at the distance between them and those ahead. Gradually, the two friends saw a dot on the horizon grow larger, occasionally vanishing after a dip in the waves, before coming back in sight, bigger and closer. It was in fact the ship mentioned by the dinghy's pilot. Between the trip and the mutiny they'd spent at most an hour getting there.

The dinghies lined up one at a time against the side of the ship, an ocean-going trawler of about thirty meters. The embarkment was done via a boarding ladder of rope and wood, requiring a little time. The not so quick were simultaneously scolded and knocked about. They had to pick up speed. '*Yallah! Yallah!* No fucking around!' The moment they stepped on board the traffickers reorganized them. Most of them went to the hold, down a metal ladder resting on the hatch. The others remained on deck, some up front, others in the back.

Preceding Semhar and Shoshana on the boarding ladder was an Arab family, a couple and their two daughters. The father went first with the younger girl in his arms, the older one in the middle, followed by the mother. Once on deck, she stopped in front of the opening, calmly rearranging her things and looking around for a place to sit, without any concern for those behind her still hanging on to the boarding ladder. Shoshana asked her to please move, they couldn't just stay there hanging on to the rope while others were waiting. The lady pretended not to hear, then not to understand. When Shoshana repeated her request, adding a gesture, the Arab woman gave her a nasty look and, in English to make sure the *zenjiyeh* would clearly understand:

'But monkeys are good at that, aren't they?'

Shoshana gave her a withering look, making a high-pitched sound that in her language signaled she was getting ready to attack, to pull the bitch's hair until she was holding a clump of it in her hand. She wasn't going to be insulted without reacting. As a child at school, in the playground, she'd made kids eat dust more than once over less than this. One of the smugglers arrived just in time to ask the lady to free up the opening—'it's in everyone's interest to move things along, dear lady'—thereby putting an end to the spat. Once the boarding was done, the dinghies turned back with the pilots and the men in uniform. They didn't even turn around to see the trawler get started and move off in the direction of Lampedusa. Force of habit, no doubt.

BETWEEN HOLD AND DECK

THE DECISION TO SET SAIL so far from Sabratha was in line with a tacit pact between the organizers and the local authorities: to permit the latter to keep up appearances for the European Union, which accused them of doing nothing to stem the tide of refugees to its shores. Before, the dinghies would leave from neighboring beaches, or even directly from the harbor, right under the nose of the coastguard. No longer. Hence the embarkation off the coast of the town that, for so many months, had been the theater of Semhar and Shoshana's disappointments. Night had fallen and a soft glow spread across the Mediterranean. The trawler's wake rippled in the light of the moon that, as it made its way slowly across the sky, seemed to be following the ship. A cool wind was blowing from the north, forcing the travelers clustered together on deck to take out blankets, sweaters, or padded jackets.

The ship was filled to the brim. More than seven hundred and fifty people as would later be learned, separated on the basis of the price they'd paid for the crossing. The majority, including Semhar and Shoshana, were relegated to the hold. Sub-Saharans for the most part—*human cargo* as one of their "handlers" had baptized them—piled one on top of the other. Like unprofitable cattle.

By a strange coincidence, the passengers on deck were Arabs, largely from the Middle East and the Maghreb. A few very rare privileged individuals had found shelter on a hideaway bed with a foam rubber mattress in the two narrow cabins right behind that of the captain. They were already going to sleep, shielded from the wind and the shrill voices of their peers, which were barely audible, anyway. The ones outside were conversing in the various accents and special characteristics of the Arabic language that, over the centuries, had branched out through these regions of the world. In one area it sounded harsh, elsewhere it resembled the softness of a caress, like the breeze swirling around its speakers. A handful of Blacks completed the number of travelers on deck. Did they come from these same countries or from south of the Sahara like Semhar and Shoshana? Other than physical appearance, nothing could help determine their geographic origin. On the other hand, one thing was certain: they'd paid a stiff price, as had all the passengers on deck.

Before their departure, the organization had made sure that each and every one had settled their account and that the group on board corresponded to the disbursed amount. A huge cargo such as this required appropriate logistics, in particular that of traffickers blending in with the mass of refugees in order to diffuse or put down any possible conflict or mutiny, plus someone else whose role it was to make sure the crossing would go smoothly. Abandoning the vessel in the middle of the Mediterranean was out of the question, as would be done with smaller embarkations of less than a hundred people, with a compass the passengers generally couldn't read, and a satellite telephone to launch an SOS once they were in international waters. It had to do with the credibility and sustainability of the enterprise. In the case of the trawler of July 16th, 2014, the organization had left nothing to chance. Besides the hired hands who had benefitted from a sizeable rebate on the price of the passage in exchange for their services, the true master on board was in the fore cabin next to the captain. An enigmatic man of few words, it was he who'd given the captain the command to start the engines. He who had the satellite phone. He knew the drill, it was his third crossing, each time with a captain hired for the occasion. The Italian contacts at their destination had provided him with the number to launch an SOS in case of trouble before they reached the coast of Lampedusa or of an encounter with the Navy. They would take responsibility for removing him from the detention center and sending him back to Libya.

Among the travelers of no specific origin were Dima and her family—she who had clashed with Shoshana upon boarding. Once the ship was on its way and everyone had somehow managed to find a small space, wedged between two pairs of legs or against the guardrail, Dina's eyes fell upon the *znuje* sitting next to her. Besides putting her in a bad mood, this unwelcome proximity brought back to her the earlier scene when they were boarding. She was still having trouble dealing with the impertinence of the *zenjiyeh*. Her face of a, of a—she was looking for the word without daring to pronounce it, although she'd done so before—was imprinted on her memory. The black woman had better not cross her path again. She'd spit in her face.

Had it not been for the moon's brightness, she wouldn't have noticed the presence of *znuje* on deck. She thought they'd all been relegated to the hold. All the way to the end, Dima thought, fate wasn't sparing her anything. It was the first time she was in such close contact with them. She'd seen a few of them in the streets of Tripoli from a reasonable distance. She didn't have anything specific against these people, but their presence bothered her. They spoke too loudly and laughed too easily. As if there was anything to laugh about being in such close quarters, one on top of the other, like camels at a Bedouin market. Sniffing the smells of rotten fish from their armpits. Dima wondered if that was their natural odor.

Alhamdulillah, from time to time the sea breeze brought some relief to her nostrils. She preferred the cold, from which you could protect yourself, than those whiffs of pork. What would she say to her daughters when they woke up? How to explain to them, who were used to the very best from the day they were born, that they had to travel under these conditions? Even during the most difficult moments of the Aleppo bombings, they hadn't experienced such a calamity.

Moreover, in the cellars Dima would sleep soundly, surrounded by neighbors whom she trusted implicitly. Despite
power cuts and sometimes a lack of food, the girls would
come and go as they pleased. But here on the deck of the
trawler packed to overflowing it was another story.

Her husband seemed to think it was normal to be seated
amid *znuje*. He'd addressed one of them in English and, Dima
had to admit, she'd responded in perfect Arabic. For now, that
would make any private conversation with Hakim impossible.
A moment later she drew her daughters into the hollow of her
arms, halfway between their bottoms and their thighs. One
never knew what might happen with these heathens around
if, dead-tired, she were to let down her guard. Children sleep
deeply no matter where they are. And she clearly couldn't
count on her husband to watch them. He, Hakim, had too
much faith in people he didn't know. She prayed to Allah—
Blessed be His holy name—not to let her drop off to sleep
so she could keep an eye on her most precious possessions.

Among the voices that rose in the night, Dima recognized
Libyan accents. The forced month-long stay in Tripoli had,
at least, made that possible. She always did have an ear for
music. For years, as a little girl and an adolescent, she'd studied music, practiced the piano. With greater determination
she could have made a career as a soloist. It had certainly
helped her to learn English and a little French with astonishing ease, while her classmates could barely put two words
together in either language. The voices began to lull her,
taking over from the gibberish of her nearby neighbors. She
let the pleasant music of the Arabic sounds carry her off. All

the more when her ears began to make out some Syrian tones that, in contrast to this journey to another place, traced a line back to her childhood, the land of her birth, the treasures left behind. But she quickly pulled herself together, this wasn't the moment to lower her guard.

★

In the back of the hold below, Shoshana was prey to other feelings. She couldn't let go of her anger at the thought of her row with the Arab woman. Really, who did she think she was, that floozy? She would have scratched her eyes out if the smuggler hadn't come to put an end to it. For a moment, her spirit was full of rage. Then other less irate thoughts had taken over, to which she was more vulnerable. Contrary to Semhar, who'd spent part of her journey to Libya locked in a container, she'd been lucky enough to travel out in the open throughout the journey. Stuck, cramped, piled up, swallowing dust, facing the scorching heat and the cold of the desert, but the sky had always been visible. Day and night. The only time she'd traveled 'locked up' was during the leg in the bush taxi that took them to Abuja. And even then, she had nothing to complain about. She had a seat near the window, and could stick out her arm, and even her head at times, through the lowered glass. As a result she didn't need to ask the driver to stop under some pretext or other. Thereafter, *Baruch Hashem*, she'd always traveled in the open air. Until tonight.

As soon as the ship left, she began to feel sick. First, the unbearable din. In the chaos of the embarkation, she'd landed not far from the motor whose noise made any conversation with Semhar impossible. Even less with the One who must not be named. Of course, she prayed—at least, she tried to—within the silence of her head and heart. But the rumbling of the motor kept her from finding the right pace and the path to Hashem. And there were people yelling loudly just trying to hear each other. It was hard for them not to talk. No doubt, they wanted to make believe they were taking a trip like any other. Or it was how they tried to shrug off their fear of crossing to the unknown. All the voices, all the mixed languages, created a nameless cacophony that collided with the floor of the deck above her head before coming back to her, amplified by a thousand clangs and intonations.

And then there were the smells. The harsh, heavy, nauseating smell of the gasoline blending with the odors of rotten fish still stuck to the framework of the hold. To every plank. Every crack. Even if washed with bleach for days on end, it would still remain saturated. Its perfume was finished off with the rancid whiffs of bodies, the mammoth breath of many because they hadn't brushed their teeth or from chomping on the acid reflux that hunger caused. Shoshana was all too familiar with it, not having had anything to eat since the revolting broth at lunch. Hard to get away from these odors. The passengers were glued to one another in an inextricable tangle. Moving proved to be impossible, not unless a titanic effort were made to extract oneself from the mass of bodies, step over them, trample on others, children, women, and men, fused into a sordid lack of privacy. Air came into the hold via the left-open hatch, but it wasn't enough to overcome this much stench.

The sense of suffocation was all the more powerful because Shoshana had always been claustrophobic. She very quickly felt trapped in spaces that were too confined without any chance of getting out in case of danger. The sense of being choked. An invisible weight would constrict her chest, tighten her ribcage. As it did now. Her hands were clammy, hot flashes welling up all over her body. Drops of sweat stood out on her forehead, her neck, dripped down her spine. Her heart started to race like a thoroughbred released into nature after weeks of being locked up in a one-by-two meter pen. She imagined it coming out of her open throat, as she gasped for air. If only she could climb out of the hold and get outside, till her heart slowed and its beat became regular again.

The first time this happened to her she must have been nine or ten years old. She was playing with some friends. She'd ended up in a cave with two of them. Everything was fine going in. They were so excited that it seemed as if they were sucked in by the mystery of the bowels of the earth. Who knew what they might find? But when they decided to turn back, it was impossible to find their way out. They were turning in circles for a good fifteen minutes, each one of which seemed like an hour to her. Rachel couldn't stop joking around while their friend, whose name she no longer remembered, took great delight in frightening them; maybe it was a boy's way of hiding his own fear. Shoshana's heart had started pounding wildly, like the ever more frenetic rhythm of women pounding grain. She felt caught in a niche with no way out, swept away by a strong sense of oppression that the cave's darkness intensified. As if the tightness of the place and its obscurity were the reverse side of the same stifling fabric. She'd started howling, panic-stricken, incapable of getting hold of herself. Her friends told her she was a wimp before, overcome with fear, they began to holler as well. A few minutes later, guided by their screams, the others outside ended up finding them and guiding them back out.

She was close to having the same feeling, there in the hold, enclosed amid hundreds of male and female bodies even more desperate than she, to the point of even bringing children with them into this hell. Some of the women were still nursing babies, who were perhaps products of being raped along the way, in the desert, in the warehouses. In an attempt to escape the sense of asphyxiation, she kept her eyes riveted on the hatch that showed a ray of moonlight, soft and warm like a laser beam. The luminous gleam crossed the crowd on deck, then the darkness of the hold, and settled on Semhar and Shoshana's little duo. The light played with their shadows as the ship progressed. It brought Shoshana some relief, the air she needed, the freedom and light required to be able to continue the journey. Without imploding. Without feeling her heart retreat inward, drawn in by the void.

Although not claustrophobic, Semhar, too, had focused on the intangible glow. As if the evening star wanted to guide them toward their destination. She looked for it in the small square of sky that came into her view. For a moment she thought she noticed a milky crescent until it hid from her gaze, like a mischievous child. But the glow stayed with them. Since their departure Semhar had said very little. To make time go by, she thought about her friend Meaza who had never come back. She refused to put a label on her disappearance. It would have made her feel as if she were leaving behind any possibility of seeing her again. Perhaps, she kept hoping, Christ would bring them face to face again one day. Wherever she would then be. The two had promised to walk side by side to the altar at each other's weddings. To be the godmother of each other's first-born child. Semhar also though about Meaza's fiancé, of whom she'd had no further news. About her parents with whom she hadn't spoken for a long time. Her brothers, one of whom loved to fish and at this very moment was perhaps at sea with their father. They must be sick with worry. What she wouldn't give to hear their voices. To reassure them. And herself.

Now Rachel absorbed Semhar's mind. A blessing she was, that Nigerian girl, whose presence she missed here on the ship with them. She would have found the words to make the ambiance in the hold less deadly, bring the missing light down there. She would have made everybody sing and dance, would have told them: 'Shit, you're alive. Think of those who couldn't leave or who died on the way. So, come on, shake those black butts of yours.' She'd had three months to get to know that ball of optimism. She'd inspired such energy, just as Meaza knew how to do.

For now, it was Shoshana who was by her side. The two girls, less chatty than their respective friends, were able to communicate without talking. They'd been holding hands ever since they came down into the hold. Like children trying to comfort each other. Semhar felt Shoshana's broad, firm, imposing buttocks against her own. Her reserves, as she called them, which even so had suffered from the lack of food these last few months. It made her smile. Shoshana would like to have shared a bit of it with her friend, whose own behind was so emaciated. So much so that in Eritrea, where women weren't always very round, some had baptized her 'cockroach bottom'. Now, since the beginning of the trek that Semhar could barely remember, it was even more true.

Indeed, what day, what date was it? She couldn't tell. She figured she'd find out upon arrival. When she would finally escape from the smugglers' claws. That's when she would set the clock of her life once again. Of course, she wouldn't be able to catch up with the days, weeks, months that were lost in the quest for a better tomorrow. But she promised herself she'd make the most of it. Live it up. While she waited, she was determined to move forward, like the ship. To look straight ahead. She let herself be drawn in by the ray of the moon passing through the hatch and across the dust to envelop her in its luminous glow. Slightly warm, and reassuring. While the trawler continued its journey toward that elsewhere of which she'd never stopped dreaming. And which she hoped above all was just the final leg before reaching Europe. Before reaching solid ground where she could finally drop the anchor of her youth.

FIRST BLOWS

PROBLEMS BEGAN in the middle of the night, after a few hours sailing on a Mediterranean that until then had been as calm as a lake. The cramped hold and poor ventilation had been the main concerns of the cargo before then. 'So far, so good,' Shoshana thought, mesmerized by her moonbeam. Her heart had given her a little reprieve. As for the passengers on deck, if they shared the same lack of privacy as those below, they also had to deal with a gradually colder wind. But most of them were equipped for it. And then, there were words around, keeping them warm. Words reverberating confusedly through the July night. Words that were whispered, vacillating, voluble, tumultuous, carried by unwavering voices steadily gaining the upper hand over the others. In the semi-darkness of the deck, Dima focused on identifying accents so she wouldn't fall asleep: Saudi, Moroccan, Palestinian,

Tunisian, Syrian—those she heard most frequently as the ship advanced. Bright, self-assured tones, quite distinct one from the other. It seemed to Dima there were two Moroccans and three Tunisians. At one point the sky was so clear that she managed to make out faces to go with the voices.

The first problems arose before the moon suddenly vanished behind the clouds. As if it were a matter of cause and effect between the moon's vanishing and the subsequent troubles. In the meantime, Dima had checked out a small group of seven or eight individuals who looked perfectly normal, bordering on the ordinary. Quite young, however, except for one who seemed well into his thirties. The others might be between twenty and twenty-five, no more. Three of them attracted Dima's attention. The first because of his face, fully covered with a luxuriant black beard in clear contrast to his prematurely white hair. The second, fresh, chubby and blond, and the third, sporting an adolescent mustache, could have almost been her sons if she'd gotten an earlier start. They'd taken shelter not far from the hatch. Carried on the sea breeze, snatches of their conversation reached Dima with some consistency. For some reason or other, the captain seemed to be in a hurry to reach their destination. He was swallowing the miles at the speed of a regatta, giving the ship an odd cadence, something between a slight swaying and a cushioned sliding.

★

Shoshana was the first to realize the moon had disappeared. It was her only link with the open air. And the moon vanished without any warning, plunging the hold into total darkness, like a schoolboy having a good time playing a cheap joke on her. Anxiety went up a notch, even among those who hadn't had the advantage of catching the radiant beam directly. The tension became palpable. Without meaning to, Shoshana squeezed Semhar's knuckles, almost crushing them. The young Eritrean got the full impact of her friend's stress. With utmost delicacy she moved the hand away from her own and placed it on her forearm instead, using a bit of pressure to let her know she was there, to calm her a little. It reminded her of moments in her childhood when, like baby animals in dire straits, her brothers, twins, would seek refuge in her arms when there was a power failure, or during a great thunder and lightning storm. She'd rely on a wealth of imagination to trick them out of their anxiety.

Shoshana gave her the same feeling. Semhar found it hard to believe, considering the Nigerian's strong build. Moreover, she wouldn't hesitate using it to impress the others and protect her from the aggression of the girls in the warehouse. But here in the dark hold, fear was making her sweat so profusely she seemed like a forlorn animal, at the heart of a thousand perils she saw coming at her from every direction. Semhar caressed her friend's arm, put a hand on her back in an affectionate gesture, like a mother reassuring her baby. She felt like saying 'I'm here' but did nothing of the sort. Instead she whispered the twenty-third Psalm in her ear: 'Yea, though I walk through the valley of the shadow of death, I will fear no evil: for thou art with me; thy rod and thy staff they comfort me.' Semhar thought that it had to be more or less the same in her Bible, perhaps with a few nuances in the translation. She felt the pressure decrease a little, Shoshana's shortness of breath diminish, finding an almost normal rhythm again. So King David's words had been useful, Semhar realized, very pleased with herself.

That's when the first lurches began—at the very moment that Shoshana was about to confront her demons, look them straight in the eyes, tell them that her God and her dream of a better life would gulp them down in one mouthful, just as Aaron's rod, changed into a serpent, had swallowed those of Pharaoh's sorcerers. With one punch the sea catapulted the boat onto heights that, from the bottom of the hold, Shoshana imagined might be head to head with the top of Kilimanjaro, before sucking it down with the same force to the water's depths. Laden with terror, a long-drawn-out 'ooooh' came pouring out from more than four hundred throats, cleaving the darkness. In the time it took for the clamor to subside the vessel had already been lifted to the crest of an even higher mountain, then driven down into an endless fall. Howling filled the hold, while the ship, indifferent, continued its momentum on the roller coaster. At times it would waltz on top of a peak, then be carelessly thrown to the bottom of a trough.

Shoshana was among the most terrified. Added to her fear of confinement, it was the first time she'd been at sea. Should the boat ever capsize, the ridiculous life vest she was carrying around her neck, with her name on it, would have trouble keeping afloat a chunk of lead like herself. She'd used part of her hidden money to buy it. Some passengers didn't have any vest at all, having no cash to buy one from the smugglers. Far from reassuring her, the vests had increased her anxiety. She saw them as a sign of inevitable shipwreck. Otherwise, if the vessel were so stable, why would they have been suggested to the passengers? The news reports of the countless boats that had gone down in the Mediterranean with all hands on board plagued her mind. Very quickly, they were joined by the images of dazed survivors that had been shown on every television screen in the world. Her pulse went back to its galloping marathon. Looking for comfort, she shielded herself with the traveler's prayer, which she soundlessly chanted to herself: 'Save us […] on the trip, […] from all kinds of punishments that rage, and come to the world.'

The trawler continued its harrowing course, scaling and hurtling down the moving mountains. Sometimes it seemed stuck, cornered between opposing waves and winds. Tenacious. The first refusing to give way to the second. Then they heard creaking on every side. Like an old nag, too heavily laden, so its bones refused to carry on. The hold was now one huge uproar, magnified in an array of sounds and languages. Sobs. Onomatopoeia, bereft of any meaning other than fear. Prayers offered in many different languages, imploring deities that were equally diverse: God, Allah, Hashem, Ashiakle, Olokun, Birkuar, Ngaan… Under the assault of the swell, bodies were tossed about only to land farther down on top of other bodies.

Miraculously, Shoshana and Semhar managed to remain embedded between the two beams where they'd found a place at the start. The agitation was so great that even Semhar was growing anxious, even though she wasn't afraid of the water at all. Her father had insisted that his children learn to swim. 'So they can race against the fish,' he'd joked. Her mother, on the other hand, looked unfavorably on her daughter, already a tomboy, skinny-dipping in the Red Sea, under the eyes of all those in the city of Massoua who wore pants. For, if she did this as a child, it would mean that she'd keep it up later on when she'd be old enough to marry.

'First of all, she's not naked,' her father had responded, 'but in a swimsuit. And then, she shouldn't be handicapped just because she's a girl. You have to be able to count on yourself before you can expect another person to help you. Besides, as the oldest she must set the example for the twins.'

Despite his wife's grumbling, her father had held his ground. 'What I'm telling you is valid under any circumstance,' he kept repeating to his daughter and so Semhar had become a veritable sea creature. She in turn taught her friends to swim if their parents saw nothing wrong with it. Once they learned, she'd dive with them from the pier when there were no boats at anchor, having left for the high seas laden with their cargoes of dreams. She and her friends would collect all sorts of objects from the depths, emerging with clumps of rubbish tossed in by human hands or carried down by the under-water current; sometimes small crabs who'd managed to survive down there, who knows how.

After a few seemingly interminable minutes the Mediterranean subsided to the calm of a placid lake. But the lull wasn't to last for long. As if the sea had rested just enough to regain its strength. To come back and thrust itself with greater fury against anything that stood in its way. The cargo were trying to regain their spirits when the ship began to dance again, starting with a slanting motion, tilting to one side, then the other. Its carcass was creaking all over, threatening to split apart at any moment. Still, it resolutely continued to chart its course across the vast body of water, resisting the assaults of ever more ferocious waves.

The hold was plunged into total darkness as soon as the moon was gone. Gusts of wind rushed in through the hatch, merging with the wails of the passengers above that could be clearly heard. 'They're afraid, too,' Shoshana thought. A sign, according to her, that the situation outside was a lot more serious than they could imagine below. Where they were buried alive. Without a sign from above. From the deck or from heaven. Her heart began to settle again, drawn in by the void. She felt she was going to faint. The only thing she wanted was to go out on deck to catch a deep breath of fresh air. But there were too many people, too much crying and sobbing all around her. She was trapped. A ball of voiceless agony, she searched for words, for a liberating breath, but couldn't find any. She was clutching on to her friend like a drowning woman to a life buoy. A few more seconds and she would faint.

The shouting from the deck intensified. Voices were being raised asking the captain to return to the point of departure. This wasn't how they'd envisioned the journey. They didn't want to leave under these conditions. In the middle of nowhere. Without a grave or a prayer. Without a last farewell to their loved ones. Without the wake interspersed with the ululations of the choir of mourners. Dima was one of them. They should have insisted more, until one of the European countries ended up by granting them the damned visa. Since there was no attendant at hand, she took it out on her husband. 'Do something. No, really, do something, for God's sake,' she repeated like a refrain without truly believing in it herself. She knew that poor Hakim wasn't up to ordering the two men in the control cabin around. Nor to appeasing the waves tall as five-storey buildings crashing into the hull, violently raining down on them each time, finally waking up the girls. The older one asked: 'What's happening, *yom*?' Her father's 'It's nothing, *habibi*' didn't convince the younger one. She began to cry, sobbing her heart out, mingling with the sobs, prayers, and desperate appeals of the passengers on the deck.

Down below, each jackhammer of the waves against the hull magnified the distress of the cargo. Shoshana managed to put a hand, clammy with fear, into her backpack and pull out her *hamsa*. If she had to perish, better do it with her hamsa, her fetish. In any case, in the dark no one was likely to identify the object. She held it clenched in one hand while the other stayed glued to Semhar's. The young Eritrean herself didn't stop kissing the crucifix around her neck. All the while the boat would lie flat on one side, straighten up under the thrust of the gigantic waves, before shifting onto its other side. Planks and joists were groaning ever more loudly, the sounds telling of the ship's struggle – a David against the Goliath of the Mediterranean. But they refused to give up. Or so it seemed to those below. The attacks of the waves against the hull persisted. Earsplitting. Until they muffled the passengers' cries. There was no longer any doubt. The water would soon shatter the planks and gush in over the cattle. Dragging them down to the bottom. The boat would sink and not one of them would survive.

MUTINY

AMID THE FURIOUS HOWLING of the wind and the ship's Saint Vitus dance, the most painful thing for Dima was the shrieking of her daughters which tore her insides to shreds. She would have given her life to reassure them, see their faces brighten up with a smile as large as the Aleppo sun, not this grimace created by her own helplessness. Having no solution, she begged Allah: 'Oh Allah, there is no ease other than what You make easy, if You please, You make the difficult easy.' May He, in His magnificence, please calm the fiery zeal of the Mediterranean! But the clamoring of the other passengers was complicating the task, both for Allah and Dima, who simply couldn't concentrate on sending her prayer up to Him. How could she calm the children when the adults right next to them were incapable of keeping their composure?

And, instead of fulfilling his duty as spouse and father and comforting his wife and daughters, her chicken of a husband was paralyzed with fear. To think she believed she'd entered married life with a man, a real man. That she could count on him under any circumstances. That he would have faced the fires of Hell to protect his family. And here, when she needed him most, she found herself face to face with a coward incapable of worrying about his own progeny, withered with panic. Like an old empty goatskin forgotten in the sun. The disgust she suddenly felt by far outweighed her wanting to vomit. She held her girls tightly under her arms like a mother hen with her chicks, as if she could thereby spare their young lives in case of a shipwreck, prevent them from sinking into the abyss. Her grip was so fierce that little Shayma's seasickness and fear of a shipwreck disappeared: 'Mama, you're hurting me,' she said. 'I'm so sorry, *rouhi*. So sorry, my love.' It was all she could say in response. While the other one, the weakling, continued to sit with his face down on his chest, back stooped over, head leaning on his arms, clutching his knees under his chin. 'No balls,' Dima chided between her teeth, far from her usual vocabulary of a well-behaved young woman.

Around her, cries and prayers rang out. The men were not to be outdone, their wailing covered that of the women and children. Pitting themselves in fits and starts against the racket of the wind, issuing orders and advice, one as useless as the other. Aware that they were faking it, they shouted all the louder. Or perhaps they believed their male hollering had the power to calm the squalls. Masses of water was washing over the deck, whipping the bodies with the regularity of a malicious metronome. Reinforcing the anxiety of the travelers, the clouds were hiding the moon, then would sometimes let it reappear just enough to expose tense faces, flesh drenched and chilled to the bone. When the ship went down for the nth time, one of the men next to Dima, who was tensely focused on protecting her brood, was catapulted toward her. By reflex, the man hung onto her neck and their faces touched. Just for a split second. No more. The *zenji* could apologize with words and gestures all he wanted, Dima was almost as disgusted with him as with her husband's spinelessness.

'What's wrong with you?' she screamed, horrified. 'Take your filthy paw off me or I'll tell my husband to chuck you overboard.'

She'd drawn the only weapon at her disposal. Aware, nevertheless, that in case of an attack she could only count on herself. And on Allah. Fully focused on his own terror, Hakim hadn't noticed anything. Had he even heard her shout her loathing at the black man's face? Dima no longer knew whether she'd rebuked him in Arabic or English. Maybe both. In any event, he understood. He must have grasped the determination in her voice and her threatening look whose lightning flashes had ripped through the darkness on the deck to strike him down. As if bitten by a poisonous snake the Sub-Saharan pulled his hand off instantly, a hand he was ready to place on Dima's shoulder in a gesture of apology to go with his words of regret. For an instant, Dima felt comforted for having spat her bile in his face, protecting her virtue, not staying fixated on her nausea and on the fear that was tightening her stomach into knots.

Dima didn't enjoy the respite for very long. Her harsh words were still hanging in the air when a group of people materialized in the middle of the deck. About a dozen of them, mostly Arabs, judging by their looks. The moon's reappearance allowed Dima to recognize two of them as *znuje*, one the poor individual who'd tried to take advantage of the boat's jolts to kiss her. They were standing with legs wide apart, holding each other's arms to keep their balance. The one at the end of the chain managed to grab the cabin in the center with one hand, waking up its occupants in the process. The others hung onto him like mussels onto their rocks. 'We want to speak with the captains,' one of them said, not really knowing which of the two men was in charge. 'With no one else.' Fear and determination stood out in their eyes. They demanded to be brought back to the point of departure. 'If the captain doesn't turn back, we'll all die,' the shameless *zenji* said. There was still time, the boat had raised anchor only a few hours earlier, they were closer to Libya than to Lampedusa, their destination. They swayed their way to the steering post, moving like sailors on solid land, passing over legs and bodies, shoving those who were in the way, in spite of themselves. Their demands met with the approval of other equally panicked passengers, who began to scream at the top of their voice:

'They're right, they're right! We paid to look for a new life, not die at sea. We want to go back to Libya.'

Their cries clashed with the howling of the wind and the waves' attacks against the hull. Dima hesitated a moment then joined her voice to theirs. She, too, was fed up with it. With the conditions of the journey, with the rolling that turned her stomach as if she were in the first weeks of pregnancy, with the unruly sea. She'd been less scared hiding like a rat in her basement in Aleppo as bombs were raining down above their heads. At least she was on dry land. She could use the breaks in the fighting to go out and breathe and stretch her legs. Here it was impossible to go anywhere. She was caged, literally and figuratively, in the middle of a raging Mediterranean, surrounded by people who didn't exactly smell like lavender. Since they couldn't ask their father, the girls asked their mother why she wanted to go back to Libya with these people, whether she didn't want to take them to Europe anymore, see all the exotic things she'd told them about. Snow, bears, and all the rest. Their questions broke her heart, but Dima couldn't afford the luxury of weeping. She answered, yes but not now, another time, my darlings. By plane, and then she joined the choir of voices again.

Throughout this time the thirty-meter long trawler was being shaken like a nutshell, its moving parts coming loose, hurtling back down into the din of water, the screeching of the wind, and the clamoring of the passengers. Tons of salty seawater came to rinse deck and bodies at regular intervals. One had to hang on with all one's might to anything within reach not to be flung overboard. Despite the seething of the elements, the group of mutineers kept moving, gradually approaching the steering post. Just then other men emerged from the edges of the hatch to block their way. Three of them were the guys who'd been such loudmouths from the start, the man with the heavy beard and white hair, the fair-haired boy, and the adolescent with the mustache. Perhaps there were other members of the pack, but Dima couldn't identify them all.

The bearded one asked the troublemakers to go back. With a peremptory gesture, he signaled them to return to their places, his arm outstretched, index finger pointing to the spot the rebels had left. He looked like he was yelling, but they couldn't hear him clearly because of the surging winds. Dima only picked up snatches of words. The mutineers disregarded the order and continued to move ahead, swaying with the rolling of the ship. The band of smugglers moved in front of them like a wall, the two groups now face to face, challenging each other's gaze, spitting words at each other's faces that couldn't have been friendly. Indifferent to human bickering, the storm kept raging. As if to cut short the exchange which had gone on too long for his taste, the bearded white-haired man pulled a knife from his sleeve, its blade a good eight inches long, shimmering in the moonlight. His sidekicks then produced their own weapons, which they had been hiding behind their backs: iron bars, a rudimentary bludgeon, a baseball bat. The rebels recoiled.

'Now, back to your place,' the man said in a strong Palestinian accent. 'We want to keep moving. And fuckers like you aren't going to stop us. We didn't come all this way for nothing. You'd better not get in our way. Take this as a piece of friendly advice.'

The mutineers understood from their looks they wouldn't back down. Worse, they seemed prepared for anything, perhaps even for murder so that the vessel could continue on its course.

Behind them, the others who wanted to go back were raising their voices over the elements. 'We want to go back to Libya. We want to go back to Libya.' In English and in Arabic. To make sure the smugglers would understand. As if all together they'd be able to change the situation, to convince the bearded one and his crew. Like the dozens of other frightened passengers, Dima was now standing, too. Trying to keep her balance on the lurching deck, holding her daughters by their shoulders to keep them from going overboard. Having materialized from his inertia, Hakim tried unsuccessfully to bring her back to reason.

'Don't get involved with this, Dima.'

'You, just be quiet. You're just waking up,' she thrust at him, flashes of disgust in her eyes, then continued to shout along with the rebels.

Encouraged by so many determined voices, the mutineers tried to force the barricade. They thought those facing them would certainly understand that all they wanted was to save their skin. They were wrong. The bearded guy grabbed one of the West Africans by the neck and before he had time to react, drove the knife into his chest. Done with the skill of a butcher tackling the animal he'd later carve up with a similar lack of feeling. The African brought his hand to his chest and sank to the ground. The mutineers were petrified. Mouth agape and eyes wide-open, thunderstruck. For more than a minute not a word came from their lips. The ones who'd witnessed the scene, Dima among them, had become mute, too, towing the silence of the others behind them. A deathly silence that, just for a moment, the stormy weather was unwilling to interrupt. When the first shock had passed, most of them went back to their place. The bearded one signaled to his cronies with a nod before he slowly wiped the blade on his sleeves. The fair-haired one and the adolescent picked up the African's body, one by the legs, the other underneath the armpits and, under the winds' obscene applause, threw him into the now raging water.

PART TWO

SEMHAR

Where a former guerilla fighter, turned into a sandal-wearing, paranoid and alcoholic watchdog, took hostage an entire population, increasing the number of disciplinary camps, the military service, targeted and random disappearances, until his country was transformed into an immense penal colony and the strongest were driven to abandon the shores of the Red Sea.

Do not fear any of those things which you are about to suffer. Indeed, the devil is about to throw some of you into prison, that you may be tested, and you will have tribulation [...]. Be faithful until death, and I will give you the crown of life.

REVELATIONS, 11-10

THE DECISION

IT HAPPENED ONE SUNDAY, Semhar remembered it very well. Although she usually wouldn't miss a Sunday service for anything in the world, she couldn't attend mass. She came from a family whose Orthodox Christian roots dated back on both sides from time immemorial. A heritage she applied with a simple unshakable faith. Between questioning her parents and looking at the photographs in the family album that was kept at the bottom of the cabinet with precious objects, she could recall every detail of the day of her baptism, chrismation, and communion all during one same ceremony. One of the prints showed her in her mother's arms in a flounced white dress with a Peter Pan collar, surrounded by her godfather and godmother, the admiring look of the three adults turned on her. It didn't include her father, who was behind the camera. Her favorite one showed all three of them: her papa, her mother, and herself, sitting between them, her face exuding a luminous smile, contrasting with the solemnity of the event. She already had the bearing of a fragile but determined reed, one that no wind could break. According to her mother, she didn't cry at all that day. Not even when the priest immersed her three times in the baptistry's water. Unlike the other babies, who'd bawled as if their throats were being slit, like that of the sacrificial lamb replacing Isaac on the pyre his father Abraham had prepared.

As a child, Sunday was a feast day for her. Easter weekend was a strange time: sad, because of the death of Christ, and beautiful because of his resurrection. A true fish in holy water. Then came adolescence, the age of awakening senses and interest in the other sex. Secret exchanges between girls, away from maternal ears. The age, too, of crazy ideas that, in the name of science, put into question the divinity of Christ as well as the mystery of the Holy Trinity. But these held no sway over her at all. Far from forsaking the path of her faith, she committed herself to it with even greater conviction, thereby living up to her nickname 'Toughy'. It had been given to her by neighborhood kids, during recess, at the playgrounds or fields of battle where she displayed her aggression on a daily basis, where she'd take on anyone stronger than she, girl or boy, returning to the attack as many times as necessary, taking the blows until she had the upper hand or her opponent gave up, tired of knocking her down. 'Stop, Toughy, I don't feel like beating you up anymore.' Thinking back to it, time had flown by with the speed of a snake in the desert. So fast it seemed someone else had lived that previous life in her skin.

Adolescence was still with her when she left to do her military service, like tens of thousands of young Eritreans, both girls and boys. The young dreaded this national service because of its indefinite duration. You know when you go in but you never know when you will come out. Officially, conscription lasted for a year and a half. In reality, however, everything depended on the country's strongman, in power since in 1993, when independence was gained from Ethiopia. Semhar's parents-to-be met that year and were just beginning to make plans for their future. From his office in Asmara, he, His Excellency Isaias Afewerki, decided on the academic direction of his conscripts. For some it was based on the needs of the State. For others on the results of the final exams that thousands of secondary school students like Semhar were taking at the Sawa military camp, in Eritrea's north-west, not far from the Sudanese border. Based also on the pleasure of Tsetse, the President's nickname because of his fondness for Mao Tse Tung and his tendency to lull the people to sleep. But this mockery was uttered quietly, even within the privacy of one's home. In short, one might find oneself training to be a geography teacher instead of taking the course in literature or science that you wanted to pursue, but which was considered too subversive by the authorities.

When Semhar left for Sawa, from Massoua, the fourth largest city in the country, where she was born and had been raised in a close-knit family, she'd dreamed of becoming an elementary school teacher. She wanted to teach children, girls in particular, open their eyes to the beauty of the world that she only knew from books, television, and the Internet, when one had access to it. And from the ships she saw arriving and leaving the port of Massoua, laden with her little girl's dreams. A childhood spent on the shores of the Red Sea had contributed to feeding her wild fantasies about crossing the sea without getting her feet wet. She dreamed of instilling her students with a sense of duty, pride in being a woman, making them understand that, without women, the country, the planet would be bland. They were the salt of the earth of which Christ spoke. Without them, it would be as flavorless as bad food that you'd want to spit out. She believed in this with all the fury of her tenacity.

After her arrival in Sawa, Semhar did everything she could to gain the right to live her dream rather than to polish Kalashnikovs, taking them apart and putting them back together again in a barracks in the middle of nowhere. Or to carry out routine tasks that served only to keep the youth under close supervision. With her characteristic determination, she worked like a madwoman, was at the beck and call of her superiors. Even if it meant looking like an ass-kisser to the other conscripts, being subjected to their surreptitious bullying, in addition to that already suffered from the non-commissioned officers. She'd bite her tongue and keep going, keeping her eyes on her dream of becoming a teacher.

It was at Camp Sawa that the rather solitary Semhar fell under the charms of Meaza. The lightning strike of friendship was reciprocal. She was approaching nineteen. Her friend was three years older, had managed to repeat her grade twice, a widespread practice in the country, with the objective of delaying the draft. Secondary school students were past masters in the art of repeating grades, even falsifying birth certificates with the sole purpose of deferring the fateful call. One day, soldiers descended on the high school of Asmara, the capital, where Meaza was studying, and took away the draft dodgers. Destination Sawa. Meaza couldn't alert her family until she was at the camp. Ever since meeting in class where they sat next to each other, the two girls never left each other's side. Meaza admired Semhar's discipline, her ability to avoid trouble. She saw the tenacity that lay behind the facade of the good little soldier. On her end, Semhar was fascinated by her friend's sense of resourcefulness and by all the things she knew about boys.

Meaza had a fiancé, Dawit, who was three years her senior. Having already passed through Sawa, he was deployed at the border with Ethiopia, as the conflict between the two countries hadn't stopped since Independence. He'd already been in the service for five years! He took advantage of his rare leaves to visit his sweetheart in Asmara, with the blessings of their respective families. Meaza's enlistment cut cruelly into the fragile equilibrium of their contact. To compensate, the two love birds exchanged texts as long as rivers, adorned with emojis of all kinds and colors. Dawit's picture was displayed on the screen of her cell phone as soon as Meaza turned it on. 'Look, look how adorable he is,' she'd crow. 'Thank God there aren't too many girls where he's posted.'

From the day she first spoke of Dawit, Semhar discovered in Meaza a coy lover who couldn't put two sentences together without mentioning her fiancé. Any occasion was good enough to bring up his name. Dawit this, Dawit that. Her hand was always on her phone, waiting for a sign from him. And it vibrated day and night. When she was on guard duty, in the evening after lights out, despite the risk of harassment. One night Meaza missed being caught by the skin of her teeth, but an air-raid siren coming from who knows where got her out of trouble. Whether a breakdown or an exercise, no matter, in any event what she was sure of was that God watched with special care over lovers who were kept apart. Meaza sometimes exchanged letters with her fiancé in the traditional way, too, which she kept at the bottom of her kit, beneath her underwear. She'd take them out during a break, at rare moments of solitude, and would reread them to the point of ruining her eyes, a beatific smile on her lips.

Meaza was the first to raise the question with her friend. Truth be told, Semhar had already heard quite a few rumors in the streets of Massoua on the subject. Rumors spread in hushed tones, for the president spent a good part of the year on the shore of the Red Sea. Countless inhabitants of Massoua had a relative or a friend among the twenty percent of the population that had fled Eritrea. Like the animals in the Aesop fable, those who hadn't yet left were dreaming of doing so. Especially the young. Amanuel, a cousin of Semhar on her mother's side, had taken advantage of his military service in Sawa to cross the border, leaving his combat fatigues and Kalashnikov behind. She didn't know how Amanuel, with whom she'd grown up and shared a deep affection, had gone about it. Through the family, she knew that he had managed to get from Sudan to Europe and was now living in Sweden as a political refugee. So when Meaza spoke of it to Semhar when they were alone during guard duty far from inquisitive ears, she was hardly surprised.

She confessed to her friend that she and Dawit had already been putting money aside for quite a while to get the hell out of the country. They had almost saved up enough. Her fiancé had very unobtrusively established contact with a network of smugglers. Judged to be traitors of the fatherland, defectors paid a steep price if they were caught. More than one had disappeared without a trace. And even if they'd managed to cross to the other side, their family might be hounded. Amanuel's family had been in trouble with the intelligence service for quite a long time before they were finally left alone. Perhaps they'd grown tired. Perhaps bribery had bought their peace. Semhar had no idea. The day she arrived in Sawa, her superiors had assembled her and the other recruits in the camp's large courtyard to forewarn them. Desertions were too frequent not to be mentioned. Better to tackle the matter head-on. They warned that those with ideas of that sort in their head should know they were being watched and that chasing rainbows was a high stakes game.

In spite of the risks, it was worth it, Meaza said. Dawit and she were fed up wasting their youth on interminable military service, and what was worse, for wretched pay. Fed up with living in this open-air prison that was Eritrea, where innumerable roadblocks and special safe-conduct officials would check passage from one town to another. Fed up with seeing no future before them at all. That was the hardest to swallow. Knowing that every horizon was blocked, not having any means by which to turn things around, even after the long period of conscription. Hope should be the last thing to die, no? Here it was completely the reverse. In such surroundings what meaning could life have? There was rage in the voice of this mere slip of a woman, even more frail than Semhar, who was barely five feet tall.

'Don't forget you're a Christian,' Semhar said. 'For us Christians, following Christ's commandments is what gives life meaning. That's where I draw my determination from.'

'I'm not forgetting that, rest assured. But we'll leave if we must. Clearing one obstacle after another, like in a 100 meter hurdle,' the sports enthusiast answered, still careful to keep her voice down. As if anyone could hear them in the dark, in the middle of nowhere.

The most difficult obstacle, she continued, was keeping the project a secret from the family. Both to protect them from potential police abuses and to avoid any leaks. 'The less your loved ones know about it, the better it is for everyone.' She hated lying about it to her folks, even if only by omission. But they had to stay strong. In the long letters exchanged with Dawit, they recounted their daily lives, renewed their promises of eternal love, as do all young people their age. The serious things they spoke of to each other via WhatsApp. Text messages mentioning the matter were deleted as soon as they'd been read, and phone storage was meticulously cleared. She was even taking a risk by telling Semhar because her fiancé had made her swear on the Bible that she wouldn't talk to anyone about it.

'And the guy won't trust you anymore if he finds out, you know. And he would be right, wouldn't he? Anyway, Dawit deserves better. It's not easy to find someone who'll have a girl that's been in Sawa. Because of all the stories you hear; you get it, right?'

Not only had she betrayed him, she'd also broken an oath. 'But let your communication be, Yea, yea; Nay, nay: for whatsoever is more than these cometh of evil,' Christ said. But it was such a heavy secret to carry. 'You can't begin to imagine.' Too heavy to bear on her shoulders alone. As an Orthodox Christian like herself, she knew Semhar wouldn't give her away. That said, if her friend wanted to join them, she could mention it to Dawit, she supposed after a moment of reflection. Meaza was one of those people whose brain is in perpetual motion, who always need to have someone around with whom to share their ruminations. Incapable of living with silence, unless they were asleep. And even then, they'll often talk in their sleep. Of course, she'd pretend not to have said anything to Semhar so that Dawit wouldn't think she'd broken her word.

'Come with us, I'd like that. And then I won't be alone. It seems there are only guys coming along.'

That's how the craving for an elsewhere had begun to take root in Semhar's mind, fusing with her childhood dreams. She started thirsting for a place where her youth would be completely free to blossom, where she could pursue the studies to become the teacher she dreamed of, and not what Tsetse and the collegial committee in Sawa would impose on her. Who knows? Maybe she would find a soul mate there. They'd walk down the street hand in hand, as they did on television. She'd never had a real boyfriend, other than a shy, pimply boy at the Massoua high school, who'd grab any opportunity to talk to her while losing himself in her eyes. He looked serious and was occasionally funny, but never dared declare himself. Although she wouldn't have said no. Perhaps she scared the boys off, as she was told by the idol of the class, who bragged about her own multiple conquests.

'You don't realize it, but you scare them, Toughy. You're too serious, you do well in class. And besides, you never give up.'

Her desire to go somewhere else wouldn't have been sufficient to make her decide, were it not for the enormous uncertainty about the length of her military service. Some women could be there until the age of forty, unless they managed to get pregnant. For Semhar it was out of the question to give herself to the first comer just to extract herself from this vipers' nest. Family was too serious a matter to envision starting one with just anybody. That being the case, she had trouble imagining she'd come to the end of her service before she was old. She took her time thinking things through without giving in to Meaza's pestering: 'So, do I talk to my fiancé or not?' The day before her decision, she spent the entire night in prayer, while around her the whole dormitory slept. When reveille sounded at dawn, she had made up her mind. She would follow in the footsteps of the thousands of other young people who'd gone before her. Whether they'd come through Sawa or not. That morning she also knew that she'd see it through all the way to the end. No matter what happened. If need be, she'd be ready to deal with the consequences.

Meaza's experience had taught her that it was better not to bring up the subject with her parents in Massoua. Even less so with her younger fourteen-year-old twin brothers, who'd soon be drafted for their military service, unless they repeated a year in school, which was never more than a deferment. Then she thought about her cousin. It would take some diplomacy to get his telephone number without raising the suspicions of both families. However, once she did, they would speak regularly via WhatsApp. Amanuel promised to advance her the money she needed to depart. But, her cousin warned, she should know from the start that it wasn't going to be a picnic. Especially for a girl—he couldn't imagine making the journey as a young woman. He knew what he was talking about. Did she trust her contacts? 'That's really important, you know. Some people have no qualms about abandoning you or turning you in to save their own skin.' But he swore he'd help her.

It wouldn't hurt if, on her end, she could get some money together as well, in addition to what he'd send via Western Union. One could never have enough for the obstacle course that awaited her. Each stage had its share of jackals to buy off. The critical thing was not to carry all of your money on you, in case you got robbed on the way and had to go home with your tail between your legs, excuse the image, cousin. In addition to surely ending up behind bars for illegally crossing the border and actively participating in hurting the country's image in the eyes of foreigners. Toughy reassured him. She was headstrong, but she wasn't stupid. She'd be careful, if only to make sure he wouldn't lose his money.

DEPARTURE NIGHT

IT TOOK ALMOST A YEAR, from the day they first talked about it to the night between Saturday and Sunday when the two young women left to join Meaza's fiancé at the Sudanese border. It was imperative that they not rush, for fear of arousing any suspicions and ruining the plan, not to mention the serious consequences that would entail. All through the year, in cooperation with Dawit, a diehard fan of Che Guevara and guerilla warfare, they drew up their departure like a battle plan. Saw to every detail without leaving anything to chance. 'The slightest mistake can turn out to be fatal,' Dawit had told them via WhatsApp. To avoid making any, the two women had to be familiar with each of their patrols; the ones before and those after, should they need to negotiate with any peers. They should take only the bare necessities, 'because you have to be able to move very fast, run if need be'. He told them where to stash it, the exact moment to move into action, and their fallback plan in case of failure. 'You must always have a plan B,' Dawit insisted.

Despite her exemplary behavior during the long period of waiting, Semhar was given just one week in all for home leave. Partly due to her mute and obstinate refusal to give in to the advances of the corporal instructor who had made his interest in her blatantly clear. Her strategy throughout was to play the idiot, on the advice of Meaza who'd already been through the same thing. She had to avoid getting his back up, lest he feel wounded in his predator's pride. 'It's a well-known fact that wounded animals are the most dangerous,' Meaza said. Semhar was well aware that funny stuff was going on at Sawa. Girls who would yield under the bullying from one day to the next. Others who'd go on leave and, as if by chance, wouldn't come back. Still others who didn't give a damn, even put on airs, without it seeming to bother anyone. Dawit was aware of it too:

'So, keep a low profile. This really isn't the time to play at being bewildered virgins and bungle everything.'

Far from bringing her down, this new adversity continued to reveal Tenacity Semhar to herself. It was impossible to catch her out. Encouraged by Meaza's athleticism, she intensified her efforts during the challenging daily exercises, which she performed without complaint. The same went for her studies, which she'd always loved, anyway. Since she was a good student, maybe the lecher would leave her alone. For once, her hard work gained her the admiration of high-ranking superiors and led her instructor to ease up on her, so he'd steer clear of getting caught harassing her. Were such incidents to become known outside the camp, it would tarnish its image even more. An image already damaged in the foreign media, which was hostile to the commander-in-chief, thanks largely to the stories told by deserters who'd left to beg for asylum in every one of the world's capitals. The corporal knew the risks he'd run if he were to cause a scandal. However, he continued to keep an eye on her. One little slip-up, justifiable in the eyes of his chain of command, one loud laugh, one whispered word after lights out—resulted in one or even two hours of jogging under the sun. Semhar endured the punishments with a stoicism that won admiration from her dormitory mates. They also provided her with an incredible endurance that placed her among the front runners of the races every time. But always one step behind Meaza. Her friend made it a point of honor not to be second:

'You wouldn't get it into your head to beat your coach, after all.'

'One day I'll make it, you'll see,' Semhar would reply, seeing their healthy competition as a way to push her own limits.

'Not even in your dreams, got that? I can be just as tenacious as you when I knuckle down. Besides, it's the only area where I can beat you. You can bet that I won't let you embarrass me.'

The week in Massoua did her immense good, regardless of the long journey. Having left at dawn, it took a whole day to get to the capital and from there two more hours by bus before she reached the town of her birth in the middle of the night. Semhar spent many hours talking with the twins. One of them, Jacob, lived only for sports, and dreamed of competing with the greatest marathon runners on the planet, of bringing back the Olympic gold for Eritrea. As his hero, the Ethiopian Haile Gebrselassie, had done for his country. He could already imagine himself riding through the streets of Asmara in the backseat of a convertible, to the wild applause of a delirious crowd, girls throwing him scented handkerchiefs, before being received at Tsetse's palace. Esau, on the other hand, had goals that were at once more modest and more ambitious: to follow in the footsteps of his father whom he accompanied on his small fishing sailboat on weekends and during school vacations. But he wanted to develop the business, 'turn it into something bigger, you know? The Red Sea is brimming with even more fish than legends, you don't even need any sleight of hand to increase their numbers'. This earned him a scolding from his older sister, who insisted he take back his blasphemy.

'Or else I won't talk to you anymore,' Semhar said, really mad.

Her mother wanted to know whether she'd met any boys up there in Sawa. Smiling broadly, Semhar said no, asserting that between her studies and her military training she had very little time for such trivialities. 'They aren't trivialities, my girl. You have to think about starting a family and that doesn't happen from one day to the next. You should find someone excellent, like your father.' Semhar already knew where she was heading. In no time she'd be telling her about the sons of various acquaintances. 'Massoua isn't without fine boys. Why look somewhere else for what you can find back home?' Sawa offered a concrete argument to lead the conversation onto another track. She was a Christian, she remarked to her mother, she owed it to herself to be an example to others, a light that enlightens the world. There wasn't any risk she'd throw herself into the arms of someone she didn't know. 'May God hear you, my girl! But hurry up anyway. When it comes to this, heaven only helps those who help themselves. If I hadn't taken things in my own hands with your father, you wouldn't be here today.' Semhar also sweetened the answers to her mother's questions about the food she consumed. 'With all the exercise they have you do that's really intended for boys, you must eat well, good quality as well as quantity, my girl. Ever since you were very small, you've always been a fussy eater. But up there you have to eat what they give you. Look at you, you're nothing but skin over bones.' Semhar didn't tell her about the diet of lentils, tea, and bullying. She did everything she could to reassure them all, forced herself to be in a good mood, a sign she had grown up. It was her turn to protect them.

As she'd agreed with Meaza, she didn't speak to them either about her plan to leave. Instead she told them how much she'd missed them, all of them, that the long months of being away had made her understand how much she loved them. How precious they were to her. It took special effort because she wasn't particularly effusive, not given to emotional outpourings. Anyway, no one in the family was when it came to expressing their affection and love. Except for

the twins perhaps who, without giving it any thought, pep-
pered their phrases with 'love you', from having watched too
many American TV series. A verbal tic that popped up all
the time. For the others, actions spoke louder than words.
Nevertheless, on one or two occasions during her week's
home leave, Semhar managed to let words take over from
action. She knew she wouldn't be seeing them again for a long
time to come. It was worth forcing her nature a little.

The night before she went back to Sawa her father gave
her some money. 'You never know, it may well be of use up
there. It's a key that opens many doors, especially in this
country,' said the almost fifty-year old. A man of few words,
a character trait reinforced by the long days of solitude at
sea, he'd added nothing else. He himself had finished his
military service a dozen years before, partly thanks to the
birth of the twins, in addition to the presence of a wife
and daughter at home. Since then, he'd picked up his work
as a fisherman, abandoned when he went into the service.
Thanks to his hard work and the sacrifices he'd made, he'd
managed to acquire a sailing ship. Now he was his own boss,
accountable to no one. Other than to the *Boss* in heaven. He
managed to provide for his family quite nicely. If it weren't
for the latent war with Ethiopia and this crappy regime,
it would be a good country to live in, he felt deep in his
heart. There wouldn't be so many young people forced to
go begging elsewhere for what they could have at home. Just
as long as his boys didn't get such ideas into their head. At
that moment it didn't even enter his mind that his daughter
might consider it.

In the morning, Semhar exchanged her father's Eritrean nakfas, and those she herself had put aside, for dollars on the local black market. Then, flanked by the twins, with their chatter and unrelenting dreams, she spent hours walking through Massoua, alley after alley, rediscovering the Pearl of the Red Sea. Alone in the afternoon, she lingered on the pier at the wharf where, far from any adult eyes, she used to challenge her friends to diving matches. Wandered around the beach as the sea breeze caressed her face. Let herself rekindle childhood memories. An era was gone, an era she wouldn't see again. As if she'd lived in a country that had been erased from the world map. Indeed, this feeling, strange for a girl her age, blended with a fear of the unknown that was opening up beneath her feet. That elsewhere which was coming towards her, so laden with mysteries. She didn't know whether she would ever see the town of her birth again. The landscapes that had shaped her, which were part of her. Of her flesh and her blood.

After that week of home leave, Semhar had no other chance to see Massoua and her family again. Every other week she'd speak to them by phone, have a few brief exchanges. Long conversations were frowned upon by the chain of command. One might just say too much. Each time she claimed she didn't have enough minutes. Just enough for her mother to ask: 'So, is there someone?' and for Semhar to respond, pretending to be offended: 'Mama!' For the twins to grab the phone from their mother's hands and say a 'love you, sister'. Time enough, too, to reassure her family: everything was fine, she was in good health. She was impatiently awaiting the end of the academic cycle and the results so she'd know whether she was staying in Sawa, being transferred to another place, or sent to Asmara to study. That would be the jackpot. In that case she'd be closer to them and could come to see them more often.

But she left a week before exams. On the night between Saturday and Sunday, she'd crossed the border of Sudan, which explained why she'd missed Sunday services. That night, Meaza had guard duty in a five-hundred meter area outside the camp. Semhar, on the other hand, had waited a solid hour after lights out to slip out of the lower bunk bed, taking care not to wake her neighbor above. To punish her, the corporal had moved her from the bunk she used to share with Meaza and banished her to the other end of the barracks. The snoring of some and the absence of any whispering from others were her signal to depart. Semhar snuck out of the camp, careful not to run into some insomniac informer. She opened the door to the right of the main gate, which tended to creak. She'd oiled it in full view of everybody the day before, interpreted by the others as an excess of zeal. 'She's close to some serious bootlicking, that one,' her harshest mocker had scoffed. That night, the door swung on its hinges without a sound, as Semhar carefully closed it behind her and strode towards where she and Meaza had agreed to meet.

There the two girls got rid of their fatigues—Semhar had kept hers on when going to bed, since she had to relieve the guard at dawn. It was a habit she'd developed a while ago to pull the wool over the others' eyes. This way she could get a few more precious minutes sleep, she explained. They put on jeans, a top, and a jacket packed in two backpacks buried the night before under a huge rock they'd moved in the dark. Besides physical strength, it took perseverance before the bulk of stone rolled away by itself. Besides what they needed to survive, they'd put a small copy of the New Testament in their backpack. Semhar had hidden her cousin's telephone number into a seam of her jeans, with a few twenty- and fifty-dollar bills she would use as a last resort. After discussing it with Dawit, Semhar had her cousin send her the money via Western Union to be paid directly to the smugglers for crossing the Sudanese border.

Borne by their faith and determination, the two women set off. The sky that night provided them with a lovely half-moon, occasionally hidden behind a few clouds. It gave them just enough light to see where to place their feet. Dawit had advised them not to bring a flashlight, as it might attract attention. They walked eagerly, making a long detour to avoid the river along whose banks nomads sometimes established their villages, their loyalty highly unpredictable. Depending on their interests or on government pressure, they might well be smugglers or informers. It was a real art to be aware of the trend of the moment and Dawit, who seemed well-informed, had counseled them to avoid these, Meaza recalled, all too happy to have a reason to talk about her fiancé without Semhar saying:

'Stop. You're making me crazy with your Dawit.'

They were lucky enough not to run into anyone. Only the cries of some nocturnal animals disturbed the night, making their blood run cold, but they carried on regardless. To give each other courage they held hands as they walked, accompanied by verses from the Bible they recited out loud, like so many shields in the face of any adversity. At times they combined them with songs, one especially, in anticipation of the last leg of their journey, the most uncertain as well as the most dangerous before their final destination. They would make it there, of course. Ardently they sang:

> *If the sea rages If the wind blows hard*
> *If the boat drags you down Do not fear death*
> *He did not say that you would drown*
> *He did not say that you would sink*
> *He said:*
> *Let us go to the other side*

After three grueling hours of trekking through the night, between a plain of stones where they often risked spraining an ankle, and more wooded hills, they were about to reach the meeting point. Some hundred meters from getting there, they heard the sound of footsteps, imperceptible to ears less sharp than theirs. Their military training had at least served that purpose. In a flash they hid in the underbrush, swift as cats. Ready to defend themselves, should the need arise. At the same time, there was no question of returning to the place of departure, Semhar had told herself privately. She recalled the promise she'd made to herself the morning she made her decision and repeated: 'All the way to the end, my dear. All the way to the end.' But, in his excitement to see them

emerge, it was Dawit who'd forgotten to give the agreed-
upon signal. 'You scared us, you idiot,' Meaza chided him as
she threw herself into his arms, under the tender gaze of her
friend, standing back from the couple's effusive greetings.
Semhar saw her friend now as a sweet, cuddly girl, far from
the little ball of nerves she could be at the camp.

Semhar didn't realize they had crossed the border about
a hundred meters from the checkpoint barrier. Before they
arrived Dawit had taken care of everything. After walking for
another two hours under a sky studded with its last stars, two
men came to meet them. Dawit spoke with them in Tigrinya,
the ethnic language of the country's majority, which was also
spoken on the other side of the border. They had another
good hour to go, as they followed the two strangers who were
leading the way. The group walked on steadily and in silence.
All that could be heard was the impact of their shoes against
the stones. Preceded by a few reddish interludes, dawn broke
at last. Then one of the men turned to the Eritreans and,
before leaving with his partner, said:

'This is it. Wait here, someone will come and get you.'

Semhar couldn't get over it, they'd made it. They were
on the other side. One step toward their destiny. Meaza was
weeping with joy. She and Dawit couldn't stop kissing, 'thank
you, my angel, thank you', they would be able to make a new
start. Follow their youthful dreams. Semhar controlled her
emotion. It was just one leg. She'd rejoice later. When she'd
reached her final goal. 'All the way to the end,' she repeated.
She didn't know it yet, but of the long obstacle course yet to
come it was the only phase where everything would go this

well. Without a hitch. She wrote a text message to her cousin to announce the happy news. Amanuel was supposed to alert his own family, who would then inform Semhar's parents of her decision to leave. As for her, she'd refrain from all contact with them, in the hope this would prevent their suffering any retaliation from the military.

THE CONTAINER

AFTER WAITING FOR several hours in the place they'd been left, Meaza's inborn impatience got the better of her. As she saw it, they'd been cheated.

'Just seeing their ugly faces, we shouldn't have followed those guys. Besides, did you hear them? "Wait here." Without any explanation, nothing. Really, who do they think we are?' It took every bit of Semhar's composure and Dawit's power of persuasion enhanced with sweet words and kisses on her neck, to bring her back to reason. It was past noon with the sun very high in the sky. The three friends found shelter under a kind of scrawny flame tree that was barely able to provide them any shade. In the distance, roughly two kilometers away, was a village whose green-edged white minaret stood out, projected over a few scattered rooftops. They could always ask for help there, Semhar suggested.

But her proposal didn't prompt any approval from the other two.

After a little while, they were hungry and had lunch, some bread and a can of sardines Dawit had brought. When they were finished, Meaza pressured her fiancé to make sure they hadn't been forgotten by the smugglers. She was sick of waiting. He wasn't just going to stay there, was he, hanging around without doing anything. He was the man, so it was up to him to find a solution and get them out of this bloody mess. This time, Semhar was careful not to intervene in what looked more and more like a lovers' quarrel. Especially when poor Dawit had the misfortune to mention he did have a number to reach his contacts, but no Sudanese SIM card. It was as if he'd handed her a stick to beat him with. His lady-love didn't miss the opportunity:

'Was it that hard to think of for the Eritrean Che Guevara?' she spat at him, ready to pounce.

'Don't worry, baby, they're sure to get here,' Dawit dodged. 'If worse comes to worst I'll do what Semhar said: I'll go over there and buy a card,' he said, pointing at what looked like a slum.

The answer didn't reassure Meaza, even though at Sawa she was used to long turns of duty that could go on for a whole night and day. She was ready again to get back on her high horse. 'If you want, we can play hide-and-seek, little girl. That way you won't notice time passing,' Semhar finally interjected, more used to keeping a lid on her worries, without ever losing sight of her objective. Her bitter irony struck home. Offended, Meaza sought refuge in her lover's arms.

The afternoon passed between fitful bouts of sleep, sitting on the ground, head against the trunk of the flame tree, and endless discussions in which the friends' dreams of the future floated up, filled with optimism, through the dry, torrid air. Meaza's good mood returned. Dusk was falling when a Toyota Land Cruiser put on the brakes close to them. The man to the right of the driver signaled them to get into the back, shouting at them in Tigrinya:

'We're going to Khartoum!'

'*Yallah! Yallah!*' he added in Arabic.

About twenty people were already in the bed of the truck, huddled together, bags between their feet or on their legs. Eritreans, Somalians, and Sudanese, judging by their physical appearance. As they got in, the others squeezed even closer to make some room. A mouse hole, where the three managed to settle in as best they could. They hadn't quite sat down yet when the vehicle lurched off at high speed. It would drive all evening and through the night on battered highways and clay roads that whipped up a thick dust, finding a haven in people's lungs. Semhar used the T-shirt she kept aside in her backpack as a face wrap. Her friends followed suit. The truck's first stop was to get gas from some people who emerged out of nowhere, heavy jerrycans filled with gas on their head. The second time they stopped to relieve their urgent needs. Everyone did, even if they had to force themselves. 'No other stop is expected, unless there's a flat tire or we're stopped by police,' the man initially beside the driver told them, now getting ready to take the wheel. Thereafter, they had to make the best of it. If you needed to puke, for example, you did it by leaning over the edge as the vehicle continued at breakneck speed. No matter if the wind blew a good part of it back into the face of other passengers.

Insofar as the sand allowed, the three kept their eyes open during the journey. Here and there a few pale stars pierced through the opaque desert night. Resting on Dawit's chest, Meaza gazed up at it, while Semhar managed to doze in fits and starts. At daybreak, she woke up on the outskirts of a large city: Khartoum. All the passengers were told to get off in front of a dilapidated old house, where two men talked with the drivers of the truck in a pidgin that Semhar, though extremely gifted in languages, didn't understand. A pack of sickly, emaciated dogs, tongues hanging out, was roaming around in a pathetic quest for something to sink their fangs into. They didn't even have the strength to bark. One of them stopped at Semhar's feet—he wouldn't have survived if she'd kicked him—sniffed at them before dragging his carcass off again.

Once the meeting ended, the travelers were taken charge of by the two new men, who looked North-Sudanese and less than reassuring. With bunches of keys and billy clubs dangling from their belts, they looked like a pair of rather unfriendly prison guards. Instinctively, Meaza sought Dawit's hand as if, with this gesture, she was refusing the separation she felt was coming. And she wasn't mistaken. In rudimentary English, the older of the men explained to them that, while they waited to pay for the trip to continue, they'd be staying in this deserted looking house, men in one room and

women in the other. 'Anyone who wants can go shopping in
Khartoum,' the younger one said sarcastically. But at their
own risk, the older one added. The police frequently checked
identity cards; aliens were incarcerated, sometimes for several
months, before they were sent back to their own country. The
falsely mellifluous tone was reminiscent of that of the corporal instructor at Sawa. Even Meaza realized that if she wanted
to get out of this rats' nest as quickly as possible it would be
in her interest to remain calm.

The travelers, he stated, would have to settle room and
board. 'This is no poor man's inn.' Semhar, who had a better
mastery of Arabic, which with English and Tigrinya was
one of the three official languages of Eritrea, translated for
her compatriots who knew it less well. The Sudanese who
did understand Tigrinya listened in as well. Of course, if
there was anyone who wanted to save some money, nothing
stopped them from fasting, even if it was long past Ramadan.

'In contrast to lodging, food is not obligatory,' the young
one declared with a sardonic laugh, displaying incisors and
canines streaked with yellow stains, the result of an excessive
use of tobacco and tea, and less regularly of a toothbrush.
They seemed a tough pair.

They gave the new arrivals a tour of the property, skipping the latrines set three or four meters back in the rear
courtyard and easily recognizable by the smell. Closer to the
walls stood a wooden trough, much like those for horses in
front of the saloons in Western films. It was half filled with
brackish water that seemed to have been stagnating for days.
'Your bathroom. Collective or individual,' the other guy felt

it useful to add, a more clearly Arab type with slicked back raven black hair. The tour over, one of them took the men to the room intended for them, the other escorted Semhar, Meaza, and three other young girls from the pick-up to the smaller room for women. Inside, Semhar lay down next to her friend on one of the rush mats flung in a heap on the ground. Time, she thought, for a chat. But drained and stiff, she collapsed like her traveling companions without even noticing that their hosts had locked the door as they were leaving.

Early in the afternoon Semhar needed the toilet. That's when she realized the door could not be opened from the inside. She banged on it loudly with her fists to call the two men, in the meantime waking up the others. The guard with the slicked back hair came running, yelling insults at her in a mix of Arabic and English, which Semhar ignored. She'd banged too hard, it could alert indiscreet neighbors, he told her, although the few small houses in the area were at some distance from theirs. Beside himself, the man said: 'In any case, the door will stay locked, that's the way it is. Especially when my colleague and I are out. It'll keep the curious from snooping around.' A little while later, they served them the last meal of the day, a kind of semolina mush and strong black tea in a filthy aluminum cup, which the two swallowed without complaint. They'd been well trained at the camp of Sawa.

Two days went by. One morning, one of the drivers who'd dropped them at the layover house appeared to update the travelers, assembled in the little courtyard. Room and board

would cost fifty dollars a week, 'a pittance, right?' On the
other hand, they had to pay up ten times as much, five hundred dollars that is, for the passage to Libya. 'For those who
have the necessary sum, there will be a departure shortly.
We'll let you know. The others will wait. The house takes
no credit. And our patience is limited,' he told them. He
left them a telephone number where he could be reached,
but only in an emergency. 'We have prepaid Sudanese SIM
cards for those of you who want to make any calls. Do I need
to add they're not free? Think about recharging your cell
phones. The electricity is on the house.' Without waiting
for any questions from them, the man sat down behind
the steering wheel of his pick-up. Immaculately white, like
his djellaba and his slippers. And shot off in a thick cloud
of dust.

Before sending the 'tourists' back to their respective
rooms, the younger guard allowed them to have a short
hour's walk just to sweeten the pill. Meaza and Dawit's
reunion was lovely,. .and frustrating because of the others
around them. They could only hold hands and gaze in each
other's eyes. 'Careful you don't drown,' Semhar teased, before
she reminded them of their goal. 'Your cooing is all very
well and good, but don't forget why we're here.' The three
friends moved off to take stock. Thanks to the SIM cards
they'd acquired at a stiff price from the managers, Semhar
sent a text to Amanuel, asking him to call her back. Dawit
wrote to his contact, a former regiment comrade settled in
England. He'd transferred his savings to him little by little,
so his friend could advance some of it to him should he run

out. None of the three traveled with large sums of money. At each stage they paid the amount needed for the rest of the journey.

Five days later, they were together in the back of a container on a truck that was leaving for Libya, in a group of about fifty Sub-Saharans. Preceded by a pick-up, the truck drove at night and stopped during the day to avoid, as the escorts explained, possible police checkpoints and robbers, their main concern. The desert route would take three interminable weeks. The smugglers, two Sudanese and three Arabs, carried Kalashnikovs under their djellabas and long clubs in their hands. With obvious delight they used them to strike the unruly who moaned about the length of the trip, the traveling conditions, the lack of food.

Semhar had a hard time quieting Meaza who, for once, found an ally in Dawit. But it would take more than that to distract her from her objective. 'If you want to bungle everything, this would be the time. Go ahead.' They were already in deep shit, she said, and they wouldn't get out of it by acting tough. They had to remain focused on their objective, not fall for the provocation of the smugglers. She reminded Meaza of her valuable advice in Sawa when she herself had to confront the corporal instructor's harassment. It was a question of principle, too: they'd embarked on this adventure together, together they would succeed. 'Or not,' she added to shock her friends to whom the idea of failure had to be horrifying. Her faith helped her find the arguments that bore some weight. She recited the verse from the *Book of Revelations* to them

that had been with her and Meaza on the leg from Sawa to
the meeting point with Dawit.

'We'll make it, friends. We'll make it,' Semhar said,
convinced.

It was the speech she gave them from all of her twenty
years, locked up in forty-five degree heat behind bales of
goods in a container whose walls were punctured here and
there by two rectangles of twenty by ten centimeters. Just
to let a little dry desert air filter through so they wouldn't
suffocate. Not enough, however, to keep a young woman
from feeling faint and creating panic among the passengers.
Being notified by desperate banging on the walls didn't please
the smuggler who'd taken the seat next to the driver, while
the others were traveling in the front of the pick-up, an air-
conditioned double cabin. The truck came to a sudden stop.
After opening the container from the outside, taking out
the bales of merchandise, which were light, to facilitate the
climbing up and coming down of that other merchandise
consisting of the travelers, and making their way through to
them, the coyotes abruptly started to beat them, shouting:

'*Soukout! Oulad Kahba!*'

'*Shut up! Sons of bitches!*'

'*Vos gueules! Fils de pute!*'

Words they could apparently utter in every language on
earth. Once the collective beating was finished, they tried
to revive the young woman who'd fainted by slapping her
hard and sprinkling her face with water. 'I hope the lesson
will be remembered,' barked the one apparently in charge.
Then they replaced the phony bales of merchandise before

furiously closing the container again. They made no further stops, despite the intensified banging and screaming, which reached them only as muffled noise.

Water was what the passengers inside the container lacked most, even more than food, which was also rationed. It was served to them in dribs and drabs, a small half-liter bottle every other day. Once only were they able to drink their fill. Maybe the smugglers were in a good mood that day. The truck stopped near an oasis to pick up a few supplies from a group of nomads who didn't seem at all surprised when the contenders for the crossing emerged from the container and threw themselves like jackals on the watering hole, fighting each other to be first. There was no other convoy or caravan on the horizon. The nomads watched their movements, their eyes burned by the desert heat.

Semhar swallowed so much water, which humans and animals drank side by side, that her stomach, shrunk from two weeks of deprivation, ejected it as soon as she'd gulped it down. An action her intestines followed immediately. She was constantly on the verge of complete dehydration, her skin tight and desiccated. One night, unable to take it any longer, she took advantage of the others being asleep and pulled down her jeans—the same pair she'd been wearing since leaving Sawa, which she'd washed when they had their layover at the wretched house—slid the now empty bottle between her legs, emptied what little fluid there seemed to be left in her bladder, and brought it to her lips. Neither the ammonia smell nor the uric acid taste could discourage her.

As dawn broke in the morning, after driving all night long, they were allowed to stretch their legs and do their business behind a sand dune, while one of the traffickers posted at the top looked on intently, Kalashnikov in hand in order to deter any potential attempt at escape. Even if people would have to be crazy to get such an idea into their head. Escape to go where? But it was a well-known fact that the desert renders people crazy. If they were lucky they would have another chance to stretch their legs at nightfall, before the vehicles started up once more. Sometimes, when it was too hot, the smugglers told them to seek a bit of shade under the truck, while they found shelter under a rudimentary tent they could easily roll up again.

One night, it must have been in the middle of the third week, Semhar woke up with a start when she felt something heavier than usual on her shoulder. They were so piled up that it was normal to find a head on your chest upon waking, an arm across your shoulder, or a pair of legs askew over your own. That night, the young boy, an adolescent of at the very most fourteen, whose head had landed against her shoulder, seemed not to want to extricate himself. When she pushed him aside very gingerly, he fell backward. Inert. Semhar uttered a shrill cry that awakened the whole container.

Since they weren't far from that morning's stopping point, the smugglers found out quickly enough. They forced Dawit and another passenger to toss the body out on the sand, then ordered them back into the container, closed the door behind them, and started up again. They drove almost all morning. Undoubtedly to put some distance between them and the corpse, so it couldn't be traced back to them in case of an investigation. Even if it was unlikely. For some time the fate of those whom the Europeans referred to as migrants or refugees had been causing a stir. But who would actually worry about it, other than some NGO's. Two days later, preceded by the pick-up, the truck dropped them off at the Libyan border.

They'd actually made it, Semhar said to the fiancés. But at what price? They must have lost six to eight kilos each. The two already frail women were barely shadows of their former selves. Semhar felt the nausea, triggered by hunger, fill her esophagus with the acid liquid she'd learned to force back down, with clenched teeth, because she couldn't spit it up inside the container. Never mind! She wanted to hold on to what was essential: they were still standing. All three of them. And even though they hadn't crossed the border yet, they'd cleared another stage. The second one, she told herself. She brought her forehead to those of her friends and for his blessings gave thanks to the 'One who is seated on the throne, the One who lives forever and ever'.

THE BEATING

AFTER THE SEMBLANCE of an inspection, with some customs officers casually walking around the truck asking the driver to open a container, one of them shoving his stick into a few of the bales of merchandise, the convoy crossed the frontier with alarming ease. It didn't take Sherlock Holmes to understand the smugglers were in cahoots with the border guards and the influential Libyan militia. In the chaos three years before, which followed the fall and the assassination of the country's former head of state, Brotherly Leader and Guide, Colonel Muammar Gaddaffi, supported by Western heads of state, with the then French President as leader of the pack, it was essential to get along with the different circles, grease the palm of a maximum number of people—which meant almost everyone—to be able to continue their lucrative trafficking. While they were stopped the occupants of the container were holding their breath. No one moved for fear of reprisals by the smugglers should the operation fail, and of their fellow travelers who would be quick to blame each other.

In the meantime, the men from the 4 x 4 came out to smoke a cigarette, drink tea, and chat with the customs officers. The check lasted no longer than that one moment of sociability and then the truck took off without any further waiting, preceded by the pick-up that once again took the lead. They drove for about an hour before stopping in the middle of nowhere. That's where the exchange took place. The day had just begun. The traffickers made the passengers get out of the container to stretch their legs and satisfy their needs under the always vigilant eyes of an armed guard. Meaza and Dawit made the most of being in the open air to gingerly touch, as if discovering each other for the first time. Amused, Semhar stood back, watching them. Then the almost fifty people were entrusted to other traffickers with whom the previous ones had been negotiating for a while. The 'leader' took his leave with words whose significance Semhar grasped immediately: 'Here you are; you're in Libya. Your fate depends on you now. And on Allah, too,' he added with a sardonic smile that seemed directed at her, with the sole purpose of lowering their spirits.

Two beige pick-ups were waiting for their passengers. Semhar and her friends found a place in the back of one of them, jackets rolled up as turbans around their heads to shield them somewhat from the sun's heat. The pick-ups were so overloaded they could barely move off. Around forty and athletic despite a bit of a belly, the new 'leader', an almost blond Berber type, had two barrels of polluted water allotted to each group, some hard old bread, and dates as dry as dromedary skin. He settled down in the front of the first 4 x 4, alone with the driver while his colleagues squeezed together in the cabin of the second one. Both cabins were fully air conditioned, of course. Once the vehicles were moving, the drivers stepped on the gas, flooring it, over alternately stony and sandy roads. Although crammed together, the passengers were tossed back and forth in every direction: front, back, sideways, thrown off their seat before providential arms held them back at the last minute. Between the potholes, the sudden braking, the large stones the drivers couldn't avoid, unless they were trying to give them an African massage, as one of the travelers called it, still brash enough to joke around, Meaza's stomach turned, and she threw up what little she had swallowed over the edge of the pick-up. Semhar hung on for dear life, clinging to an arm, a leg, a waist, a shoulder, the edge of the pick-up, like a last hope.

The first time the pick-ups stopped near a group of nomads to fill up on gas, Semhar knew once and for all whom she was dealing with. Seated beside her, a Sudanese man had been talking to himself for at least half an hour. Looking at the others without seeing them, he kept rocking back and forth, like a Jew at prayer. He seemed to be in another world. The only link that still connected him to the rest of the group seemed to be rambling words even his fellow Sudanese had trouble making out. Initially, Semhar tried to pay attention to him, speaking to him in English, then in Arabic, but the young man didn't see her any more than he did the rest. Reluctantly, she let it go but continued to watch him from the corner of her eye in the hope he'd finally regain his senses and give her a tangible sign that he was back with them. That was when the vehicles stopped for gas.

The Sudanese threw himself off the bed of the pick-up and began to run straight ahead, his body bent forward as if, with every step, he was going to fall flat on his face. His strides were doing battle with the sand in which his feet would disappear, then pull out with difficulty, scattering the grains behind him. He hadn't even gone fifty meters when one of the smugglers caught him and so it began. Blows were raining down on him everywhere: head, shoulders, stomach, knees. The young Sudanese screamed, struggling, arms across his face in an attempt to fend off the punches. Then he stopped resisting and roaring, dropped to the ground, his body rolled into a ball. The smuggler managed to loosen an arm from his chest and drag him behind like a hunter returning with game.

Stopping near the group, he handed the club to another Sudanese and told him in Arabic: 'Beat him'. The man didn't understand, or pretended not to, whereupon he received a violent blow from the butt of a Kalashnikov on his shoulder blade, another on his chest that made him double over before he stood up and grabbed the club. He held it in his hand, stunned, not knowing what to do. 'Beat him,' the smuggler repeated. '*Yallah!*' The Sudanese struck him half-heartedly. The other shoved him and bellowed: 'Harder!' Then the Sudanese began to really hit his compatriot who lay curled up on the ground. 'Harder!' And he struck. 'Harder!' And he struck with increasing fury, as if mesmerized by the command. Tight lips and tears in his eyes. Under the uproarious laughter of the traffickers, the scathing look of the nomads, and the petrified gaze of the other passengers. After a few minutes, the leader motioned with his hand. The smuggler restrained the raised arm of the Sudanese and took away the club and the leader gave the signal for departure. The vehicles started up, leaving the bloody body behind in the burning sand.

At that point Semhar, who'd witnessed the scene while biting her tongue, flew off the handle. It was the first time she broke her own rule: never to swerve from her goal, no matter what. But such treatment of any human being disturbed her deeply. Even more disturbing to her was the fact that the Sudanese was paying doubly since his dreams were coming to an end in the desert where he might perish without any help from anyone. It was both cruel and unjust. Her father had always stopped her mother from hitting them. 'There are other ways to correct and educate a child,' he'd say. He who could be so strict with them. As she remembered his words, tears of anger filled her eyes. 'Too much, this is too much,' she thought. If no one was going to rebel, these vultures would end up by killing one of them. And there would be no justice to hold them accountable. She started to strike the side of the vehicle with her fists, and shouted in Arabic with all the strength her frail chest was capable of:

'You've got no right to do this. He paid like everyone else. You've got no right.'

The two 4 x 4's braked sharply, the leader the first to step out. Still, he was taking his time as he walked straight over to Semhar. Thanks to the rearview mirror he'd noticed from the front of his vehicle where the shouting was coming from. Reaching her, his blue eyes shot piercing looks at the *kahloucha*, dealt her a powerful blow with the back of his hand, heavy rings on every finger except for the thumb. The young woman's head went flying against her chest. She hadn't quite straightened up yet when she caught another one in the opposite direction. A veritable whiplash. Her left cheekbone was pouring blood, splattering the Berber's butter-colored djellaba. Its soiling fueled his anger tenfold. Blows came down on Semhar's head and chest as if she were a punching-bag.

Unable to just watch and not react any longer, Meaza and Dawit jumped up without exchanging a word, intending to come between their compatriot and her tormentor. Before he could even open his mouth, Dawit received a blow from a gun butt against his temple; Meaza was immobilized by the barrel of an assault rifle pointed against her face. Some watched the scene in silence. Others turned their head or eyes away in embarrassment. Until the leader himself decided to stop the beating. Despite their anger and their sense of injustice, the three friends knew they were no match. Meaza soaked her tee-shirt in some water and dabbed her friend's injuries first, then Dawit's, who refused her help. He was livid, given the smuggler's cowardly act and his own helplessness. All the more since it was he who'd led the girls into the adventure. And here he sat, unable to defend them, to prevent the horrifying scene that was playing out before his eyes. It was worse than if he'd been an accessory to it.

Moving off, the man said in English, loudly and clearly so everyone would hear:

'We have no right to do what? Beat him up? Ditch him? You're the ones who have no rights at all. Get that into your *qird* heads: none at all. You belong to us. If you insist on going where no one is waiting for you, you'll do what we tell you to do. Period.'

That night at the bivouac, the Berber stood before them flanked by one of his armed gorillas. He grabbed Semhar by the wrist. She was so tiny that he didn't need much effort to drag her off behind him. While the young *kahloucha* put up a struggle, his associate kept a gun on Meaza and Dawit. He knew the rest wouldn't intervene, since fear is always a good counselor. Dawit, on the other hand, was a bomb within an inch of exploding. Meaza sensed it and, for once, had wisdom on her side. She gently grasped his hand, letting him know there was nothing he could do. Besides being doomed to fail, his reaction would only run the risk of making things worse, bringing the traffickers to focus even more on Semhar and the two of them. After a few minutes that to the couple seemed like an eternity, one of his colleagues came to replace their guard so he could join the leader behind the dune. Three other sidekicks were already there, spectators waiting excitedly to participate in the feast.

Semhar was no longer struggling or shouting. She wouldn't give them that pleasure. Hold on, she told herself, jaws clenched. Hold on. She called on the verses from her not so distant childhood for help. 'Dogs surround me, a pack of villains encircles me [...]. They divide my clothes among them and cast lots for my garment. But you, LORD, do not be far from me. You are my strength; come quickly to help me! Deliver me from the sword, my precious life from the power of the dogs. Rescue me from the mouth of the lions; save me from the horns of the wild oxen.' The smugglers took possession of a cold, frigid body. Of a cadaver. Stiffening only to remove any other form of satisfaction besides that spit of cum with which they were defiling her body. Somewhere in the Libyan desert that night, Semhar lost her virginity and, with it, much of her innocence.

The rest of the journey proceeded without any further incident, other than the few whacks the smugglers dealt out just to let off steam, but without any great conviction. All that time, Semhar and her two friends remained fused to each other, almost forming one compact block. Although not particularly demonstrative and not much given to hugs, Semhar had never before accepted being fussed over this much. Without ever divulging to Meaza what had happened behind the dunes. Anyway, her friend needed no words from her to figure it out. Semhar never wept in front of her tormentors either, other than when the impenetrable darkness of the desert allowed it. When pain rekindled through her body, when her mind was doing a balancing act on the edge of madness. But she took infinite care not to break the silence and thereby alarm her friends. The trip, which took three days in all, brought them to the suburbs of Sabratha, after a detour via Benghazi where other desperate folks expanded the number of those seeking to depart. Seeking a life to live.

DISAPPEARANCE

WHEN THEY ARRIVED by the end of the day at the new layover, the three Eritreans were separated once again, women
to one side, men to the other. About thirty meters apart, the
two buildings where they would be staying were just as dilapidated, but far more imposing than the place in Khartoum
where they'd been lodged. Each was a vast warehouse that
that at first glance seemed abandoned. Surrounded by thick,
three-meter-high walls topped by a double row of barbed
wire, the whole looked exactly like a private prison, even if
there wasn't anyone in uniform visible around. No watch-
tower either from where prison guards armed with sniper
rifles could take down fugitives like rabbits. In the asphalted
courtyard, next to barrels that should hold reserve water,
was a small group of men conversing loudly, some standing,
others slumped in white plastic chairs, smoking, or tapping

into their cell phones as their sole activity. At first glance, they didn't seem armed other than with a club and a pair of handcuffs, which they carried conspicuously on their belt. Perhaps they kept their Kalashnikovs hidden, to be taken out only in case of an escape attempt or mutiny.

Semhar and Meaza were pushed into an immense hangar, even though it could barely contain the large number of tightly packed women, a few privileged individuals on mats, most of the others right on the floor. Chance had it that they ended up beside two Nigerian women, who'd been confined there for six months as they waited to emigrate to Europe. One of them, Shoshana, who was quite chubby, explained the ways and customs of the place, the attitude to take to prevent the all too frequent physical punishments. To be made into an example, the most recalcitrant were whipped in the courtyard, in front of the others who'd be assembled and forced to watch. She pointed out which guards to avoid looking in the eye at all costs, an act that was interpreted as a lack of respect; which guards some girls were getting favors from in return for... She was looking for the right words, then simply said:

'Well, you know what I mean.'

'The jackpot is to become the favorite of one of the guards, if you don't want to be called upon by his henchmen,' her friend Rachel added, whose sassiness immediately pleased Semhar. 'But, whatever you do, you won't escape from the dirty stuff these sons of bitches—with all due respect to female dogs—will take you to do on the outside. They rent your ass out to other guys, and they take all the money.'

That wasn't all. These pigs were crazy about unnatural practices. 'They visit every orifice. Might as well get used to it,' she said in rather blunt English, rattled off like an AK-47. Frankly, compared to her, Meaza was the Holy Virgin. If Semhar and her friend had something to hide, she continued, they'd better put it somewhere else. Assuming that in this shithole there even was a place to hide anything. The two Eritreans promised themselves to treasure the advice of the Nigerian women. Though it wouldn't exempt them from the cynicism and cruelty of the jailers.

Without any news of Dawit, Meaza and Semhar spent the following days learning how the place functioned. Almost every morning the guards would collect some girls for destinations that changed from one day to the next. They'd pick them out in groups of ten or twelve, the choice depending on their mood of the moment, before they tossed them in the back of a 4 x 4, identical to the one that had brought Semhar to Sabratha. The most attractive ones worked all day long as sex slaves servicing an entire herd of men with wide-ranging tastes, who'd come and go without a break until nightfall. On the way back, the girls had nothing left but their eyes for weeping or, a slight balm on their injuries, finding refuge in the arms of a friend who'd been spared that day. The ones who were less appealing in the eyes of the guards were split up into two groups: the first were sent to slave away as maids in the opulent homes of Sabratha and its environs. The second group, Semhar among them, were sent to be dishwashers in restaurants, where one of the rare advantages consisted of swiping the leftovers from the customers' plates, otherwise

THE MEDITERRANEAN WALL

intended for the trashcan or for wandering dogs. For Semhar
those days were a true feast. The handlers would frequently
forget to give them food, or else only give them some meager
fare every twenty-four or even thirty-six hours.

Working themselves to the bone in restaurants, where
the pay was but a paltry sum of which three-quarters landed
in the pockets of the organization, had another advantage: a
certain amount of freedom. However, that didn't make it easy
to escape. More than one before Semhar had tried and been
caught, turned in by restaurant owners, or by the locals who
were either hostile or simply disturbed by the comings and
goings of people who were from another culture and didn't
speak their language. Sometimes, believing they were getting
away, they'd wind up going from the frying pan into the fire,
that is, into the traps of networks of competing, even more
savage, traffickers. It was rumored in the warehouse that they
were better off having to deal with the smugglers associated
with the militia of the Uncle, the most powerful patron of
Sabratha. Nobody knew the exact reason for this. Maybe
his enterprise was more reliable. Maybe he'd succeeded in
getting more people across the Mediterranean. In any event,
those who benefited from the protection of the 'Doctor' or
the 'al-Bible' were less popular. It was a good thing, Shoshana
had explained to Semhar, that their hangar was in the Uncle's
territory.

On the outside, Semhar did her utmost to renew contact first with her cousin, then with Dawit's army buddy at
Meaza's request, who had recommended she memorize the
phone number, just in case. 'You never know, little sister, you

174

might need it someday. He's cute, you know. I've seen his picture. If he also has Dawit's temperament and good heart, who knows? Once you're there.' Their phones had been confiscated upon arrival. In contrast to the Sudanese the previous week, the Libyans distrusted anything that represented a potential danger for the organization. With a cell phone, they could not only talk, but take photographs, film, record their conversations and send them to the outside. The few times the Eritreans had access to them was on the express order of the traffickers to ask their family to make an extra payment for the crossing, the price of which kept increasing. Better than Wall Street and the stock exchanges of London, Tokyo, and Paris combined. Semhar concealed as best she could what they had to endure on a daily basis. She doctored it up, twisted things. She wasn't keen on conveying any alarming news, even unintentionally, to the person on the line.

Dawit's friend did the same on his end. Via Semhar, he told her that her fiancé had found a job in the building. He was careful not to add forced labour, which he could have done; that more than once when night came Dawit felt he'd been flattened by a steamroller. He'd go back in the morning only to avoid being awakened by kicks or doused with water in the face, a game the bodyguards in the men's warehouse were particularly fond of. In short, Dawit was holding on, a euphemism to keep hidden the other abuses of which he was a victim, being forced one night to sodomize a fellow prisoner who'd attempted to escape. But his friend was hopeful. The job would serve to pay off part of the past and future debt. Together, the two of them would manage to collect the money needed for the crossing. Thus the engaged couple exchanged some news although they never spoke, although the hangars faced each other, although each of them could see the other warehouse on the days they went to work. The latrines and what was supposed to pass for a shower were set up in such a way that the men and women wouldn't run into each other. Unless it was the women running into the guards.

And then, one night, Meaza didn't come back. She'd been in high demand recently. Who knew why? It was a month and a half since they'd arrived, maybe more, Semhar had lost all sense of time. For some reason, hardly a day went by that Meaza wasn't taken out of the hangar. She'd made it a habit not to drag her feet, to get up the very second the guard pointed at her, to rush out so that he didn't have to waste his precious time. She was struck fewer times, fewer blows with clubs and boots, all of them abuses that had become the girls' everyday plight, served like clockwork in the morning when they woke up and at night before they went to bed. Like the collective showers with the garden hose, administered right in the room where they'd then have to sleep without the floor being dried first. To give them a wash, the guard would say snickering: 'It smells like rancid pussy down there.' To spend even a single day without being beaten would be a miracle. A blessing from the Almighty, was Semhar's conviction.

Nevertheless, Meaza had managed it. She could go for days on end without being the victim of any mistreatment. It was her turn to explain to Semhar and the two Nigerian women how to do it. You had to obey orders very fast. Be ahead of the handlers' expectations. Even if it meant being rebuffed, with words like 'we didn't ring for you, Negress'.

'It's what they call making the best of a rotten deal. Resisting serves no purpose at all, girls.'

As the news from Dawit grew more and more scarce, Meaza became more distant. From then on, she looked like a visibly wilting plant. Dawit was her alpha and her omega, whose trust and love had endured, despite everything she'd suffered in Sawa. And who would forgive her what she was experiencing here, too, once she'd told him. She told him everything, her Dawit. Holding on without him made no sense at all, without Dawit life didn't seem worth living. So she brooded two, three days long. Then as she woke up one morning her exuberant side emerged again. Together with Rachel she managed for hours on end to make the two others laugh until they were crying. It was as if life, in its odd ways, had taken the upper hand over Meaza's feigned pragmatism. Her false cynicism. The persistent hunger that twisted her innards like the braids on Rachel's head. The filth. The heavy, fetid air. Life, stronger than everything else. Stronger than the abuses and the imagination of their torturers.

Until the night that she didn't return. It had happened before to others. Without anyone knowing whether they'd been thrown on a boat leaving for Europe, whether they'd succumbed to the cruel treatments, whether they'd been buried in a communal grave around this prison with no name. Or whether the traffickers had delivered their corpses to the sand and the hyenas of the desert, as rumors making the rounds in the hangar had it. Semhar remembered that the night before Meaza had a slight temperature. They'd all had that experience, often after the collective showers. A result also of the change between the scorching heat of the day and the chill of the night. Without any blanket other than the body of a friend coming closer just to warm up. Usually the fever would leave the way it had come. Occasionally, it could be eased a little with some tea with lemon and honey, some paracetamol obtained when outside. Or thanks to a small favor bestowed on a guard.

The previous evening, Meaza had come back limping more than usual. She was clearly holding her lower belly and buttocks. A strange thing for her to do. She didn't 'feel like talking very much, not tonight, girls', despite the insistence of Semhar and the Nigerians. Even stranger for a chatterbox like her. But she'd sworn to her fellow victims that it was nothing serious. In any case, nothing more than what they themselves had already experienced, too. That night she fell asleep in Semhar's arms who rocked her with verses from the New Testament. Obviously, the Christian formula had worked well. At dawn, she was in top form again with enough energy to leap like a goat, go stand by the door once the jailer had pointed to her.

'You, *habiba*,' the demonic pig had grimaced.

She was ready to go back to work. Semhar watched her move off all perky. Meaza waved at her like someone who's leaving home to go to work after a restful night and a solid breakfast. Still, Semhar caught a glimpse of something else, a glimmer of sadness in her gaze, at odds with her little birdlike jumps. Since she herself wasn't working that day, she had plenty of time to think about it. But couldn't find a convincing answer.

The following night Meaza didn't come back. As reassurance, Semhar told herself she might have been with some people who had specific requirements, who preferred nocturnal frolics, in the dark so they wouldn't have to look at her jet-black skin. That she'd be back later. Then the next day. After three days, she began to worry in earnest. Since she'd been there, Semhar knew that the smugglers didn't necessarily announce your departure in advance. They'd show up one day and collect girls as usual. Some in the group would go to work, but others would find themselves on a boat that very night, destination Lampedusa or another Mediterranean shore.

Semhar wanted to believe that Meaza, so maternal toward her, would never leave her without any news. She was the only one who'd detected the moments of panic and fear behind her apparent calm, the demons that worked her body since adolescence, since a small five-year old cousin she was watching had drowned in the Red Sea under her eyes. Without her, whom her father had trained to swim like a dolphin, being able to save him. And that blasted Red Sea never returned the body. One morning before leaving for work, Semhar with her most enticing look asked the jailer in Arabic if he knew anything about her friend, the little Eritrean girl whom he'd taken five days earlier. She hadn't come back since. His only answer: 'Mind your own ass, Negress,' a thick spurt of black spit chucked at her feet.

It would take a lot more than that to discourage Toughy Semhar. Taking advantage of a moment when she was leaving work, she managed to contact Dawit's army buddy. She asked if he'd had any news from the young couple, since it was now five days that Meaza hadn't come back to the warehouse. He hadn't but he would find out. He'd move heaven and earth to know. Two more days went by. The answer Semhar dreaded came, a curt no. Dawit didn't know anything about it either. Thereafter she didn't know anymore to which saint she should devote herself. Meaza gone, she would have arranged one way or another to contact them. She was too resourceful not to have thought of that. Unless the boat hadn't reached its destination yet. Sometimes they wandered at sea for weeks before they were rescued by a gunboat from Malta, Italy, or an NGO. Unless the ship hadn't arrived at all. Unless Meaza hadn't left Libyan soil. Unless...

Semhar was afraid to think of the irrevocable. She deepened her praying, helped by Shoshana. Even if they didn't have the same faith. The Almighty, Semhar was convinced of it, was one and the same. No matter what name he was given beneath these heavens or any others. The absences of Meaza and Rachel, equally missed, brought the two young women closer. Three years older, Shoshana knew how to show solidarity. Together they processed the shock as best they could, and many more besides. As time went by, when neither of them was working outside, they told each other their personal stories. The day they made the decision. The departure. Their itinerary. Their hopes as well. Raised each other's morale when either was at her lowest point.

A few weeks later, Dawit's friend confessed to Semhar that he no longer had any news from him either. He'd tried in vain to contact the smuggler with whom he'd been in touch. It was not a good sign. But he hadn't lost hope to get him on the phone one day. In which case, he'd keep her posted. As for her, if she needed anything at all, he'd be there for her. Insofar as he was able. He was eager for her to know that. Once she was in Europe, if she didn't know where to go, she shouldn't hesitate to call him. There were possibilities here in Germany. In the winter, nights are three times as long as the days. But the people are welcoming. And besides, it would make him happy. He'd grown used to waiting for her calls. He was interested in getting to know her in reality. In seeing if she resembled her voice.

Semhar would never know what happened to the young couple from Asmara. She was hoping. Praying for her soul sister to come back. From the realm of the dead, like Lazarus. Until the day she embarked on a trawler for Europe. With her new friend, thank God. There, too, she'd held on to a last sprig of hope of finding Meaza among the passengers. They would recognize each other at the very same moment, throw themselves into each other's arms, crying. Laughing, too, because they would have their future opening up before them. Like the Red Sea at the feet of the children of Israel, Shoshana suggested, with whom Semhar now shared her most intimate thoughts. The two would tell each other all about the months they spent so far away from one another. Over and over again. Crying and laughing. Laughing and crying.

ON BOARD
THE TRAWLER

Et la mer à la ronde roule son bruit de crânes sur les grèves,
Et que toutes choses au monde lui soient vaines, c'est ce
qu'un soir, au bord du monde, nous contèrent
Les milices du vent dans les sables d'exil...

SAINT-JOHN PERSE

And the rounding sea in her noise of skulls on the shores,
And all things in the world to her are in vain,
so we heard one night at the world's edge
From the wind's militias in the sands of exile...

(TR. DENIS DEVLIN)

NAUSEA

IN THE GRIP OF their own worries, the passengers in the hold knew nothing, or almost nothing, about the clashes taking place on deck with the more agitated passengers. How could they imagine, even for an instant, that the 'privileged' overhead could be having as hard a time, if not harder? Depending on the direction of the gusting wind or the angle of the boat, huge torrents rushing in through the open trapdoor left them very little time to think about the situation of those more affluent. And then the roaring of the winds, colliding at the hatch, like a herd of camels forced through the eye of a needle, wedged in place unable to either move forward or pull back; those that followed pushing with all their might, intensified by the powerful crush of the ones all the way at the end. After a few minutes of desperate struggle, the winds up front were flung forward, opening the way for the rest that, once set free, penetrated the hatch triumphantly. It generated such astounding noises, alternately fluid, continuous, and choppy, sounds whose magnitude was exaggerated by not knowing what was happening above. And so everyone's imagination was working a form of sabotage.

Along with the fury of the winds came the never-ending assault of waves targeting the hull. In the corner where she'd found refuge, Semhar felt every blow reverberate in her back, visualizing them as battering rams pounding against the gates of one of those cities long ago, driven by a ferocious and determined foe. Waves struck the trawler at mid-flank where, under the duress of their onslaught, the hull was threatening to give way. For Semhar there was no doubt: at some point or other it would cave in. The only question was when. To delay that possibility, to prevent it from happening, she prayed with all her soul, one hand almost crushing the crucifix around her neck, the other clinging to something: Shoshana's leg, an unfamiliar arm, a joist…

From time to time the waves would retreat, providing a breather, but it never lasted for long, unfortunately. Not even long enough to feel relief. Or to forget about them. In fact, they'd retreat only to recharge their batteries far away, then come back even more aggressively, beating against the hull, over and over again. Beating and beating as if possessed. Beating without taking a breath, roaring to rend eardrums, congeal bodies, and send hearts into their throats. Stomachs emptied their bile, intestines let go. The screams of terror swelled. The end seemed ever closer. It would come with the next wave. The next surge. Like the exterminating Angel carrying out its duty of death. Relentless. Utterly indiscriminate. Even those on deck would go through it. Such was the thinking of the terrified below. The chaotic distribution had placed Semhar and Shoshana at the level of the bow's recess, an absurd positioning: half upright, buttocks compressed between two pieces of wood, legs propped up by other bodies, thereby preventing them from falling backward with every shockwave. As a result, despite the water in the hold, their bottoms got wet only when the trawler leaned too much to their side. But it was impossible to escape the feeling of being caught inside the drum of a washing machine, the spin cycle at full speed gone off the rails, or to get away from the mounting nausea.

These dreadful sensations reminded Shoshana of an experience that, until this crossing, she had thought of as the worst moment of her young life. For some time, unbeknownst to her parents, she'd been seeing a guy with whom she was madly in love. She'd even been thinking about facing the fury of her father who would rather be damned than welcome a goy into the family. Actually, she never did discuss it with him. But she'd heard him many times, as an elder of the synagogue, sharply lecturing those who professed somewhat more liberal ideas on the subject, even without acting on them. She certainly would not have found an ally in her mother, guardian of traditions and her father's sounding board. Nevertheless, none of this kept her from falling in love with this guy, five or eight years older than her. Crouched in the back of the hold as it took on water through the hatch, Shoshana realized she hadn't known the exact age of the man she'd loved so inordinately, who'd wound her around his little finger that much. And she still didn't know.

She'd planned to flee with her goy. To Abuja or Lagos or somewhere else. Nigeria was a huge country that offered a thousand places where she could live her great love overtly. Far from family pressures and the community's rude stares. She was ready to leave her birth land, follow him to the ends of the earth, if need be. It was the first time the idea of leaving for a foreign country had entered her mind. Rachel was the only one who knew about her plan. 'Has he brainwashed you, that guy, or what? You're losing your marbles, little sister,' her friend said, laughing. She also knew about the pressure of the demands Shoshana's boyfriend was making. 'A man has needs,' he told her. 'And besides, it would be the real proof that you love me.' She was nineteen, she hesitated. It went against everything she'd been taught at home. Even Rachel who at her age had already seen a thing or two, wasn't very eager for her to prove her love to him in that way.

'Once he's gotten that proof, he'll be treating you like a doormat or worse, sis. Hold on to what you have,' she told her, 'so that no one will take your crown.'

Shoshana didn't like hearing her friend repeat this phrase at every opportunity to girls tempted to prove their love like this, the only valid criteria in the eyes of their boyfriends.

'Stop your blaspheming,' she said. 'Just because it comes from another religion doesn't mean you should mix it up with all this sex business. And besides, Jesus was a Jew, I'll have you know. So, just stop.'

Besides being a goy, her lover had another flaw; he'd never worked a day in his life. Without any particular education, he was living with his old mother—his father had disappeared ages ago into the blue—and off money that his younger sister sent from England via Western Union. He was always well dressed, like a movie star. 'All that money,' Rachel said. Never a speck of dust on his cowboy boots. His perfume—Invictus by Paco Rabanne—broadcast his arrival from ten meters away. He was the one to start a style or stop it. All the young men in the village conformed to his way of dressing and would recreate their wardrobe once he'd moved on to something else. His garish side had ended up by seducing Shoshana, together with other girls with whom he was rumored to be having affairs. But Shoshana couldn't care less. Anyway, people always found fault with things. Now, she was angry with herself for having been so gullible.

She was so much in love that in the end she gave into the guy's increasingly strong pressure. He resorted to every plausible trick, which ran from teary-eyed pleading to blackmailing her with a break-up, playing at being offended, or the veiled threat of taking up with someone else who wouldn't equivocate so much. Yes one day, no the next. Because then she'd love him for real. Shoshana did it twice, maybe three times, she couldn't remember anymore. But she had a vague memory of something rough when her boyfriend's mother had gone to the market. Anything but romantic, none of the stars she'd expected to see in broad daylight. What she remembered specifically was the morning sickness a few weeks later. Her growing distress as the thing inside was taking root. How would she present the matter to her parents? That was when she started thinking about fleeing with him. The day Shoshana spoke to him about it, he answered that they needed to think it through. Yet, at the same time looking for a last quickie. When Shoshana refused, he said that maybe there was another solution.

'We can't just leave like that, on a whim. Without a penny in our pocket. Where would we go?'

'We love each other, don't we?'

'Of course we do, babe. But that isn't enough. Give me some time to think about it.'

Then he disappeared, from one day to the next. Without any further sign of life. Just as his father before him had done to his mother. Leaving Shoshana in a jam. With the nausea that threatened to give it away to her parents. She had to invent a thousand excuses to explain her lack of appetite, her sometimes odd cravings, her fatigue, which she blamed on having to study for her final exams. Shoshana's father didn't suspect a thing and became all the more attentive to her, as opposed to her mother whose sly allusions made it clear she suspected the reason for the nausea. In the end, Rachel convinced her to get rid of the thing. 'You'll see, it will pass smoothly. And no one will be the wiser. Trust my experience, I tell you.' Rather than confront the paternal wrath, Shoshana thanked her childhood friend, who took care of finding the money and the clinic in Onitsha, where they went in the middle of the week under the false pretext of getting information for their future university studies. And the nausea came to an end.

It was the most horrible experience of her life. Until this bloody awful crossing. Thinking back on it, Shoshana wondered how she could have been so very stupid. Just for that alone, she didn't regret having left. Putting distance between herself and her naivete. But even more than the ferocious noises, the total darkness enveloping the hold for a while now was upsetting her. At first she told herself it would pass, the moon would reappear, she'd keep her eyes riveted on its reflection until the dawn returned and would save her. But the moon seemed to have vanished for good. Like her bastard boyfriend who'd made her stop ever wanting to fall in love again. The darkness only increased her sense of suffocation.

Were they going to hold out? Would all of them hold out? Shoshana felt the apprehension in the hand Semhar held out to her. That young Eritrean, so calm until then, who had imbued her with part of her serenity. 'We're going to make it,' Shoshana told herself to raise her morale. She tried to think of the interminable stay in the desert of the children of Israel before they settled in the Promised Land. An otherwise more painful ordeal. The one who must not be named was in the throes of probing her faith. As He had done with Job. As He did with Balaam and Jonah. 'We'll make it,' she reassured herself, muttering the traveler's prayer for the nth

time. Engulfed by her anxiety, Shoshana didn't hear the first grumblings beginning to rise around her.

Most of the refugees were finding that time was passing ever more slowly. They'd been told the crossing would take six hours at most. Even if the smugglers had been careful to add: 'Depending on the weather.' But the trawler had been suffering the storm's assaults for about ten hours, if not more. They realized they had no choice. They were left abandoned in the darkness, shaken as if they were in a blender. If the boat were to capsize, they'd be stuck down below without being able to find their way to the trapdoor and get up to the surface. Prisoners of the hold and of the Mediterranean. How could they even know they were going in the right direction? No one had come to talk to them. That might have reassured them perhaps. Or not. Between two lulls, doubts were going from mouth to ear in a variety of languages, translating the same fears, the same intensifying need to see the light at the end of the tunnel.

The decision came after yet another lurch, lasting even longer than the preceding ones. Semhar felt an inert body below her, the body of a boy at most ten years old. She'd seen him when they were going down into the hold. He was accompanied by a man he called uncle. The two, who seemed to have a very close bond, had found a place next to Shoshana and herself. Semhar palpated him in the dark, took his pulse, and discovered to her horror there wasn't any. She had no time to mention it to her friend and, evidently, she wasn't the only one in this situation. Other voices were whispering in the semi-darkness, more than one of them with a dead body nearby. They didn't shout, as if they were trying to hide a shameful disease. Moans coming from different corners of the hold met with muffled echoes, which turned gradually to sobs, then to anger.

'If we stay here, we'll all die,' some voices cried out. Repeated in every African language, the phrase went through the hold like wildfire. The rumbling swelled, went from mouth to mouth. Whispered gravely. Hummed, chanted, hollered. 'We'll all die. We'll all die.' Neither Shoshana nor Semhar could have said who started it, nor from what section the impetus originated. In spite of the dark to which their eyes had grown somewhat accustomed, they realized that a huge roar was moving toward the hatch, trying to get through in the opposite direction to the winds. The two women joined in, carried by the momentum of the others and their own desire. That of Toughy Semhar, riveted to her objective, even if she had to die for it. That of Shoshana, the leader, whose small army had been dissolved along the way. With dozens, hundreds of the damned of the African earth, they went on the attack.

BRAWL

TRUTH BE TOLD, the two friends had no idea what was happening, either about the source or the cause of the mass action. They'd been swept up in the frenzy, ready for any eventuality, which in their situation was most likely the beginning of a shipwreck. In any case, they needed to be up on deck, among the first to disembark if ever help was to arrive. Or to jump overboard and not be trapped underneath the trawler's inverted hull. The worst possible scenario for Shoshana whose heart was beating thunderously. With pointed elbows and some extra shoving she led the way, Semhar clutching her waist. Without a word, the two had decided to make it out together. Shoshana still remembered the heartrending farewell with Rachel, while for Semhar it was the memory of Meaza's disappearance. It was unthinkable that either would lose yet another sister-friend. Hereafter it was till death do us part for each of them. Such were their thoughts as they forged their path amid the panic-stricken refugees.

The boat was pitching under their feet. Because of the moving crowd? The rough sea? The moon had reappeared. Despite the bodies rushing to the hatch and clutching the ladder, visibility had improved a bit. The hold was upside down. People were pushing and trampling each other in a pandemonium of screams, sobs, and nervous hysteria. Shouting matches came raining down in linguistic confusion worthy of the Tower of Babel, hateful looks and an intensity of voices substituting for simultaneous translation. Shoshana's solid build and her five-foot-eight frame allowed her to control their situation somewhat. Her head back, Semhar was searching for a breath of air without letting go of the other one's waist. Because the crowd was so compressed, they were actually standing still, motionless.

It felt like gridlock in Lagos where one could spend two hours to move five hundred meters, every driver sticking to their lopsided position under the dispassionate look of the police. It could happen any time of the day or night; a permanent rush hour, which an impromptu demonstration or the exit from a soccer match would render even more impenetrable. Shoshana had gone there once during her adolescence and returned in a state of shock. And to think she'd envisioned settling there with her secret love. But the day after her boyfriend ran out on her, she swore 'on the Torah and on Jerusalem' never to set foot there again. Even if there was no other place to go in the whole wide world.

'Remind me of that if I ever change my mind,' she'd told Rachel.

Suddenly, the process was reversed. Bodies tumbling backward in a monstrous tangle. The thrust of those who were in front now collapsing on those behind, trampled, and no one to rescue them. Others were dropping off the ladder, off the deck, driven back by kicking boots, blows with clubs and iron bars. Shrieks, calls for help, rang out from every direction. Soon no one was attacking the hatch any longer. The last two had been ejected like ripe fruit from a shaken tree. In the aftermath, the ladder was pulled up, hoisted up to the deck, and the trapdoor slammed shut. The *cargo* were back in complete darkness, not a single ray of light from outside. A young Senegalese took a cell phone wrapped in a plastic bag from his pocket and turned it on. Several passengers followed suit. The light reflections cut through the dark and focused on the bleeding body of the uncle of the boy who'd died just a few hours earlier.

The two young women noticed him at the same time. Shoshana couldn't hold back a cry of dismay nor the tears that welled up in her eyes. The man was bleeding so profusely that his shirt no longer had its original color. Blood spurted erratically from his mouth like a geyser. He'd been brutally stabbed twice: once in the chest, once in the abdomen. He was lying in a crimson mess, stretched out on his back, panting, his arms slack alongside his body. He didn't even have the strength to bring them up to his wounds to try to stop the hemorrhaging. Perhaps he felt all effort was futile. Death, it seems, never comes as a surprise to anyone. On the contrary, it always heralds its arrival. It wants to be noticed head on. To see the fear in our ashen human eyes.

As best she could, Semhar rushed over to the man lying in the back of the hold. 'Air, air,' she said in English, in Arabic, and in the little French she knew. All of it with a composure that stirred Shoshana's admiration. But since the hatch had been closed there was very little air. Yet her voice was so firm that everyone obeyed, pressing against each other in the already jam-packed hold. She knelt down near the body, yanked off the shirt, called for a piece of fabric and some water, clean water if possible. Some of the other passengers kept their phone lights on so she could see what she was doing. Someone gave her a bandana, another a head scarf, whose ends she tied together. She motioned Shoshana to turn the injured man on his side, 'gently' she commanded, then to lift him carefully so she could slip the fabric under the body and create a bandage, hoping thereby to stop the bleeding. Solemn and compassionate, she repeated the steps she'd learned in the army, all her energy focused on the attempt to save this life.

It wasn't enough. In all likelihood, the stabbing had damaged vital organs. The body's temperature seemed hotter than that in the hold. The man had lost a great deal of blood— too much blood. He was becoming delirious in a language most of the refugees around him didn't know. At the height of his delirium he kept repeating the words 'Tolegba' and 'Danbala'. Someone in the group, obviously of the same ethnicity, said it was Fon. The injured man must be Beninese, Togolese, or Nigerian. From one of the regions of the former Kingdom of

Dahomey, in any case. Sensing that he didn't have much time left, he asked his ancestral spirits to receive him benevolently. The interpreter chanted with him what must have been a funeral song. When they stopped chanting, the dying man sputtered in a last breath: 'Deliver me, Lord, from eternal death on that awful day, when the heavens and the earth shall be shaken and thou shalt come to judge the world by fire... Here I am, trembling and full of fear..., before the approaching judgment and the ire that must come.' A few seconds later he gave up the ghost, his hand in the hand of his countrywoman.

As she closed his eyes, Semhar made the sign of the orthodox cross, from right to left, thumb joined to index and middle fingers, the two free fingers to the palm, while chanting: '*Requiem aeternam dona ei, Domine, et lux perpetua luceat ei.*' In turn, a few Senegalese, close by the head of the deceased, recited the *Salat al-Janaza*: 'Oh God! Forgive our living and our dead [...] Oh Allah! ... whoever You cause to die, cause him to die with faith.' A breach of orthodoxy since the deceased was not a Muslim. So overcome by the violence of the death, it had come to them quite sponta-neously. After all, it came from a good place. Any Muslim in their situation would have done the same. Allah, in His infinite goodness, would understand and forgive them. As for Shoshana, she was hesitant about what attitude to take. Certainly, Judaism would allow her to pray for a Gentile. But intolerant as he was, what would her father think if he saw a woman pray for the eternal rest of the soul of a goy? And what was worse, doing so without a *minyan*, the quorum of ten men, indispensable to the prayer's realiza-tion. A moment later, unable to stop herself, in the silence of her heart she finally spoke the *Kaddish Avelim*: '*Yitgadal v'yitkadash sh'mei raba* / […] Magnified and sanctified is the great name of God…'

The trawler was continuing its journey across a less stormy sea. On deck, almost as bright as day thanks to the moon, Dima was still in shock from the spectacle she'd just wit-nessed. When the *znuje*, the Blacks down below, burst onto the deck headfirst, like rats emerging from their hole, it took some time for the travelers around her to figure out what was going on. Weren't they supposed to stay in their subterranean world and they themselves in theirs, up above, till the end of the journey? It was the pack with the bearded white-haired Palestinian, who had knifed the African and thrown his body into the sea with the help of his accomplices, who were quickest to react. The three men with Tunisian accents had joined the group. Two of them, who looked as if they were approaching forty, led the gang to meet the cattle from the hold who were demanding to stay on deck. They were suffo-cating down below. Since the boat was shaking less, the two groups were face to face in no time.

Those on deck tried to push the refugees back into their rathole. Pushing hard against their chests, they shoved the leaders with both hands. Larger in number, the *znuje* proved more determined. This time they weren't going to give way. No words were exchanged. The deck gang had drawn their knives and clubs. A ferocious hand-to-hand encounter ensued. The blows fell violently, hitting skulls, faces, shoulders, ribs, bellies. Consisting of fairly young men, the vanguard of the hold retaliated. At first it seemed the deck gang was retreating, at one point with their backs to the railing. A sudden movement of the ship and too heavy a charge by their adversaries, landed several of them in the water. Cornered, they fought back and got the upper hand again.

At the end of the brutal and merciless confrontation, three Sub-Saharans were left on the deck. The rest were pushed back into the hold, the ladder raised, the hatch slammed shut. The bloody bodies—Dima couldn't tell whether they were still alive or not—suffered the same fate as the earlier victim. They were picked up by the four members of the group and thrown into the swirling waters of the Mediterranean which swallowed them up. Perhaps the sea would leave them as fodder for its animal population, or perhaps it would hold them close until they were an integral part of its own moving body.

The bearded one wore a macho grin: his group had won. Just some negligible scratches in their ranks. He himself had suffered a nasty uppercut in his ribs that was hurting like hell. It would pass, he was used to it. It would take more than that to get the better of a tough customer like him. The eyebrow of the blond boy was split wide open. One of the older men, whose ears stuck out more than those of Mickey and Will Smith combined, tried to stop the bleeding with a piece of cotton that appeared from nowhere. Then he pulled a dressing from his pocket and put it on the wound under the impenetrable gaze of another older man with a military haircut, who'd kept himself out of the fray, and said to the blond youth:

'You're a warrior, big boy. Your mama would be proud of you. You put up a good fight. It'll be fine.'

Dima was as stunned as the other travelers who'd been present at the brawl. While the ship continued its course, the group of men sat down at the hatch opening, clearing off those already there, and began to talk as if nothing had happened. The one with the army haircut rolled a cigarette, lit it, and then took a long drag before handing it to the blond boy. Judging by the smell, it was something other than tobacco. Dima couldn't get over it. 'And these people call themselves Muslims,' she thought. 'They can't stop tossing "*Inshallah*" and "*Alhamdulillah*" into everything they say. In her eyes, it was adding blasphemy to crime.

She turned her eyes away from these heathens—there was no other word for them—and looked at her daughters. Hana and Shayma were sleeping the sleep of the just. Allah is great, she said to herself. He hadn't allowed her angels to be witnesses to these atrocious scenes. What sort of men were these who could kill the way you slit the throat of a pig and then go back to talking as if nothing had happened? Perhaps the ones they'd thrown overboard without any feeling were true Muslims. The Mediterranean was dead calm again and the trawler continued at a less erratic pace. The winds, too, had stopped blowing. No longer washed by any more waves, the girls had fallen back asleep as if they were in bed. It's crazy, the way children can sleep under any circumstances.

Hakim hadn't budged. Dima couldn't tell whether he, too, was sleeping or whether he was pretending so he wouldn't have to deal with her rebuke.

Just to get to Lampedusa, she prayed. To get away from this assortment of types, the destitute and the Africans. She didn't know what the island was like, but she was sure that she'd be better off there than on this ship of horrors. Just to stop rubbing elbows with killers. Just to have the torment come to an end. These horrendous scenes might reoccur, and she had no desire whatsoever to watch them again. And then, if those below were to make a new attempt—they weren't safe from their reappearance, Dima thought with dismay—who knows if they wouldn't be successful in forcing the barricade the traffickers had set up at the trapdoor? With the stuff they were smoking just before they must have lost their clarity. It would be child's play to knock them down. And once the *znuje* had made it, then what? Would they send the deck travelers down to the hold in their place? Would they toss them into the Mediterranean as the others had done with the members of their race? One doesn't know what these people are capable of. Well, yes, one does. She'd seen reports on television that attested to their barbarity, even among themselves. She didn't dare imagine it.

And then there was that weakling, asleep next to her. So sluggish, he was snoring like a chainsaw. Once they were in Europe, would she be able to continue living with this man who'd revealed his true face to her? The face of a self-centred coward, not even capable of watching over his own daughters, or of being with her out of simple solidarity since she couldn't sleep. To pass the time, they would have evoked their previous life in Aleppo and Damascus. The future opening before them, holding so much that was unknown. Neither of them had any family in Europe. A few vague acquaintances if they looked carefully, but that was it. Dima had never felt so alone in her life. She'd like to shove a well-aimed elbow into Hakim's ribs to wake him up. Ask him to behave like a man worthy of the name. Not like a coward. This, this... But she stopped herself, choosing to keep an eye on the *znuje* sitting next to them. So close to her daughters.

CHORUS OF THE SLAVES

SHAYMA, DIMA'S YOUNGEST, woke up just as the wind began to blow again. She was shivering, despite a part of her father's jacket lying aslant across her chest, in addition to her own parka and the woolen scarf around her neck that her mother had bought for her at the Tripoli Shopping Center, together with a pair of gloves in a synthetic fabric. She knew her to be sensitive to the cold and also that, even in mid-July, it might be chilly at sea. All that gear didn't keep little Shayma from trembling when she woke up. She needed to urinate. She wanted to know where the toilet was. Dima met the request like a punch in the stomach. How to explain to a little kid her age that nothing of the sort was planned for on board? That she'd have to relieve herself in full view of everyone. Like an animal. A miracle—*Alhamdulillah*—that the girls hadn't felt the need for a toilet any sooner. The overcrowding and the stress of the bad weather must have upset them, and, in that sense, sleep had been of invaluable help.

The smugglers who had come for them at the hotel in Tripoli the night before had spoken of a six-hour crossing. It was the passengers' responsibility to control themselves for the length of the trip. 'Just a little while,' one of them had said, holding up his thumb and index finger parallel to each other. It wouldn't kill them. Of course, there would be buckets available in case of a very urgent need, but not enough for everyone. Nor could they place them everywhere. That wouldn't leave enough space for travelers. And they would have been forced, very much against their will, to charge more for the seats, you understand? But may Madame be reassured! It would only be for six hours maximum. Maybe less, *Inshallah*. That was without adding the natural elements that had decided to prolong the journey beyond the predictable. Unless the man had sold them a bill of goods, which was highly probable: 'Those people will do anything for money.' Add to that a captain whose skills, for those who knew, attested to an extremely limited knowledge of the art of navigation. Without a doubt, the organizers had entrusted the helm to a second-rate car mechanic, chosen for his availability and a fee that was lower than that of the competition.

Dima was pulled back from her thoughts by her younger one whose need was more and more urgent. Regaining her overprotective maternal instinct, she got up, took each of her daughters by the hand, after waking the older one so she wouldn't be left unattended next to the *znuje* while her inconsiderate husband was sleeping, stepped over the bodies piled up on the deck, and went swaying toward the group of traffickers. Once there, she addressed herself to the older man with the military haircut. She picked him because she'd seen him stay in the background during the brawl and subsequently direct the debriefing, dispensing good and bad points. The typical attitude of a leader who lets his subordinates do the dirty work. She spoke to him straight away without any 'hello' or 'good evening', any 'how are you? how's the family?'

'The girls need to pee, maybe more. They haven't been to the toilet since we left and can't hold it any longer.'

She adopted a deliberately imperious tone, her way of saying that she was a woman to be reckoned with. She insisted on making it clear that they didn't come from the same world. He remained silent for a while. When he finally raised his head, which he'd kept lowered all that time as if Dima were addressing someone else, he had a vicious smile on his lips. First, he turned to his aides, taking them as witnesses with his look. Then, unflappable, he retorted in his funny Tunisian accent that he was not the toilet attendant. Having said that, if it were she, he would have rushed to accompany her and help her lower her little silk panties. With his teeth if need be. The others greeted his words with a greasy laugh. The old man looked as if he'd anticipated that reaction from his mates. He paused for a moment to let their snickering fan out into the air. Like a ham actor who takes his time before each response, waiting for the applause from a devoted public. Once the laughter stopped, the Tunisian continued. Since it involved children and she had asked him so nicely, she could go behind the middle cabin where there were two buckets available for people in need. The guy had sensed the class disdain in the Syrian woman's voice and took pleasure in adding:

'Don't forget to empty the bucket into the sea. There is no *kahloucha* maid here.'

Dima was visibly shaken. Followed by her daughters and the sneering, she went around the cabin looking for the buckets, praying to Allah and the Prophet there would not be any men awake in the area. Fortunately, two families were settled not far from the separate containers leaning against the cabin, emitting a strong smell of piss and excrement that the sea breeze couldn't chase away. Perplexed, the older one asked: 'Is that it, Mama?' 'Yes, my sweetheart. Only for the trip. Soon it will be over,' she lied. It wouldn't do to tell her child, who had experience with the hard times of war, that she should take it in her stride. The women helped stand guard while the girls did their business. Dima couldn't stop thanking them—'Allah will reward you'—and swallowing her shame. She had never been so humiliated in her life. Tears came spontaneously, more of anger than anything else. But she kept herself from sobbing so she wouldn't worry her little ones. She suppressed her tears, cursed Hakim and his entire ancestry back to the fifteenth generation. And even part of his descendants if ever he were to have children with another woman.

Once the trapdoor had been slammed shut on them, the *cargo* in the hold were even more agitated, Shoshana the most anxious of them all. She felt like a caged wild animal. No one could have talked her out of feeling that she was alone in the world. The only one facing a horde of demons. She shut her eyes, seeking the sleep that kept trying to get away from her. As long as her eyes were closed, she thought, she wouldn't have to think about it. She'd ignore the confinement as well as the suffocation that the darkness provoked. If Hashem, in His boundless goodness, would send her sleep, she wouldn't have to fight this battle, which was costing her so much energy. She'd wake up at daybreak when the European coast would be within sight. At least for those above. But sleep continued to elude her. After some time she stopped pretending. She was aware that it was just a way to stop her racing heart.

At the same time, she refused to lose her grip. In her family that wasn't done. In her own way she, too, was tenacious. She found another means to try to control her rebellious heart. She focused on breathing in through her nose and filling her lungs, holding her breath for about ten seconds, then slowly exhaling through her mouth. She repeated the exercise several times with closed eyes, in the hope her heart would slow down until it found its normal rhythm. She couldn't have said how long this self-deception continued and had to admit it didn't work either. Her heart was still an untamed foal left to its stampedes, its zigzagging in the wild, which she attempted to catch with tricks, one more half-baked than the next.

Then the only song she knew came into her head, one that seemed to fit the situation perfectly. She'd learned it in middle school from an Italian teacher. At the time, Dante's language was popular among those of her generation, because of the migration of the previous twenty years. Many of her compatriots, whose daughters had ended up in the claws of the Italo-Nigerian mafia, had found fertile ground in the

Belpaese to sow the seeds of hope for a better life. There were also thousands of apprentice soccer players who were dreaming of a golden career with Juventus of Turin, Inter, or AC of Milan. Italian soccer may well have been the shadow of its former self in the 1990's, it still continued to nurture the dreams of the youth on the other side of the Mediterranean. Before transferring his fantasies of glory and wealth to music, Ariel used to see himself as the new George Weah, the sole African winner of the Ballon d'Or. Everybody knew the saga of the Nigerian players Kanu, Taribo West, and Martins who made a fortune in soccer. Boys as well as girls.

Very early on, Shoshana was a fan of soccer, a veritable religion in her country. She, too, dreamed of one day wearing the jersey of the national women's team, the *Super Falcons*. Even if women's soccer players earned a lot less money. So, like thousands of young Nigerians, she'd taken up Italian. But in contrast to the others she didn't picture herself living in Italy. To do what? Basically, she was convinced—no doubt out of ignorance—that there was no greater, no more beautiful country in the world than Nigeria. It had everything to offer for everyone to live really well. Wanting it alone was sufficient. The massive departures to foreign countries were a trend that would go away with time. When she was younger, she couldn't see herself settle anywhere else. Italy didn't make her dream any more than England, France, or the United States. China or Australia even less. Not even South Africa, which was closer and where a number of her compatriots were up against all sorts of prejudices, as they tried to create a better future for themselves. If she'd ever thought about another

country it was Israel. Not to make her *Aliyah*, the final move
to the Holy Land, as some members of the community had
envisioned it when the matter came up of finding a location
to escape from the drought and the climatic vagaries. But
rather to visit, to set foot on the Promised Land of which the
Torah speaks, that land where the marvelous stories that had
populated her childish imagination had taken place.

In short, she'd chosen Italian as her first language because of
her love for *calcio*. And also to fit in. She was already different
enough where she lived. It was the right move. She thought it
was a language of indescribable beauty. She was in her third
year when she learned the song that came to mind now to try
and suppress her dread of imprisonment and darkness. The
teacher, a young well-tanned Roman with dreads bound up
in a net, a silver star in his left ear, and dark green eyes, was
as beautiful as an angel. That had motivated her even more.
She would have loved it if he'd been her first, instead of that
other bum. She became a teacher's pet in Italian class. She
knew the lyrics the teacher had made them translate by heart.
The melody from *Nabucco* that she first heard in class, then
looped at home, had seduced her even more since it evoked
the exile and slavery of the Hebrews. The banks of the Jordan
along which she dreamed of wandering as a child. It would
have been a foretaste of Paradise if she'd been able to visit
Jerusalem, then go to the river to bathe her feet, despite her
reserve, her entire body in the stream of the mythical river.

Shut inside the hold's obscurity, her eyes closed, Shoshana
began to hum the *Va' Pensiero*. The words of the 'Slaves'
Chorus' came back to her with unnerving ease. She didn't try

to stop the tears that were flowing slowly down her cheeks. She felt completely alone in the world. Anyway, no one would see her in the dark. She hummed very quietly but loudly inside her head and heart, as the boat started its drunken rolling again and the waves came back once more to hit the hull with the same violence.

Va, Pensiero, sull'ali dorate;
Va, ti posa sui clivi, sui colli,
Ove olezzano tepide e molli
L'aure dolci del suolo natal!

The waves could batter as much as they wanted, Shoshana no longer heard them. She was somewhere else. The 'Slaves' Chorus' inside her head, and in her thoughts took her far from the cesspit where her hope for a better life was wasting away. Shortly before leaving the land of her childhood, once she knew that the drop-off point would be Lampedusa, she'd felt the need to hear the song again. She'd downloaded the YouTube video and watched it, singing along at the top of her voice. Grasping each detail, every nuance, every sound. The scene takes place on a square in an Italian town. She didn't remember anymore whether it was Naples, Verona, or Rome. No matter. The public, won over before it started, applauded as the first notes began. That's how she imagined the opera, performed outdoors, opening out over the hills and the golden valleys of freedom, of which *Va' pensiero* speaks. Prompting tears of emotion, in spite of yourself. Preventing you from hearing the deadly assaults of the waves against the trawler.

Del Giordano le rive saluta,
Di Sionne le torri atterrate.
Oh mia patria si bella e perduta!
Oh membranza si cara e fatal!

As she sang, Shoshana imagined the Hebrews in captivity in Babylon. What does being banished from your native soil do to you? Being reduced into slavery? Far from your people, your mother tongue, the landscapes and smells of your childhood? What do you feel? Does exile make the lost homeland dearer to your heart? Does servitude invite you to curse the oppressor and his descendants forever? Does it lead to self-contempt? Shoshana had no answers to all these questions that as long as the song lasted were colonizing her mind. Questions borne by the powerful melody and verses of Verdi's *Nabucco*. While each clash between the trawler and the Mediterranean was carrying her farther away from her homeland, and from the ashes of a love story in which she all too often felt she was the only protagonist, so much so that she sometimes wondered if she'd actually experienced it or just dreamed it. Fortunately, the song was there, inspired by the Lord to give her the strength to endure her suffering.

O simile di Solima ai fati
Traggi un suono di crudo lamento,
O t'ispiri il Signore un concerto
Che ne infonda al patire virtù!

DROWNINGS

THE *VA' PENSIERO* brought Shoshana some relief but, sadly, not for long. The time it took for it to go through her head twice or more was enough to bring its soothing effect to an end. Cunningly, her heart had caught on to the ploy. It, in turn, had retreated, like the waves going out to sea to regain strength before coming back with even greater fury. It now started up like a bull let loose in the arena. Dashing off, rearing up, suddenly stopping. With the clear intention of throwing off its adversary and, once he was on the ground, wiping off its hooves on his chest. Here it was racing again just as fast. Clambering up the steps to challenge the spectators with its gaze. Turning the tables, seeing in their eyes fear changing sides. Shoshana's heart was in her throat now, was going to come out of her mouth, fall on her thighs, pulsing blood. Close to giving in to an adversary stronger than she,

she tried yet another diversion. 'Are you sleeping?' she asked Semhar. It had been a while since the two had spoken. In the reality of the hold of a vessel battling a stormy sea, it could have been a century. She needed to hear a friendly voice to shut up the demon that had taken possession of her mind and was whispering sick thoughts to her. She wanted to know about the Red Sea. Was it really red?

'What?' Semhar asked.

'Red. Is the Red Sea really red? Blood red. Peony red. Poppy red.'

'It is the most beautiful of any sea. It is... *wonderful*, as you say in English.'

'That's not what I was asking.'

'I know. But...'

'So, spit it out.'

Anxiety had made Shoshana aggressive. Tenacious but perceptive, Semhar picked up on it. In her country, she replied, they called it the Eritrean Sea. It was a very beautiful blue-green. The only one of its kind. 'The postcard images of the Maldives and the Caribbean Islands can't compare, they're nothing, you understand?' Having said that, she had seen it be red. Oh, not very often, but she'd actually seen it red. And that could go on for weeks. Then one day the sea would go back to its original color. As a child, she believed unequivocally that it got its temporary coloring from sharks feasting on the flesh of reckless humans who had ventured too far into their territory. Which was plausible, no?

'By the way, why do sharks have this nasty reputation while they're not the only sea creatures that love human flesh?'

'Go on,' Shoshana said impatiently. She was afraid her friend, who couldn't speak in a straight line, would go off on another tangent. With her, one digression led to another. Like Talmudic nitpickers. In the end, she'd lose the thread of the conversation. So, how does the sea turn red?

'Like rare meat,' she said, should Shoshana be looking for a comparison. She knew that her Nigerian friend hated raw meat. It was one way for her to continue her narration as she pleased. However, the story was more complicated. Very few parents, her father among them, allowed their children to swim in the sea. They were terrified of drowning. 'You can count on the fingers of one hand the people who know how to swim there. And I'm not exaggerating.' So, they had invented the legend of sharks whose favorite dish was the tender flesh of children which they would sever in one fell swoop with their hundreds of teeth before swallowing them without even bothering to chew. The red coloring in which the sea would occasionally drape itself, came from the blood of disobedient children. She, too, had believed it. Then one day at school— she was in the early stage of high school—a natural science teacher had explained to them that the Eritrean Sea took on that ochre color when a certain, rather special variety of endemic algae was blooming. She couldn't recall its name, 'a difficult thing to remember, something in Latin, you under-stand?' Still, that's no reason to disobey your parents, the teacher warned, for the Red Sea was, indeed, infested with sharks. Semhar kept talking for quite a while. And didn't need to be begged. 'A real chatterbox,' her father used to say. When she was small, it was impossible to stop her once she got going. Not until she was in the army did she learn to respect the orders of silence. Was forced to. Otherwise she'd be harassed. That made her tolerate it even less. Besides, she also had her goal: not to stagnate in any army barracks until she was forty. Or pursue a profession her superiors imposed on her. 'It's like entering into a marriage arranged by your parents and ending your life with that same guy, you understand? The horror of it all.'

In the darkness of the hold, Semhar sensed that Shoshana was still in need of hearing a friendly voice. So she continued. Talked about her brothers, the twins Jacob and Esau, one of whom was following in the footsteps of his father, the fisherman. They didn't like to ask him to help them with their lessons. Poor kids, even if it meant reviewing a year of math or all of English grammar in one afternoon. They were essentially her guinea pigs. Had she told Shoshana that she wanted to be a teacher? Preferably with girls. The day their teacher explained the Red Sea to them was the day she knew she wanted to become one herself. 'A little like accepting a vocation, you understand?' Jacob, the athlete, had the greatest difficulty in school. Fled from it like the plague. When he really couldn't abscond from her apprentice-teacher lessons, he'd cover her with kisses right in the middle of a session to shush her.

As soon as she was settled in Europe, she would apply for the twins to join her to release them from their military service. Have them discover that the world didn't stop at the Red Sea. No matter how beautiful it was. That the horizon was a great deal wider than what they could see from the pier of their city. Jacob would also have a better chance of realizing his dream of an Olympic gold medal, even if it meant running under the colors of a different nation. However, knowing him it would be Eritrea or nothing. But she didn't know whether in an official competition the dictatorship would allow an exile to represent the country. It would set a bad precedent for those inside the country. On the other hand, for her parents it was all over: they wouldn't want to join her. Their future lay behind them they said. She understood, even if it was hard to accept.

After talking for a long time, Semhar took a more solemn tone to tell Shoshana about her faith in one Creator. 'Whether you call him God, as we Christians do, Yahweh, Allah, or even Architect of the Universe.' He was good and compassionate. She was convinced He would bring them to the other shore. As when Jesus was caught with his disciples in a horrible storm on a precarious boat and He calmed the wind and the sea. He would bring them across safe and sound. Whatever happened. It was just an ordeal to get through. Semhar's words for her friend were what she herself would have liked to hear to alleviate her own anxiety, which she was doing her best to keep hidden from her. Nevertheless, they were sincere words in which she believed as well.

Semhar's comments were interrupted by an enormous noise, following a violent shock. There could be no doubt, the trawler had hit a gigantic reef. They were both wary, certain the hull was going to open right where the hammering sounds came from and the water would rush into the hold. It did not happen. Even after the long minutes during which they were holding their breath. In fact, the shock was the result of a clash with a wave even more violent than the previous ones. For a while the onslaughts continued. From inside the hold, howls were merging with the wind on the Mediterranean. The vessel repeated its mad, drunken choreography of cavernous backwashes and mountainous ascents, like Golgotha, as Semhar put it. Plunging to port and starboard. The passengers' screams of panic started up again, too. Women's strident voices and children's heartrending sounds mixing with the harsh tones of the men. All expressing the same terror. The fear of ending up as flesh for sharks and other creatures of the sea.

Dawn couldn't be far off. Pinkish specks were streaking the dark sky. Dima checked the time on her waterproof watch, bought in Tripoli the night before their departure, which was working wonderfully well despite being endlessly doused in seawater. It had been a lucky hunch. Just for that alone, she justified the price of the purchase. The gusts' return brought back the nightmares of the previous hours. Aghast, the passengers watched the trawler disappear into the sea, emerge again unscathed, playing leapfrog with the swells. Sometimes it couldn't avoid them nor surf on top. Then it would take them full flank and reel under the attack. Other times the charge would arrive in front, the vessel would recoil, leap, reel backward. All things that had been hidden from Dima during the night. At one point, the water was flush with her buttocks because the ship was lying on its side, the fear in the travelers' eyes multiplied by ten. But the ship continued on its way. Despite the creaking. Gradually more audible scraping led them to believe the ship would split in two, right in the middle. And the Mediterranean would engulf them all, one after another. The best swimmers would be under the illusion they could pull through, but in the cold water of this raging sea, Dima thought, it was impossible to survive.

★

The girls woke up and clamored for something to eat, cutting short their mother's ruminations. They were hungry. It was seven o'clock. The sky now clear and cloudless. They hadn't put anything in their mouths for fifteen hours. In fact, not since the preceding day's afternoon snack. Excitement of the departure, then stress over the bad weather, had taken away their appetite. Now their stomachs were demanding their due. After two weeks in Tripoli, Dima realized her contacts didn't control the deal from beginning to end. The departure promised with every encounter did not depend on these men, who looked more like henchmen than anything else. They had no damned reason to provide any credible explanation for the long wait. From three days they'd changed their story to five, then seven. *Inshallah*. And so on. As if Allah were obliged. So, in addition to a few bottles of water, Dima had kept in reserve two cartons of milk and three of juice, some cookies, brioches, dates—and a small flask of 90% alcohol, 'it can always come in handy'. Whatever happened, she would be ready for D-day. It was a good thing that she'd thought of it. Imagine the scenario otherwise: nature up to its own tricks, people yelling around her, the girls crying with hunger... Hakim hurried to serve them. As if he really wanted to be forgiven for sleeping through it all. 'At sea you shouldn't have an empty stomach, my darlings.' He didn't have anything himself. He would later admit to Dima that he'd been afraid they might run out before the end of the journey, which to him wasn't in sight yet. He could deal with hunger, his daughters could not.

While Hakim was encouraging his children to eat, the wind doubled in strength, trumpeting like ten thousand angry elephants. The waves were boiling around the trawler, which once again was going nowhere. Perhaps it was moving forward. Impossible to notice with the naked eye, at any rate. Suddenly, the ship on its right side, the waves snatched a lady and her son. They didn't even have time to scream, call for help. Her husband rushed to the railing, grasped it with both hands, his chest tilting forward. Two burly men had to grab him to prevent him from plummeting into the raging waters as well. He tried to resist, but the two were stronger than he and managed to hold him back. They only allowed him to turn his head, hoping he'd see his wife and boy emerge. Instead, two orange objects—life jackets—ripped off by the waves, came to the surface. They appeared on the water, disappeared, only to reappear farther on, in a taunting, sadistic dance. The man screamed. Gasped that he'd agreed to the sacrifices and taken all these risks so he could provide his family, his son, with a future. Far from the war in Libya. That the French president, Sarkozy, and his Western supporters had turned his country into shit. They were the ones who'd forced them to leave. It was because of them that his wife and his boy were dead now.

'All of it for this to happen,' he repeated over and over again. 'All of it for this. What does life mean to me now?'

Then he stayed motionless, flanked by the two body-guards attending to him, his eyes riveted on the unending space of the Mediterranean. Shocked by the scene, some travelers raised their voice again demanding they turn back. One stocky guy, about thirty with a paunch, turned directly to the old man with the army haircut, whom Dima had asked about the toilets. The old man didn't even glance at him but kept talking with his clique as they were passing a joint around. The more time passed, the more assured the unrelenting voices became. A frail, bespectacled young man, idealism in his eyes, wanted to know why they had closed the hatch.

'How can they even breathe, those poor wretches in the hold? They could be asphyxiated down there. They paid for the crossing, too, didn't they?'

Other voices rose to support his argument.

'What he said is right. You don't treat human beings like that,' the first man to speak added.

'It's unfair,' a woman said.

'You can't do this,' someone else spoke up. 'We'll report you when we arrive.'

At the word 'report', the old man stood up as if propelled by a spring. He leaned against the center cabin so the wind and the lurching of the ship wouldn't sweep him away. Everyone on deck fell silent to hear what he had to say. He took a final puff, slipped the joint to one of his buddies, took his time exhaling with his head slightly backward, the picture of ecstasy. Then he turned to the protesters, his strong voice overriding the wind.

'If you're so concerned about their fate, nothing is stopping you from giving them your seats,' he said, causing hilarious laughter among his group. 'As for you, nerd, you want to play the righter of wrongs? Under different circumstances I'd make you pay for your impudence for less than this. But since I'm not in the mood to deal with any bullshit, I'll just explain. If we leave the hatch open, it will let water into the hold. And do you know what could happen then? If you want to die, throw your fucking selves into the sea. Not me. As long as I'm here nobody opens that hatch.'

His words didn't convince everyone. 'The hatch was open before the brawl,' one woman grumbled. 'Such cynicism,' another one muttered. 'It's no way to treat Muslims like them. Even if they weren't,' said the man with the glasses, not letting it go. As soon as the old man sat back down, voices began to demand once more that they turn back. The deck was divided into two camps: those who wanted to return to Sabratha and the rest, the majority, that wanted to keep going. Against all odds. Short of confronting each other, insults went flying in every direction. The old man and his group went back to their business. As long as it didn't threaten the vessel's security, which was their own, they could all curse at each other as much as they wanted. Anyway, even the loudmouths wouldn't budge. They had seen how the two earlier fights had ended.

'Just let them babble,' the old man finished disapprovingly.

'EVERYONE DOES
THAT OVER THERE'

DIMA WOULD LIKE TO have had four hands to plug her daughters' ears and spare them the coarseness and blaspheming flying around on deck. But she knew it was a useless battle. That scum was shouting so loudly their voices defied the clamoring of the winds and waves combined. Besides, there was something more urgent: protecting them from possible drowning. The previous unfortunate episode rang like a warning. She had to double her vigilance. After being forced to relinquish her home, her land, she wouldn't survive losing her daughters, her most precious possessions. She reassured them with both words and caresses. She shouldn't let anything show that might increase their fear. Shayma had found shelter in her father's arms, her head against his chest, eyes closed, her left thumb in her mouth. A sign of growing insecurity for her. Hana, her older one, was glancing around, looking like an anxious animal, turning her head like a periscope, simultaneously fascinated and terrified by the roaring of the winds, the force and turmoil of the waves, the shocking screeches of the trawler, resisting the fury of the elements again and again. Dima kept praying in silence. She knew that Allah 'always answers the anxious when he invokes Him and [...] He takes away evil'.

Suddenly their young Moroccan neighbor burst into tears, even though he couldn't stop smiling at the girls a few hours earlier, trying to get them to understand his words and strange accent. Dima hadn't been able to place their origin and that bothered her. Since she was also a good judge of faces, she decided to guess his age instead. He must have been close to twenty-five, twenty-six at most. A pleasant face, despite his somewhat unsightly teeth. In the end, when she could hold back no longer, she asked him where he came from, after first telling him that she herself was Syrian. That's how she found out his name was Hassan. Unintentionally, the young man had helped Dima draw the girls' attention away from the immediate danger, keeping them from posing questions to which she had no answer.

When the storm picked up again, he curled himself up into a ball, his back rounded forward, his head between his legs, his arms hugging them. He'd not spoken another word. Hadn't looked at the girls anymore. And there he was now, sobbing like a kid realizing his helplessness in the face of the world's injustice. His nerves had obviously given way. His shoulders were shaking with spasms he tried to control, to no avail. But he couldn't hide his distress. Without letting go of his younger daughter, Hakim put an arm around his shoulder, whispering words of comfort into his ear. Maybe afraid he seemed like a wimp, the Moroccan sputtered between two hiccups:

'You have to understand, I'm not afraid of dying. The only thing I regret is that I won't see my little girl just one last time; she's only two.'

'God forbid!' Dima intervened. 'Your daughter, where is she?'

'With her mother,' the young man replied.

Having come to Italy illegally at the age of thirteen, in the wake of a paternal uncle, Hassan had married his little Aisha's mother, a pretty woman from Calabria, twelve years his senior, a human rights activist and a volunteer with a reception center network for migrants. 'She looks like our Maghrebin women,' he said with a bitter smile. He pulled a little plastic bag from his pocket, took out a cell phone and showed them the picture of the two women in his life, being very careful to protect the phone from the water spraying everywhere. It showed a plump lady, her eyes the same raven black as her hair, holding a sweet smiling little face in her arms. They'd met in Milan where, like so many Calabrians, his wife had landed in search of a job.

'There isn't much work to be found in Calabria. According to her it's worse than where I come from, in the Maghreb.'

He didn't have time to get to know that region, which his wife described as a paradise that couldn't feed its children. A few weeks after their daughter was born, they caught up with him over a petty theft he'd committed as a teenager. A kind of initiation ritual that would let him join a gang, not knowing he'd be made to pay the price years later. It happened during an ordinary police check for having run a red light. 'Everyone does that over there.' Without it leading to anything more than a verbal reprimand. When the *carabiniere* wasn't in a good mood, you'd get a ticket. But not so in his case, he had the bad luck to get picked up that day. And even though he spoke Italian with a strong Milanese accent—thanks to which he'd gotten out of quite a few bad situations—and even though he'd spent half his life in the country, since the massive 2008 sorting out of illegal immigrants, all he had was a resident's permit given to him on humanitarian grounds, renewable every two years. They were married when Aisha was born. He hadn't any time to obtain Italian citizenship. The *sbirro* proved to be intractable and had refused to consider the fact that their daughter, a little Italian, would grow up without her father. Ultimately, he had to take the rap. Immediate deportation to Morocco and banned from setting foot in Italy again for ten years.

For three long years he'd been fighting to try to return. Various appeals to the Italian Consulate in Morocco had produced nothing. His wife had moved heaven and earth, without any success. He'd immigrated to Tunisia where dinghies for Lampedusa were departing frequently. His Calabrian wife was against the idea. But he couldn't stand being so far away from them any longer. And besides, it was fast. One night and one day's sailing and you'd reach the steep coast of

Lampedusa. Closer to the Tunisian and Libyan shores than to Italy, the island was the port of entry to Europe for those who came from Africa. Between the money he'd collected thanks to a bunch of shitty jobs, 'excuse the expression', and what his wife sent him, he managed to get on board one of them. Teeming with illegals, the dinghy had arrived in the middle of the night in front of what, seen from the sea, appeared to be an island. In any case, it was inhabited, considering the large number of shimmering reflections they could see in a twinkling ballet under the effect of the tide, as they came closer to the coast. It was Lampedusa, a minuscule, arid island where you would quickly start to feel claustrophobic. He'd made it, he couldn't believe it. The first time in his adult life that he wept: he was going to be back with his wife and his daughter.

'If you're here now, then it means you didn't succeed,' Dima said gently.

'*Già*,' the young man said, whose Italian was more fluent than his Arabic. Hence his incomprehensible accent. 'Indeed,' he repeated several times, without any further explanation.

'And Lampedusa, what's it like? The reception? The people? How do they see us?' Dima started again, sensing it would do him good to talk and help a little to rid him of his anxiety.

Hassan continued as if he were talking to himself. The overloaded dinghy, whose motor had died a few miles from shore, was rescued by a fishing boat, then escorted by a naval gunboat. As soon as their arrival was announced, human rights activists came flocking to the landing area. Smiling, they were holding up hurriedly made signs welcoming the refugees. One of the women, an LGBT activist covered in piercings and tattoos, had scribbled in rainbow-colored letters: *'Welcome, migrant friends. Thank you for not leaving us among the Italians.'* They'd brought barrels of mint tea and packs of mineral water, which they distributed to the survivors as they came off the dinghy. The migrants, as they were called, were taken to a retention center away from the center of town. Thanks to an opening in the metal fence, the less timid came and went as they pleased, although officially it was forbidden. Since it was January, and the tourist season—the island's main activity—was still far off, the town hall and the police looked the other way. They could mix with the local population, contact the NGO's, and the refugee aid organizations.

Since he spoke Italian it was easy for him. After the first major shipwrecks of the early 2000's, some covered in detail by the international press, Lampedusa collected the bulk of the refugees. According to the rumors, for more than a few the concentration of people was good business. The budget supplied by the government and the European Union was relieved of several million along the way—and the toll points were many—before the remainder was allocated to the management of the center to improve the conditions for the refugees. Go figure. On the whole, things with the local people went well. 'I remember the times when we, too, would go to Tunisia with our fishing boats. We were welcomed like friends. We'd stay three or four days before going back to sea,' a little old man had told him. He'd made a room available to Hassan where he had twice spent time with his family during his stay on the island. His Calabrian wife couldn't bear knowing he was so close without visiting him. On the other hand, there was no way for him to leave the island and go to Sicily.

According to his wife and to what he himself had picked up from the Internet, things had changed lately. Without a doubt because of television, which throughout the day was airing slander about the refugees: allegedly, they were rapists, unscrupulous cutthroats, carriers of disease. On site, two or three pariahs had committed some petty theft, nothing worse, and often just to feed themselves. Although not hostile, the population became less welcoming. Some dangerous elements of a small group known as *Generazione identitaria*, joined by extreme rightwing allies from Poland, Hungary, Austria, the Netherlands, and France, were talking about chartering a ship to block the rescue of migrants on the Mediterranean by Doctors Without Borders and similar organizations. In the medium term, it was their dream to erect a wall in the Mediterranean to block Muslim invaders from the South, as was already being done in other regions of the world who had the future of their own citizens at heart. According to their spokesman, there was nothing utopian about it. One just needed the will to do it. Furthermore, such a technological feat would demonstrate the superiority of European civilization over the others.

In any event, after three months at the Lampedusa retention center, Hassan was taken to Palermo, then deported back to Morocco again. This time he didn't return to Tunisia. For some time, the Tunisian coastguard had been showing greater zeal to put most of the dinghies out of action. Rumors had it that the Italian Minister of the Interior had signed an agreement with the local authorities in Tunis, whose ins and outs eluded the average citizen. Since then, those who managed to slip through the net were fewer and fewer. The coastguard made life hard for them, they knew they were risking a lot if they were to get caught. Consequently, prices had skyrocketed. One had to wait for the right time slot, which could be postponed from one day to the next. Without knowing if it was true or if the smugglers were playing mind games with the applicants for departure in order to increase the cost of the crossing.

Thus, Hassan had settled on Libya, 'quite an odyssey, you have no idea,' he recapped for Dima. Even so, compared to the Africans he considered himself lucky, he said, as if he came from a different continent. They had a much harder time getting onto one of these boats. Especially in Libya. He'd seen some horrible things, blatant acts of racism, contempt, and cruelty. Dima received the allusion to the *znuje* in embarrassed silence. The altercation with the two snooty women when they came aboard reawakened some disagreeable thoughts in her head. Anyway, Hassan said, he wasn't planning on spending ten years apart from his daughter. His wife had proposed coming to Morocco with little Aisha during her vacation. He appreciated the thought, but it would have been a stopgap measure. 'You realize? What father would accept seeing his daughter only once a year? I didn't kill anybody, as far as I know.' His Calabrian wife didn't have the means to travel more often. Neither one of them had a future in

Morocco. He'd advised her to save her vacation money to finance his crossing. Sooner or later he would find an opportunity. Which was what happened. He'd waited six months before he could get on this boat.

'But it will all have been for nothing,' he sobbed.

'Allah is great,' Dima said gently. 'He will let us arrive at our destination. Soon you'll be able to kiss your little girl.'

This was the right time, she assured him. He would slip through the net. That was how life worked. 'You spend your time running after something you can't get. Then one day, just when you least expect it, the situation sorts itself out.' She could feel it, everything would work out for him. Dima seemed convinced. As if piloting the boat, controlling the elements, the administrative decisions once arrived at their destination, as if all of it were solely up to her. So that the young Moroccan regained a semblance of serenity and began to smile at the girls again. Taking advantage of another lull while the vessel moved on, Dima wondered what kind of a reception would be waiting for them there, for her and her family. Would she be received with gobs of spit? Displays of hostility? Or, on the contrary, would she run into people as generous as the old man who had lent Hassan a hand? That first name, Hassan, reminded her of a long-ago piece of her story she wanted to forget. She held her older daughter close to her heart and stared at the horizon.

THE IDEA

SHOSHANA AND SEMHAR would have been incapable of saying how long ago the trawler had left the coast of Sabratha. Whether it was day or night outside. They'd lost count of the hours. At sea time seemed so long, even more so under their traveling conditions. All they knew, or rather tangibly felt, was that after a brief lull the waves had come back hard. They were not letting the boat move nice and slow at its own pace on its Mediterranean path. The break allowed time for them and their companions in misfortune to catch their breath. Have the illusion of taking a trip like any other, despite the discomfort of the situation. In contrast, the water had started to beat persistently against the hull again, while the wind roared outside. Just like the storm suffered by the boat that Jonas had taken to flee to Tarshish instead of going to Nineveh as God had commanded him to do.

As the hours went by the temperature kept rising, the heat was unbearable. Not a breath of wind passed through the cracks in the hatch to bring in some fresh air. The hot, nervous breath of the cargo made the atmosphere all the heavier, generating sweatiness and a tingling all over. Like when you are stressed and feel hot flushes running through your body. At first, Shoshana was too focused on her heart's whims to pay it any attention. Then the temperature in the hold began to feel like a sauna. Sweat started to bead on everyone's foreheads and the two women were drenched.

Shoshana felt a first drop slither down between her breasts. She'd taken off the jacket she was wearing when she arrived, thinking naively she'd be traveling on deck. You could be a leader and still be ingenuous, she derided herself. Here she was, her shirt soaked through and literally glued to her skin. She wanted to take it off, undo her bra, stay topless. But even in the dark, buried in the belly of the trawler, she didn't dare. The weight of her upbringing. She imagined her father's glare cutting through the dark to hurl his disapproval at her. Like Hashem's condemnation of Cain hiding in his tomb after killing his brother. What if he'd been in the Sabratha warehouse! The smell of her own skin was unbearable to her. She could separate it from the prevailing stench. Unless it was the equally pestilential smell of the others.

Semhar, on the other hand, couldn't stop wiping herself. She dabbed herself with the back of her hand, her forearm, her jacket. She needed to get rid of it quickly before the salty sweat would sting her eyes, blurring her vision. The more she wiped, the more emerged from her body. She was sweating like a pig now. She was about to faint but miraculously pulled herself together. It reminded her of the strong heatwave at Massoua when even the Red Sea was boiling. 'No use cooking the fish we caught today,' Esau would joke, 'they're already cooked.' If this were to continue, they'd all die long before getting to Europe. Without air it wasn't viable. Even for her, who'd done turn after turn of guard duty under extremely grueling weather conditions. They had to do something. Perhaps there was a way to negotiate with the smugglers so they'd open the trapdoor. 'We can do all things through Christ who strengthens us,' she told herself, paraphrasing Paul the Apostle in his *Letter to the Philippians*. Being given a leg up, someone could knock on the hatch and explain to them that it was untenable. That they were all about to perish down there. That's what they needed to be told. They didn't seem to understand. It wouldn't be good for them either if they disembarked in Lampedusa with a pile of corpses in the hold. They'd be held responsible and end up in prison. Maybe they didn't care. In that case, they had to have accomplices on site who would help them to make it through without a hitch, escape the trial for human trafficking she'd heard about when smugglers were identified. Be that as it may, it was up to those below to intervene, take their destiny in hand by making a lot of noise. The idea had already been going through her head for quite a while.

'Sometimes you need to have the courage and the strength to shout so as to be heard. Don't you?'

After a moment, Semhar realized she was talking to herself. Shoshana was neither agreeing nor disagreeing with her.

She who was always so quick with a comeback, never going along with other people's suggestions. Semhar would have liked to get her opinion. Hard to know what she was thinking if she didn't answer. If she could see her face, she might at least read a message there. She seemed to be somewhere else. Had sought refuge in her inner universe. Or else something had happened to her. Semhar grabbed her friend's wrist, felt her pulse. From time to time it was beating regularly, staccato at other times. Sometimes it stopped before starting up again in a rush, as if to make up for lost time. Shoshana didn't react. Maybe she was sleeping, Semhar told herself. If she'd fainted how would she know? Semhar began to get panicked, a rare thing for her. But this was different. In addition to her friend's silence, there was that other thought going through her mind.

She had to help Shoshana regain her senses. Talk to someone to make sure it would be a good initiative. For it concerned everyone in the hold. Especially the men who would have to give someone a leg up. She couldn't decide on her own. Maybe Shoshana, who claimed to be a leader, would have done it without consulting anyone else. Suppressed sobs reinforced her idea. The passengers in the hold were at the end of their tether. Of everything. Of the scorching heat. Of the stress. Of their strength in their quest of hope. And soon at the end of their lives unless they did something about it.

Even slaves on the slave ships knew how to rebel. She'd seen it in the film *Amistad*. She must have been fourteen or fifteen. She'd gone wild over the main actor, Djimon Hounsou of Benin, with the body of a gladiator. She was torn between anger, because of the film's subject, and love for Cinqué-Djimon. Watching him tighten his muscles to free himself from his chains and break those of his comrades, she'd felt shivers running through her body. He was the first man who'd ever aroused such turmoil in her. Why the hell had Shoshana chosen this exact moment to fall into such a deep sleep? The more time passed, the more chance that the irrevocable might happen. They had to act. Now.

PART THREE

DIMA

Where for years a deluge of the most unlikely bombs beat down on Aleppo the White, expunging the imprints of silk and the homes of marble from all human memory, before throwing its inhabitants out onto the paths of exile. In search of peace and hope.

Thee only we serve;
to Thee alone we pray for succor.

SURA I, 5

THE BEGINNING OF THE END

WITH THE ELEMENTS seething around her, although less violently than in the preceding hours, Dima reflected on the past twenty-nine months. A long, tortuous route to now find herself here, leaning against the guardrail of this ship bound for exile. A word whose impact was hard for her to grasp, viscerally attached as she was to her native land. A word devoid of any meaning for her since she'd never participated in politics. Even at the university where the braggarts were confident enough to blame al-Assad father and son for every evil on earth, albeit under their breath. Running around talking about dictatorship. Most of them weren't born and bred in Aleppo, as Dima was. Her family still owned real estate in the old city and had moved two generations ago to the more elite west where she was born, while newcomers belonged to the population living in the east of Aleppo only for the past generation. Among them was a certain Hassan whose appearance, features, and speech betrayed a modest social background. The poor man thought briefly that he might go out with her. Such arrogance! At semester's end she heard nothing more about him. Disappeared! As if, when all was said and done, studying wasn't all that important. There were rumors that, after a detour via a prison cell, he and his buddies had been banished.

Dima had never been particularly interested in any of this. Not in the endless debates to learn who had control over the country, whether among the politically or the religiously powerful. Or if, in the name of their respective interests, there'd been a pact between the two to subjugate the population. As such, the university seemed to her a place of pointless chatter, where more than one man would push ahead in order to satisfy his desire for class vengeance. She would have bet her favorite Louis Vuitton purse—the Asty model in beige-pink—that this Hassan was one of these opportunists. After studying psychology for two years, she left the Department of Human Sciences for a much more concrete training in the field of chemistry. In that area jobs were plentiful, especially in Aleppo, which provided more than half of the country's medicinal needs. Her parents could find no fault with it. What was crucial to them was that she go to university.

'Times change,' her father often repeated—may his soul be at peace! 'If there's one thing that al-Assad father and son have contributed to Syria, it is the liberation of women. That's far from the case in the countries around us. You'd be wrong not to take advantage of it.'

Had the al-Assads really contributed to the emancipation of women as her father believed? Or was it the fruit of the struggle by the country's progressive women and men, which, in order to outdo the imams, the Baathist regime had been forced to come to terms with? She didn't know a damn thing about it. But she did intend to take advantage of it, and now. Since her earliest years that's all she'd ever done.

The youngest of three siblings, she turned up when her parents least expected it and her family pampered her all the more because of it. A housewife, her mother was approaching forty-five and her father, an agricultural engineer, was ten years older. The entire family greeted her arrival as a blessing from Allah. Her brother and sister, seventeen and fifteen years her senior, would constantly spoil her as a child and into the early days of her adolescence. She was a princess at home, where her wishes came true almost before they were uttered. Until Adnan, the oldest, settled in Damascus to work for a state organization; and her sister Lamia settled in the eastern part of the city, after marrying a penniless member of the Salafi movement, who completely turned her head around, stuffing her brain with outlandish ideas. A shock to Dima.

This mismatch alienated the two sisters. The definitive break came when her older sibling started to wear a veil and dress completely in black like a giant fly, although Syrian women are known for their elegance and for wearing dazzling colors. Although they didn't practice a hardline Islam, Dima had certainly grown up in a family that respected the Prophet's precepts. They shared their lamb at Eid with the very poor.

They observed Ramadan to the end except under special circumstances, as when her grandmother broke her hip at the same time that her sister chose to go into labor. Her father—may Allah welcome him into His dwelling!—would like to have made the pilgrimage to Mecca but his life was cut short. Two years later, his pious, gentle wife followed him, as if incapable of living without the man to whom she'd linked her destiny for sixty years. Despite this tutelage, Dima never walked the twisted path of her sister. A good Muslim, yes; a bigot, no.

In short, she'd always kept her distance from politics and therefore didn't see the huge shake-up coming. It was like a cancer that in three years destroyed life, gnawing from every corner at the social fabric. In many regions the country became unlivable, including in her city of Aleppo. From what Dima would later learn, everything had started off in the wake of the famous 'Arab Spring'. She'd heard it being talked about every so often. On the internet or, less frequently, on the State TV. In any case, the economic situation of Aleppo had nothing to do with that of the country. The city had less than 5% unemployment before all this chaos. One had to be lazy to the extreme, be bone idle, like the family Lamia had taken up with, in order to not find a job. Isn't that at the bottom of it all? When people have nothing to keep them busy, they get some strange ideas. Just twiddling their thumbs, you know. Afterward they blame the government, the affluent, fate, or even Allah. Anyhow, between her work and her two girls she had plenty to do, even if she had the Ethiopian *zenjiyeh* to help her with the house and the cooking. In need of a change of scenery after her father's death, her mother moved in and also lent a hand for a while.

That was the moment it happened. Friday, February 10th, 2012, Dima remembered it very well indeed. First came the two car bomb attacks, causing dozens of deaths and hundreds of wounded. The State TV had shown images of the survivors, faces covered with blood, wandering the streets. Bewildered. Intending to win the population over to their side, each clan accused the others of being at the source of the conflict. That very day, her mother went to join her father. Dima would never know if it was because of the slaughter or of the grief accumulated over two years without her deceased husband. She would often sit for hours, staring into space outside her own body. Still, Dima had taken her in. It was Hakim's idea, to keep an eye on her. She was too old to live alone, anyway. But wouldn't admit it. She increased the number of chores to pull the wool over her eyes. Gave the *zenjiyeh* a hard time to let her cook instead. Told stories to the girls, stopping in the middle without remembering what came next. Sometimes, not even what story she was telling. Added to these repeated memory losses were the various aches and pains she routinely complained about more and more. Hakim hoped that, by pestering her with their questions, the girls would gradually turn her away from the excessive sadness that overwhelmed her when she was alone. Hana and Shayma seemed aware of it and some nights would refuse to get out of their *jidda*'s bed. It wasn't enough. She departed two years later, happy to join her love.

Consequently, Dima would never know whether her mother had left out of sorrow over the loss of her husband or because of the twin attacks committed on the day of prayer in a city, which since the beginning of the rebellions had been spared. As if Aleppo were the last bastion of a Syria that was no more: the heavenly Syria of her childhood and early youth. The Syria she would never see again, she reflected emotionally. Without knowing whether her last thought came from the physical separation from the land of her birth or from the irrevocable fleeing of time. The fact remained that her older brother came rushing over from Damascus for the funeral. As did her sister, who lived in one of the family homes on the east side of old Aleppo, with her mullah and her slew of kids. If she couldn't take the bloody pill, all she had to do was fuck less, Dima objected, even though she despised any form of vulgarity. Or not at all, how about that. It would be better for everyone.

After that bloody Friday, life in the city was no longer the same. Aleppo's inhabitants walked around looking over their shoulder, gave a wide berth to any car parked too long in the same place, with or without a driver behind the wheel. The women of Aleppo forgot about their leisurely strolls, which would bring men to instantly stop whatever they were doing just to watch them go by. Fortunately, her parents were no longer around to witness this. At first Dima regretted her mother's departure at just eighty-one years of age. She could have held on another twelve years or so, Dima thought. As did her husband. The girls would have benefited a little more from her presence, despite her neurons going into a tailspin. Later, in view of the way things developed, she told herself: so much the better. Allah does what He does, and He does it well. Indeed. Neither of her parents could have endured watching their city being reduced to rubble, its people torn to pieces, as in the African countries where the *znuje* used machetes to mutilate each other.

Suddenly an atmosphere of suspicion grew among the people of Aleppo and for Dima that was the most heartrending. People who the previous day would look for each other on the street to have a little chat, invite neighbors over for tea and cookies, now no longer trusted each other. Worse, with their eyes, sometimes with cutting words, they accused each other of belonging to one or the other of the enemy camps. Those who lived in the east section of the city proved to be increasingly intrepid. They'd strut about, noisily laughing, in the large public garden of the station district, the Al-Sabil Park, or at the Shahba shopping mall where they couldn't even afford to buy much of anything, but merely paraded their idleness past the various stores. One day, one of them made a gesture with his thumb of slitting a neck in the direction of Dima and Hakim who in their air-conditioned SUV were stopped at a red light. It still made her break out in a cold sweat when she thought about it. The last time they saw each other, Lamia was talking just like those thugs. From what Hakim reported to her, on the internet minds were heating up, talking about democracy, about the need to put an end to the hereditary dictatorship. She had better things to do than spend her time reading this drivel. She and her husband would discuss it in bed at night. Or rather, Dima would listen to him without understanding the reason for so much hate.

Five months after the car bombing, the rebels attacked Aleppo from the southern district of Salaheddine. The authorities reacted by deploying troops, tanks, and armored vehicles in the city. In all her life Dima had never seen so many weapons of war. Then the Russians, Iranians, and Western powers interfered. The most unlikely bombs began to rain down from the sky like fireballs announcing the end of the world. Planes and helicopters roared overhead, but nobody knew any more who had sent them. What power, and by what right. Were they from Al-Shaitan or Allah?

Added to that, renegades of Daesh were infiltrating everywhere; army rebels were defecting with their heavy arms and tanks; alliances and counter alliances multiplied so quickly that she lost track of it all. The Israelis, too, were in on it and fired their missiles at Aleppo to lay into Hezbollah, so they said. The population was sniped at from all sides, like common wild boars or other haram animals. Dima didn't understand anything anymore.

ON THE ROAD
TO DAMASCUS

A YEAR AND A HALF had gone by since the events began. The city was split in two. The west, where Dima and her family had always lived, came under control of the government forces, while the east was controlled by various rival groups, each with its own allies. It meant that any hope for peace was gone. The factions were firing mortars at each other from morning to night, as if exchanging sweet nothings. They had to teach the girls to go to the cellar for shelter at the first alert. Burrowed like rats, the family stayed there without seeing sunlight for an entire week, without knowing whether it was daytime or if Aleppo's brilliant stars, nowhere to be seen anywhere else in the world, had come out. When Hana and Shayma were tired of bickering with each other just to pass the time, they'd hound her with questions:

'When will this be over, *yom*?'

'Very soon, *Inshallah*, very soon.'

'Yes, but that's what you said yesterday, too,' Hana, the younger one, insisted.

'Today it's very soon.'

'Even sooner?'

'Yes, my darling.'

But it didn't stop. For the first time in their lives, the girls had to get used to shortages, to make do with what their father brought back between one bombing and the next. Until then, all they'd known was abundance, an embarrassment of choices. Now they had to be content with what was on their plate. Either that or starve. But their adaptability surprised their mother. Dima didn't know if she would have reacted so sensibly at their age. When your horizon is reduced to the humid walls of a basement. Surrounded by neighbors whose homes were partly or completely destroyed, by others afraid to be alone, with whom you didn't always have anything in common. With whom you had to overcome mistrust and stick together. Forced cohabitation produced more racket, more kids whose mood swings, carelessness, fears, and hunger had to be managed. For you couldn't just feed your own children and pretend not to notice the others next to you drooling with envy.

Protest didn't come from the kids alone. In the cellars, tongues loosened. To keep boredom and terror at bay, to try to find an explanation for what was happening up there, which was beyond all comprehension. Some held what they called the dictatorship responsible for the tumultuous situation. Others blamed the Islamists, traitors who were using religion to take over the secular power. It was always the same, they'd always divided the country. Then they took it out on their compatriots who'd let themselves get carried away by foreigners with their so-called democracy when these same people were wholeheartedly supporting the bloody monarchies of the Gulf.

'They don't give a damn about their country,' a close neighbor of Dima and Hakim's shouted. 'All they care about is their economic interests. And besides, every nation should pave its own way, at its own rhythm, without accepting any lessons from those who were colonizing them only yesterday, regardless of the standards they're preaching today.'

It was all very well and good for Obama to talk about a 'red line' and 'enormous consequences' should there be any chemical warfare, and then not give a damn. Go and give his famous speech in Cairo addressing the Arab and Muslim world, pretending to want to change the order in this region of the world before siding with Israel, like his predecessors. And worse yet, to accept the Nobel Peace Prize without any hint of embarrassment, without having done anything concrete.

'Do you know any folks who would have refused a million dollars?' Hakim asked. 'It's those who awarded him the prize you should be criticizing.'

The heated discussions were beginning to feel like trench warfare, just like the bedlam outside. It was a political initiation for Dima. That's when she started to become intolerant of being locked in unless it were short-lived and inside a moving vehicle. Any unchanging situation in an enclosed space where she couldn't leave of her own will, left her feeling trapped. She was beginning to need air, felt she was going to faint on the inside, as if with each inhalation her life were draining out. An anxiety she unwittingly shared with the *zenjiyeh* who'd given her a piece of her mind when they were boarding. The few times during this period that a lull lasted long enough for them to sleep in their own bed or when, that night, she simply couldn't stand being buried in the cellar and decided to go back to her bedroom, placing everything in the hands of the Prophet and Allah, Dima would take the side facing the door, forcing her husband to leave it open. Poor Hakim had to wait for his daughters to be fast asleep so he could suggest making love. Often fruitlessly because, as soon as her head hit the pillow, she'd be comatose in an unconscious attempt to make up a little for the sleep she'd lost.

With his resourcefulness at the time, Hakim was able to bring electricity into the cellar. A privilege constantly sabotaged by ill-timed power cuts. As a result of this, they could watch a movie on the computer, keep the kids occupied, in addition to not rotting away in darkness twenty-four-seven. Some days they'd catch some television. With intermittent Internet, they'd know where and when to get fresh supplies in the city. The first weeks, *Hamdullah*, they had enough to eat; not that it was anything luxurious. But the food situation began to grow worse too. Much worse. One day, a neighbor caught one of the enormous rats that wandered through the cellar without paying any attention to them, becoming aggressive if they were chased. Their way, no doubt, of claiming priority over the space. The creature was the size of a young rabbit. The neighbor would have cooked it had the idea not been so revolting to the children, while an elder intervened: 'Rats, it's like *halouf*, it's *haram*.'

With each more or less prolonged respite, the men would go out looking for food, Hakim included. To succeed in bringing back some provisions, they had to take the 'passage of death' that linked west and east Aleppo. It meant crossing the checkpoints set up by each clan after negotiation with the guards. Bribes, entreaties, family relationships, friends served as bargaining chips. On the route between two road-blocks, one had to avoid being fired on by snipers hiding in the gutted buildings. 'You'd think we were in Sarajevo under siege,' Hakim reported to Dima who feared for her husband every time he went out. Leaving at dawn, the round-trip would sometimes take the men an entire day, not knowing whether or not they'd make it back by nightfall. On occasion they'd spend the night on the other side without being able to let the women know, since phones worked only half the time. Those nights Dima would fall asleep with lead in her stomach at the thought that her girls could wake up as orphans, and she a widow. Such momentous risks only to see the men return the following day with very little, or even nothing at all. The despair in their eyes was pitiful to see. The adults would then do without, in favor of the children and the elderly.

When the supply was damaged by a mortar or in some other mysterious way and there was no running water, Hakim would connect a rubber hose to the nearest fire hydrant. He'd always find a solution, Hakim. Always. If that weren't possible, he'd go all across the west of Aleppo with other men until he came back with water-filled jerricans. To relieve themselves there were buckets, half full of water they would take upstairs to be emptied in the toilets at daybreak. At the same time, an adult would accompany the children outside where they could stretch their legs, shout at the top of their voices, let off steam as much as they wanted before returning to the dankness of the cellar. The unbearable lack of privacy. The whining of the smallest ones. The smells, too, when the buckets couldn't be emptied. The dull sounds that came down from outside causing recurring tremors in the bowels of the buildings. So many things, which finding herself on this dubious trawler en route to Lampedusa made her remember in spite of herself.

Dima had no idea how they could have handled such a long period of deprivation. Like rats, human beings must be able to adjust to anything. Nevertheless, after eighteen months of it they no longer had the strength. They knew their time to leave the city had arrived. Like tens of thousands of others before them. They turned off the light, closed the door, and left. Taking only what was strictly needed: official documents, bank books, title deeds, some family photographs. Others kept them on a flash drive. Two or three pieces of clothing. They would recreate their wardrobe in Damascus. Not forgetting their cell phone. Everything that could fit into one suitcase, two at most.

Dima insisted on leaving on a Friday, the day of prayer. Even if, partly or completely demolished, most of the city's mosques had closed their doors. That was her only non-negotiable condition. Hakim didn't see anything wrong with it. And what if the bombings were too intense for them to leave on the projected day? Too bad: they'd leave the following Friday. In any case, on the day of prayer, to erase that fateful Friday from her memory when she'd witnessed the city of her birth descend into madness. Witnessed her mother's leaving to join her father. She wanted to put their departure under the best of auspices. After that, she would be sure to come back and pick life up again as before.

They didn't wait for the following Friday. On Thursday, the warring parties instituted a forty-eight hour truce under the aegis of the UN and some members of the Security Council. The next morning, the cellar assembled for prayer, men in front, women in back. At the end, Dima and her family said goodbye to the diehards and the undecided. They went, leaving a wounded Aleppo behind. Mangled to its core. To her great regret she couldn't let her sister know, who was blockaded in the east of the city. Even if they were cool toward each other because of her damned mullah, they had come out of the same womb. Her deceased mother—may Allah welcome her into His paradise—would not have appreciated Dima leaving without a farewell. But that day no phone calls were going through. She left a message with a neighboring family that was still hesitant to move, should her older sister or her mullah husband manage to cross the demarcation line and come to make inquiries about them.

THE DECISION

ONCE THE DECISION to leave Aleppo was made, Dima and her family found refuge at her brother Adnan's house. The civil war had spared the capital until then. Large convoys of Syrians were going there for shelter, leaving by any available means of transportation. Until, they hoped, the hostilities would come to an end so they could go home and pick up their previous life or, for the more pessimistic, leave the country. Adnan lived in a spacious apartment in the posh district of Basha, with his Aleppo born wife Qamar, whom he'd known since adolescence, then lost from sight before being reunited in Damascus a few years later. Their two boys, of whom one had been working for three years while the other was finishing university, shared a three-room apartment in the same street as their parents. The one condition on which Dima's sister-in-law would let her sons leave home. In fact, independence under supervision proved to have its good sides, for they'd stop in almost daily, for dinner, or to bring laundry to be washed and ironed. Or for the pure and simple joy of being with their family. Sometimes on a weekend they'd spend the night if they didn't have a date or plans to go out with friends to some trendy Damascus club.

Ultimately, their limited emancipation allowed Hana and Shayma to each have their own room and not get in each other's way. After the long interlude in the cellars of Aleppo, they needed that, Dima exulted and couldn't stop thanking her sister-in-law. 'Allah will reward you.' 'For what?' Qamar asked. 'What else is family for?' Hakim and his wife stayed in the guestroom. The boys hunkered down on the sofa bed in the living room on nights when the whole little group decided to stay up together to listen to Dima and Adnan's childhood memories, enveloped in the aroma of Qamar's dishes, as she was a more than skillful cook.

'Why do you think I married her?' her husband would tease, his own culinary talents limited to the preparation of *zhourat*, a flower tea, but very proud of the compliments his house guests had for his wife.

'You terrible macho!' Qamar answered, tossing her napkin in his face. 'Is that the example you set for your sons?'

'Don't let him mess with you, my sister. Adnan, you old pig, you didn't do the cooking, I'll have you know,' Dima cut in while Hakim diplomatically kept a low profile, an affable smile on his lips.

The girls were the joy of Auntie Qamar, who was not totally at peace with the loss of her two boys. Having no grandchildren, Uncle Adnan would at the slightest opportunity suggest a drive into town and so they discovered Mount Qasioun, perched at more than a thousand meters altitude, where at night, bundled up in duffel coats as protection from the deceptive breeze, they had the lights of Damascus at their feet. The weekend after they arrived, Adnan took them to visit the Cave of Magharat al-Damm—the Cave of Blood—where Kabil committed the first killing of a human being on earth when he took the life of his brother Habil. The story both fascinated and frightened the two sisters. Narrated in this magical place, it took on a symbolic significance in their eyes. Next came the excursion to the Al-Hamadiyeh Souk, 'the largest and most beautiful one in the world', their uncle said proudly, more chauvinist than a lifelong Damascene. There the sisters hoarded colors and smells, dug their hands and nose into the stands of the merchants who, to their never-ending delight, offered them snacks and trinkets as they passed. They stuffed themselves with *bouza*, orange flower and pistachio flavored ice cream, so that when it came time for dinner they were no longer hungry. Their eyes wide open in wonder at the mountains of dried vegetables, fruits, spices, and their ears equally astonished at the thousand and one sounds coming from everywhere, under the amused look of their host, this time accompanied by their dad while Dima and Qamar had gone out together for some window-shopping and a little private talk between sisters-in-law.

Even before they arrived, the sisters were registered at the local school, thanks to Qamar who had also taken care to tell the mothers of their respective classes, so they'd be welcomed kindly by their classmates. They picked up a semblance of normal life, with well-defined routines as children of their age require. Three weeks after their arrival, they felt at home. Aleppo had become a memory they'd bring up from time to time when others asked, but almost never among themselves anymore. Still, in Dima's mind things were clear: all of this was temporary. Just until, she hoped, as did thousands of other migrants, the combatants dealt with their problems and let the family return to their native town.

One way or another, this damned war would surely come to an end. Even the Iran-Iraq conflict had ended after eight long years of ruthless combat. She remembered as a child seeing streams of refugees pouring into the streets of Syria. They were on television, faces without any expression, bunches of kids following in their wake. In old Aleppo, where between the solidarity of some and the contempt of others who accused them of stealing their bread and their jobs, many had failed as had their pipe dreams of going home. In Syria's case, Dima tried to convince herself, the government forces would take over sooner or later, supported by the Russians and the neighboring Iranians. In the worst case, they'd arrange an honorable peace with the moderate factions that the West supported. Together they'd dismantle the fanatics of Daesh.

Not for anything in the world did Dima want to hear talk about these renegades enthusiastically exploding the country's most beautiful sites, places of which the entire world was envious. Destroying mosques as if they were crushing an annoying mosquito, tarnishing the image of Islam in the eyes of the world. And besides, she was too attached to her freedom as a woman to confer any virtue on their *niqab*, the veil in colors of mourning, which reminded her too much of her sister and her mullah. The government was playing on this image with the intention of rallying to its cause the fringe of the population that remained attached to a certain very relative secularism. Be that as it may, Dima was full of hope, *Inshallah*, that reason would prevail. Absolutely.

Six months later, Hakim's wife grew disheartened: the war, very much present, was gradually approaching Damascus. In the rest of Syria the situation had deteriorated even more. However, the television broadcast nothing but victories of the loyalist army, presenting them as humiliating defeats of the enemies of peace and progress, hiding from the population the advances made by the rebels and the troops of Daesh that were no more than a hundred and fifty kilometers away from the capital. Thus, the war played out on the internet, each party vying to take control and change it into a vehicle of propaganda. The news came from other, informal, sources as well: mail, telephone, cell or grapevine. Even carrier pigeon, Hakim joked in the face of the avalanche of news 'from well-informed sources' that came from everywhere.

Dima had seen the archeological site of Palmyra and its two thousand-year old temples shattered, which she had visited with her parents as an adolescent. Centuries of history wiped off the map in the snap of a finger. During that time, her fellow-citizens continued to flee the burning country in their tens, their hundreds of thousands, out onto the highways of the world. Just like those Africans whose poverty was displayed throughout the day on every TV and computer screen on the planet. That was the moment Dima knew that in her native land there was no longer any future for her and her family. Sooner or later Daesh, the rebels, or the Westerners would arrive in Damascus. And since al-Assad's son was hanging onto his throne, it would be war there as well. Better get out while there was still time. A conclusion she reached with a heavy heart. What remained to be done was to discuss it with her husband.

One night in bed when the whole house was asleep, she talked about it with Hakim. It had always been the setting for their most constructive dialogues. Often after making love. Far removed from the commotion and tensions of everyday life, in any case. Non-smokers, nestled in each other's arms, they'd take advantage of this time of relaxation to talk. They'd made it a habit to whisper, even though there was no risk of any indiscreet ear hearing them. As if it were the best way to listen to each other. Or to prevent a mischievous djinn from stealing their words as they passed from the lips of one to the ears of the other. That particular night Dima opened her heart to her husband. She told him about her doubts, her fears. The fear that the war would come right to their doorstep. Tear their family apart. Take away their loved ones. She didn't know if she could survive such a loss. Losing her parents, despite the immense grief, was part of the natural order of things. But burying one of the girls would destroy her. She told him about her yearning to go back to a normal life again, without worrying about the next day. To do ordinary things.

Go to the movies, for instance, to a restaurant, a concert. At first Hakim was quiet.

'We're doing all that in Damascus already, aren't we? What is there anywhere else that we can't have here?'

'Yes, but for how much longer?'

'In the end things will surely settle down, *rouhi*. Besides, we're at home here. It's our country, we have no other. You don't emigrate when you're over forty,'—he was forty-one, she thirty-eight. 'And where would we go?'

'Wherever we're welcome,' she answered. 'Where we can offer a future to the girls.'

That was the argument that convinced Hakim. Hana and Shayma were the apples of his eye. Wasn't it his duty as father to protect them against all odds? Including offering them exile as an inheritance. Far from their native sun, their schoolfriends, their early memories. If anything happened to one of his daughters, he would never forgive himself. And if something happened to him and Dima, what would become of them? Of course, they could count on Adnan and Qamar. All he had to do was look at the way those two were indulging the girls. Every now and then Hakim had to intervene to get things back on track or else he'd have two spoiled little brats on his hands.

It was already not so easy with Dima. Not to get him wrong, he loved her very much, his Dima. She could be anything, even a great deal of fun when she wanted to be, but easy she was not. She had a tough character, after all. So having to manage two princesses in addition to the queen mother... In short, children should have boundaries. Qamar and Adnan were not their biological parents, perhaps that's why they hesitated to reprimand them.

Other than that, the time was beginning to drag for him as well. For six months now he hadn't really accomplished much of anything: some small computer jobs suggested by his brother-in-law or some of his friends. He couldn't call that working. He was getting depressed going round in circles in the apartment. And as long as they had the possibility of doing things differently they couldn't feel happy drawing on their savings, which weren't bottomless. The truth was that they had one foot in Aleppo and the other in Damascus. They were no longer there while they couldn't make up their minds to be here. Being here would imply actively looking for a job, for each of them, which so far they'd refused to do, for fear of starting a new life in Damascus that would make a return to Aleppo difficult. They'd rather pretend they were waiting. And yet none of it depended on them. Hakim knew it. Plus the news that reached them from Aleppo was hardly reassuring. In the end, it didn't take him long to see eye to eye with his wife. The muezzin's grating voice hadn't ripped through the air yet to call for the al-Fajr prayer when they had come to an agreement on the decision to be made and fallen asleep in each other's arms.

EXPLORATIONS

THE NEXT DAY the couple began to gather information about visa applications for refugees at various consulates. They didn't investigate Australia, which was too far from everything. Canada and the United States were brushed aside as well. Distance was not the only reason; the American dream, so fascinating to so many Syrians, did not inspire them. The same held for Africa, even with the Maghreb as their target. Hakim knew his wife too well not to realize she'd break out in hives at the mere mention of that continent. For them it was Europe or nowhere. With the exception of the Eastern European countries where xenophobia, especially with its Islamophobic face, had become so commonplace it was frightening. The coming to power of the extreme right in several of those formerly communist nations had exacerbated the rejection of the other. The scum of Al-Qaeda and Daesh were offering them the excuses for their need to hate on a silver platter. A practicing Muslim, Dima only wore the veil inside the mosque, as the holy Koran advocated. Outside, she liked nothing less than letting her lovely ebony curls fall freely on her shoulders, but that didn't mean she was prepared to serve as a scapegoat for frustrated and perverse ignoramuses.

The couple also struck France from the list of potential lands of exile. According to some friends who'd settled in Belgium, while ordinary citizens, often those of very modest means, could be enormously generous toward foreigners, the politicians spent their time reveling in mere words: country of human rights, land of welcome… Why not beacon of humanity, while they were at it? As soon as they couldn't resolve some social tension, they threw in the issue of immigration as food for popular vindictiveness, picked up by cautious intellectuals arrogant in their speech but well versed in the art of being courteous. Under the pretext of being even-handed, they remained more inclined to welcome deposed dictators than their victims. Or else artists and intellectuals whose fame would serve to perpetuate the myth of a land of welcome.

'Too bad,' Dima said, 'The girls would have loved to live in the city of the Eiffel Tower, the Champs-Elysées, the Arc-de-Triomphe.'

'France isn't just Paris, you know.'

'Don't worry. We'd visit Versailles as well, Mont-Saint-Michel, the chateaux of the Loire, the Côte d'Azur,' she summed up a list of stereotypes. 'It must be a beautiful country, even if their cuisine will never be equal to ours.'

'I understand,' her husband answered. 'But we have to be realistic, *habiba*. You said it yourself: we'll go where we're wanted. And that, according to the information I've been able to gather, as well as what the "Belgians" said, is obviously not the case in France.'

That assessment made, the choice of destinations available to Dima and Hakim was reduced to at most a dozen countries where they could expect their qualifications to be recognized, perhaps after some further study, find work, and have a decent standard of living. Enthusiastically and naively they threw themselves into the search for the precious 'open sesame' that would provide them with the right to leave Syria and move to Europe legally. They had professional skills, some savings, they wouldn't be a burden on the society that received them. All four of them spoke English and, in Dima's case, a little French, always useful in countries like Switzerland, Belgium, or Luxembourg. Their profile was that of the perfect war refugee.

Their application was refused everywhere. Often without any real explanation. Perhaps their file hadn't been truly analyzed, Dima said. 'They must be getting thousands of them,' her husband soothed her. 'How can they take every one of them into account? How can they handle them all with empathy and objectivity?' Had Dima been interested in the United States, he might have played the green card lottery. They might have had better luck. Those government officials who were compassionate advised them to try their luck again at a later time. 'In six months or a year. Who knows?' It was the only word of comfort they were given by the most sympathetic of them. For now, they didn't comply with all the conditions needed for a refugee status, and even less for that of political exiles. The European economy was convalescing, and the old continent couldn't receive the world's hardship all by itself.

'I'm sure you can understand. We're very sorry.'

As they waited, the war was advancing on Damascus with great strides. Dima felt its threatening breath down her back. One day, it took the form of a car bomb assassination attempt, either the rebels or Daesh claiming responsibility. A week later, scattered bombings came down on the capital's periphery, so that it awakened the memory of the dark days in Aleppo for Dima.

In her dreams she saw her country rediscover its harmony and she was back in her Aleppo home, miraculously spared from the bombs. She'd started working again. In the evening, she came home, sat down at the table with her family to have dinner, prepared by the Ethiopian *zenjiyeh* who in their absence had watched over their house. It wasn't too much to ask, good heavens! But in the morning, she'd wake up in Damascus, in her brother's guestroom, wanting to weep, but having to suppress it so as not to bother Hakim.

After all their futile steps, stressful, energy-consuming, and all in all quite costly, the couple finally contacted a network of smugglers that assured them they could help the family enter Europe, starting from Tripoli. 'We'll discuss money later.' For now, they should think about getting there with their own resources. Which in these times of conflict was no small matter. Most international airline companies were avoiding Syria. In partnership with their countries' governments, they used it as a way to put pressure on al-Assad, in the hope he would finally clear out. With the dictator out of the way, it would be easier from the Western point of view to negotiate a peace that would exclude the Islamists, their bête noire.

Among the solutions they considered for getting to the Libyan capital, Dima and her husband thought of leaving for Lebanon by car. Like tens of thousands of refugees before them. From there they would take a plane to Tripoli. In normal times it would take two hours to drive from Damascus to Beirut. But with the hundreds of thousands of Syrians already there or trying to enter, the official Lebanese channels ran the risk of being swamped. The tiny state of Lebanon, weighed down under the waves of refugees from the region, could decide to close its borders at any moment. And if for some reason they were stuck there, how would they get to Tripoli by car?

'All said and done, it's not a good idea,' Hakim concluded.

After another night of productive dialogue, the couple agreed to fly to Algiers and leave from there for the Libyan capital. Thanks to the Internet, Hakim had studied the situation. The advantage of going via Algeria was that they wouldn't need a visa. It was time and money saved. From then on, they should expect tortuous detours and several short hops; many airline companies were avoiding Libya, highly chaotic since the fall of Colonel Gaddafi. In the worst case, they'd find a way to cross the thousand-kilometer border between the two countries there. In just a few weeks, Dima became cognizant of the innumerable conflicts in the region and the difficulty in leaving Syria, even for people like them. It tore her morale to shreds. Nevertheless, Hakim was committed to persuading his wife that the family should go to Tripoli. Having been apprised of their plan, Adnan timidly tried to dissuade his sister and brother-in-law from leaving:

'It's risky,' he said. 'The press has daily reports of boats capsizing in the Mediterranean. That sea has become one gigantic cemetery.'

It would break his heart to receive news of their disappearance. Without a trace. Without his being able to identify their bodies. Give them a burial. Say the *Salat Janaza* for the peace of their soul. He'd never get over it. He would be angry with himself for the rest of his life for having allowed them and their daughters to run that risk. As her big brother it was his duty to draw their attention to the perils of their plan. The more Adnan talked, the less convincing his voice became. Deep inside he thought they were right. Had Qamar and he been younger... But you don't attempt an adventure like this at fifty-five, an age when you have more memories than future. And if their boys were to announce their departure tomorrow, he didn't know how he'd react. If he'd give them the blessing, the *bismillah*, in the name of Allah, the Clement and Merciful; maybe with a heavy heart, but he was almost sure he'd do it.

Faced with their determination, he recommended that his sister and brother-in-law be discreet. He was working for a government enterprise. If this came to be known the family would risk paying the price. They'd be seen as adversaries, seeking to discredit the regime, when all they were trying to do was save their skin. Adnan also warned them against the swindlers for the crossing, traffickers who'd prey on the despair of people in their situation, holding out the prospect of the Promised Land. Upon arrival they'd be stripped of all they had. Once these details were openly discussed, they agreed that Adnan would transfer money as things evolved, according to their needs, before sending them the bulk of their savings once they were settled. *Allahou akbar!* He would guide them there safe and sound.

Those were the words Dima had hoped to hear. They did her good, comforted her in her decision. Once she and Hakim had agreed to leave, they would have left anyway. Better to go with her older brother's blessing, she thought. Deeply touched, she embraced Adnan, covered him with kisses, as if he'd been alone in planning and financing their project. 'Thank you,' she whispered to him.

DEPARTURE

IF IT WAS HARD to tell the girls they had to leave once again and go still farther away, what Dima dreaded even more was her inability to find the right words to explain the reasons why. In Aleppo there'd been no need for a discussion. The reality of the war was right there. Tangible and brutal. With its confinement, its daily deprivations, its nightmares, its fears. Its hatred of human beings ad nauseam repeating the fratricidal myth of Kabil and Habil. Its explosions, the blasts of its firearms of every sort, of every caliber—medium, small, heavy—sophisticated or home-made, automatic or radio-controlled. As long as death spewed pure hell and mowed down lives. With its incessant roar of planes and helicopters, the whistling of missiles ripping through the night, the day. The ground quaking continually in advance of the tanks. Buildings collapsing with a crash of concrete and dust, their

battered steel skeletons giving way. The calls for help from
people to whom no help of any kind could be offered. The
sirens of ambulances coming closer, rising and falling, then
suddenly dying out, reducing the heralded hope to nothing.
Then silence. Crushing with mysteries and anguish. Like
gigantic dark clouds stacking up in the sky, presaging torren-
tial rains and devastating floods.

Hana and Shayma were familiar with it all. Dima and
her husband hadn't had any trouble telling them why it was
necessary to go and take shelter at Uncle Adnan and Auntie
Qamar's house in Damascus. The months of confinement
under such strange conditions felt like anything but a game,
as Hakim had initially tried to make them believe for their
protection. When your stomach growls, hunger makes you
writhe in pain, and you sometimes hear yourself saying 'a
sleep is as good as a meal'; when you wake up screaming
from a nightmare in which huge steel caterpillar vehicles
came charging at you to swallow you alive, you may be only
six and eight years old but you understand a whole host of
things. You wonder if one day you'll be the age of your parents. If you, too, will know the joys of love and will give birth.
If you'll see your children grow up. And to protect them will
invent stories that even three-year old toddlers wouldn't
believe, as yours are doing with you. In your misfortune, it
might even happen that you'll doubt the existence of Allah
and of His Prophet.

The little one had started to wet her bed. Against their will,
she and her older sister had embraced the idea that the horror
wasn't going to end overnight, with a wave of a magic wand.

And the night when Dima announced that the family was leaving for the capital the next day, it seemed perfectly logical to them. For what they had known for almost a year and a half wasn't living. That evening, Shayma's only worry was knowing whether she'd come back home—their house had been spared until then—to get her favorite toys and see her friends. When it was all over. For the two sisters it was obvious, but only as an interlude between two other places. They couldn't really imagine life without their return to Aleppo.

This was a completely different story. They had adapted with astonishing speed to life in Damascus and hadn't brought up Aleppo again with their mother. It seemed that in their eyes that was ancient history. A page turned forever. Like water incapable of going back to its source. It had made Dima sad. For her Aleppo represented their roots. And like trees, humans cannot live without roots. That's how they hang on in the great adventure of life. That's how they manage leaving, even for very far away, and coming back without getting lost. Otherwise you wither on the vine until you waste away. That was the reason Dima was having a hard time molding herself to that painful word exile, to which she came inexorably closer with every mile the broken-down trawler traveled.

The girls had created a new home with new habits, new friends, while the language and the cultural universe were still the same. Although in Dima's eyes it would have been absurd to compare Damascus to her native city, which had been the country's economic lifeblood ever since the Silk Road. Proud Aleppo, the Vienna of the Levant with its multiple gates, its ancient monuments: the fortified Citadel, the Junblatt Palace, the clocktower of Bab-al-Faraj, the Forty Martyrs Cathedral... and here they were, having to pack their bags once again. This time for some place elsewhere, inconceivable for them to understand. Where they'd have to speak another language, change their perception of the world, build other relationships with their environment.

Even if the war had hastened their understanding of life, Dima was aware that at their age she couldn't tell them everything. Or else she would have to use such simple words that they might not understand anything at all. How to explain to them, for instance, that they shouldn't divulge the news of their departure to their classmates to prevent putting Uncle Adnan and the rest of the family in danger? How to justify all the roundabout routes to get to Europe which they weren't even sure they'd be able to enter? Illegality, what's that? After yet another night of discussion with Hakim, they agreed to say as little as possible, as late as possible. 'The less they know, the better,' her husband concluded.

However, every now and then Dima couldn't keep herself from alluding to a possible place outside Syria. Watching a film on television with the family that showed images of Germany, Italy, England, she asked them if they wouldn't like to visit those countries someday. Thereby she'd piqued the curiosity of the two sisters who, eager to know more, pounced on the Internet and the enormous encyclopedias in the living room cabinets. Then, on the world map, they were able to locate the Coliseum, the Imperial Forum, the Brandenburg Gate, and Big Ben. Some of the monuments reminded them of the Temple of Jupiter or the Roman Arc in Damascus, the ruins of Palmyra that were constantly shown on TV. On the other hand, Dima was very careful not to tell them about the conditions under which they would be traveling. 'We'll make it up as we go along,' she thought, and Hakim agreed.

Three days before their departure, she really had to tell the girls they were leaving for Europe, for the countries whose images they'd been looking at the past few weeks. In her immense desire to protect them, she might risk their rebelling against any thought of leaving. 'Again? I'm fed up with all this. Why can't we stay here like our friends? They're not leaving.' But the news didn't upset the girls beyond what was reasonable. Ever since the time their mama had been talking to them about Europe, it had seemed natural that they would go there in the end. The little one wanted to know if they would see Father Christmas; the older one asked about the snow, the bears, all those exotic things. Dima said 'maybe', without committing herself:

'It depends how long it takes us to get there.'

'Is it that far? As far as America?' Hana asked.

'Farther than the moon?' Shayma asked in turn.

'Not that far,' Dima said. 'But we have to have a layover in Algiers, then a stop on the way in Tripoli, the capital of a country called Libya.'

'What's a layover?'

'It's when you stop and wait to change planes in an airport.'

'And why do we have a layover?'

'Because there's no direct flight from Damascus to Libya.'

'Where is Libya?'

'In Africa, *rouhi*.'

'So they're black then.'

'They're very much like us, my kitten.'

'How can that be?'

'It's a long story.'

'Will you tell us some day?'

'Yes, yes, sweetheart.'

'Do they speak African in Tripoli?'

'They speak Arabic, my girl.'

'Why?'

'And why are we going there?' It was Hana speaking now, without giving Dima any time to answer her sister's question.

'Papa and mama have things to do there.'

'Can't you do that later, or ask Uncle Adnan to do it for you? That way we can get to Europe faster, without any layover.'

'Impossible, sweetheart. We have to be there ourselves, all of us together.'

'And then we'll go back home?' Shayma asked.

'Don't worry, angel. Auntie Qamar and Uncle Adnan will be here waiting for us.'

'Not here. The other house we left behind.'

Since they left Aleppo, Shayma hadn't talked about that anymore. Dima had been convinced, erroneously, that her younger one had left the city of her early childhood behind. And here she was, bringing the subject up again. At the most inopportune moment because Dima had no answer for her. She felt a twinge of sadness. Deep in her heart perhaps, her daughter had sensed they were leaving for good. In that case, why had she broached the matter at that precise moment? In her panic, Dima didn't know what to say. After a brief silence, so doubt couldn't seep into Shayma's mind, she muttered something like 'we'll talk about it again tomorrow' or 'later, when Papa comes home'. She didn't remember anymore. As luck would have it, her little one hadn't insisted and moved on to something else. In bed that night, Hakim suggested raising the topic in stages without going into any details.

'Children live in the moment. They easily forget yesterday, and just as easily adapt to today, without planning for the future too much. When it comes to that, they're much more flexible than adults. That's also why they suffer less from migraine,' Hakim dodged, before turning his back and falling asleep.

The crossing was to cost three thousand dollars per person. For that price, the smugglers would get them into Europe, and that was it. The rest, consisting of the leg to Tripoli, the costs of lodging and food there, would be their own responsibility. In truth, money was not a problem. As far back as Dima could remember, the couple had never lacked for money. They'd both been working for a good fifteen years already. Hakim a bit longer, since he hadn't lost time changing from one university department to another. Indeed, Hakim, had always known what he wanted! They'd had time to save money. In addition to what they had inherited from their respective parents, they had no debts to pay off. The house in which they lived in Aleppo belonged to Dima's family.

Initially a technician in the pharmaceutical industry, she had settled for a job as a medical secretary, which left her time in which she hoped to create a family. She had always wanted children. Also from an affluent family, Hakim was a software engineer.

They came to know each other thanks to her profession. They first met in Dima's clinic where Hakim came to be treated for a gastric ulcer. He was scared stiff of the endoscopy, although it was just a minor procedure. That day, she still remembered it, he wasn't very impressive, far from the dashing young man of a fine background, handsome, boisterous, and with a bright future whom she subsequently discovered. He demanded general anesthesia for what was a painless test that many a patient endured without any anesthesia at all. He couldn't be dissuaded. Dima understood he was afraid and, touched, reassured him as if he were a child. As they talked, she managed to convince him to have the procedure under local anesthesia. A compromise that would become the trademark of their relationship. In addition to being a handsome man and an established professional, Dima thought at the time, Hakim could also be flexible. She was sick and tired of cheap macho men who refused to change with the times.

Having said that, she didn't throw herself into his arms, much less his bed, like some desperate old maid ready to give herself to the first comer. That's when the guy takes you for an easy lay. Therefore not marriageable material. And should he ever accept to marry you, it's only so you can become his cleaning woman. None of that for her. For now she'd let him stew in his own juice. For a moment, her mother, her cousins, her women friends were all afraid she was going to let this good catch slip away. They treated her like a capricious princess straight from *A Thousand and One Nights*. Her older sister, brought up-to-date by their mother, blamed her for always having been daddy's little girl, spoilt rotten since her earliest childhood. Preceding her by many years, she was sorry she'd participated in this endeavor, with the result today that no suitor would ever be good enough for Mademoiselle. In any case, the emotional tie to her older sibling had started to unravel until it broke at the death of their mother, who had always served as the link between the two sisters.

Dima knew very well where she wanted to go with her suitor. She'd known from the beginning that he was the right one. He was the one, she was sure of that. Her heart would go into a spin as soon as she saw him, to the point that she'd always stop for five or ten minutes on her way to see him so she could pull herself together before each date. But she shouldn't let Hakim believe that he was all she was waiting for, that if she'd made it to twenty-six without a fiancé it wasn't because no one wanted her. Or because she had a nasty temper. That frightens men off. He, in particular, was the type you had to reassure. She'd known that since the endoscopy episode. Several boys, including that scoundrel Hassan, had approached Dima and, one after another, she'd sent them packing. Until Hakim showed up. She let him come, granted him the basics so he wouldn't lose patience and leave, but not as much as he desired. Dima was very good at that little game. With her alluring smile and her flattering words, when she wanted to she was the queen of trickery. Skilled at getting on the good side of father, brother, cousins, friends, who all let themselves be lured into her trap and ask for more. Indeed, what the young woman wished for was to be loved as in the European and American films, which she devoured every evening and on weekends in the Aleppo movie houses. She preferred dark places with small screens, which before the war the city was replete with. And it happened just as the princess desired: Hakim increased his visits, brought her flowers non-stop, took her out to restaurants, gave her DVD's of the international classics until their engagement was officially announced.

He kept it up after they married because he loved his Dima. Her heavy jet-black curls. Her lustful gait that conveyed a curbed sensuality, despite herself. Her face that would light up when she burst into unguarded laughter. That was actually what had seduced Hakim in the end. He continued also because she'd threatened him with every possible and imaginable reprisal if Monsieur were to change his good habits. 'Don't think that now that we sleep in the same bed you can behave like a clod.' If need be, she knew how to let him cool his heels, postpone his yearning for fatherhood. Her young husband had to guarantee her that he was ready to assume a progeny, which she wanted as much as he, if not more. And not only to prove to his friends and to society that he had balls. Her objective in life wasn't to support the patriarchal wishes of a Syrian male. Was Hakim sure he could look after his children when the time came? Give them the attention they needed? 'A kid is not a shrub, it doesn't grow by itself. And even shrubs need a hand to water them now and then.' It was out of the question for Monsieur to spend his free time hanging out in cafés with his friends and leave them, her and the women of both families, in charge of his own offspring.

Before that, however, she wanted to take advantage of her youth and travel with him. Gradually she succeeded in getting him to be the man she dreamed of. Her friends never stopped praising Hakim's inner qualities that contrasted sharply with those of the males they had at home, about whom they complained all the time. Half-mocking and half-proud, Dima would reply: 'It's your own fault. You didn't train them well. This one is custom-made. Between the *zenjiyeh* and him, I have ample time to take care of myself.' Today she was ready to go to the end of the world, to face hell or high water with her Hakim.

The Saturday of their departure, she wasn't particularly nervous: Hakim was beside her. Well, almost, separated only by the girls who really wanted to be between their parents for this occasion. To wander around delightedly through the hall of the international airport of Damascus, three-quarters empty so that their steps resonated on the stone. They'd been discussing it for an entire day, asked a thousand and one technical questions that their father was happy to answer. 'How do planes stay in the air?' 'When you go to the toilet, does it fall on the heads of the people below?' Shayma asked. 'What is autopilot?' Dima was certainly turning an important page of her life, but the four of them were together.

Adnan and Qamar came to the airport with their two sons. It was an emotional farewell, but no more. The main things had been said and done at home the night before after they left the mosque and that morning over family breakfast. Hugs, effusive and kind words, the umpteenth warning, good luck wishes: 'May Allah in His benevolence be with you.' Tears, too. With all of her six years, Shayma reminded them all that they weren't going to a funeral, but they were going to see bears and Father Christmas. That made the whole clan laugh. The boys, who'd spent the night at the house to be with them, brought down the baggage while the family joined them downstairs. Adnan drove the ten-seat minivan they'd rented so they could all be together till the end, rather than taking two separate cars. After checking the luggage at the airport, they waited until the very last moment before going through security. A final kiss as they held hands, then Dima and Hakim were gone, holding back the tears they felt welling in their eyes. Being dragged along by their impatient daughters whose gaze was already turned toward the bears and Father Christmas. Toward another place. Toward tomorrow.

ON BOARD
THE TRAWLER

Where are your monuments, your battles, martyrs?
Where is your tribal memory? Sirs,
in that grey vault. The sea. The sea
has locked them up.

DEREK WALCOTT

THE ONSLAUGHT

SEMHAR KEPT THINKING about how to get her companions in misfortune to attack the hatch. Tiny gleams filtering through the trapdoor suggested it was daytime. Besides the overall layout of the hold, they allowed her to make out a jumble of silhouettes, but without diminishing the heat, as dense as ever, the lack of air, or the feeling of suffocation. It would be the perfect moment to launch an attack, the soldier in her thought. People were at the end of their tether, on the verge of losing everything—their time, their money, their dreams. The sacrifices they'd made to succeed. If you added life itself, the list was complete. Pressing down on the lever she was convinced she'd trigger a reaction from them. Those on deck had no notion of what those down below were suffering. They were like the stones of the proverb, nice and cool in the riverbed that couldn't care less about the stones exposed to the heat of the sun. They had to realize that under these conditions those below wouldn't hold up. Did they want them dead or what? In that case, might as well die fighting. 'Better to die standing than to live on your knees,' she said, quoting Che Guevara. An ideological slogan she had retained from her time in the army when the government in Asmara was embracing socialist tendencies.

Shoshana, on the other hand, was trying to rein in her heart, to cope with the heat, the stickiness clinging to her skin. She was on the brink of exploding. She felt like screaming out her last breath to eject the demon devouring her entrails. The little energy she had left, her spirit, her entire being was turned toward this hand-to-hand battle with the evil inside her, the ultimate battle she owed it to herself to win. For herself. For Hiram. To help him, once she was in Europe, to leave the hell of Sabratha. She wouldn't give up. That was it, she wouldn't give up. Whatever happened. Even at the cost of her life. 'No, no, what are you talking about?' the angel inside her head whispered. 'You have to stay alive. Alive, you hear?' For her parents as well. To honor their self-sacrifice. So they could be proud of her. She repeated these phrases like a refrain, while wiping huge drops of sweat from her neck and face, which sprung back with the speed of the carnivorous plants in animated films. Faster in any case than she was able to get rid of them. To give herself courage, she chanted, alone in her corner, '*Oh! Jonah. Oh! Jonah. Go down to Nineveh.*' An old gospel song with a lively beat and lyrics. She'd first heard it sung by an a cappella men's quartet and downloaded it as the ringtone on her cell phone. She loved a cappella men's choirs. For her, it was music in its barest essentials. She'd listened to the song ad infinitum, as she did every time she really liked something. She couldn't help it. Shoshana's love was insatiable. Even if, after her distressing experience with that jackass, she'd vowed to stop.

Up above, the passengers were struggling once again with the wind's fury. It would leave, then come back escorted by waves that would brutally wash over them. Toss the boat from side to side. Straighten it up like a nimble puppet in the hands of a destructive Golem. When the wind withdrew, the ship's hull would take over, groaning enough to shatter the hearts with foreboding. From time to time, supporters of a more humane treatment of the cargo in the hold and the others, the as-long-as-it-doesn't-affect-me group, would insult each other, more to vent their alarm than out of a conviction they could win their opponents over to their side. While the traffickers remained wholly indifferent to all of it.

Dima and Hakim had picked up their conversation again. A way to muzzle their own anxieties. To pull the wool over the girls' eyes. They, too, were on different sides of the fence. The one-month wait, sequestered in a hotel room in Tripoli, the problems of the crossing that was more dangerous than anticipated, the uncertainty about the future: had they been right to bring the girls along into this predicament? Hakim's irresponsible sleeping during the brawl with the *znuje*, all these ordeals had brought the flaws in their relationship to light. Revealed the unspoken truths that had accumulated over the months, the years, like so many layers of dust under a Persian rug, behind the fine façade of a cohesive couple, envied or taken as a model by their entourage.

When her husband had the misfortune to ask her what she thought of the business of the people in the hold, everything came to the surface. Still, Dima tried to control herself. She answered curtly—so she wouldn't blow a fuse—that what mattered to her was getting her daughters to safety.

'To me as well, protecting the family comes before all else,' Hakim replied. 'What are you talking about, *habibi*?'

'And how do you expect to do that? By snoring like an old chainsaw while terrible things are going on? Nice way to protect us. Really,' Dima mocked.

'You think this is a good time to be arguing?' Hakim uttered between his teeth so the girls wouldn't hear.

'Listen, to each his own. You, you'd rather that this band of *znuje* come bursting onto the deck and come straight into our midst to slit our daughters' throats! Not me. You and your big ideas!' (As she spoke those words, Dima thought again of the two African women at embarkation, whose insolence she had trouble processing. That kind came into her house only as servants. And even then. Just because the circumstances had put them on the same boat didn't mean they could permit themselves to order her around. Really, what were they thinking, those two?)

'Still,' Hakim said after some reflection. 'It's no way to treat any human being. That's not what Islam says.'

'Let's talk about that. What does Islam say? That a man should drink on the sly? Like when I caught you by surprise drinking alcohol in Damascus? Who knows how many times you lied to me about that? Maybe you were already doing it in Aleppo. You hid your little game well, didn't you? Who knows how many other things you lied about to me.'

'Islam doesn't formally forbid drinking. That's not how it's written in the Koran.'

'You just interpret it as you want to. You're nothing but a good talker. And to think that I let myself be taken in by your sweet talk. You really bamboozled me, and how. No really, what an idiot I was.'

'Anyway, this is neither the time nor the place to be talking about these things. This conversation is of no interest to the girls.'

'Right. With you it's never the right time to have a serious conversation,' Dima taunted, always needing to have the last word.

Hakim didn't respond anymore. He withdrew into one of his typical silences, only disrupted by the raging elements alternating with the shouting matches of the other travelers. He, too, was thinking of Aleppo again, of everything he'd left behind. And especially of the future that was awaiting them on the other side of the Mediterranean. Once their savings were spent, what would they live on? How much time would it take for him to learn the language of the country that would agree to receive them? To get his qualifications recognized, if possible. Apparently, English-speaking computer scientists had a better chance than others, which was good since it was the language in which he'd mastered all the technical jargon of his training. Or else, study for a new profession? Yes, but which one? To tell the truth, he was no longer sure at all he'd made the right choice with Dima. Maybe he should have left alone and then, once he was settled somewhere, apply for the family to join him. Instead of having them run these risks. Maybe they should have stayed and faced the situation there. Maybe they would have died like the tens of thousands of others killed by one of the factions that occupied the land. So what? The same fate could await them now, if they were shipwrecked. And he wouldn't even be able to save his daughters. How long can you last without any food or water in the middle of the Mediterranean, attached to a life preserver? That story about people surviving at sea without eating or drinking for days on end, clutching a part of a plank, was merely a fable. According to his calculations, it would just be a matter of hours, not days. And death with its hideous eyes would come, enfolding their voiceless wails in its liquid cloak.

In the meantime, Semhar had decided to move on to the attack without consulting anyone else. Not even Shoshana who, once she'd surfaced from her strange sleep so similar to a black-out, had taken shelter in her world of chanting and humming. Semhar, propped up slightly better on the side of the hull, began to pontificate to her companions in misfortune. One had to wonder how such a powerful voice and such determination could come out of such a scrawny body. Out of this tiny bit of a woman who, when seen from the back, could be easily taken for a little girl. Her face, features, and sweetness were those of a child. She told them in English—simultaneously translating into Tigrinya because of the large number of Eritreans, Ethiopians, and Sudanese in the hold—'We are all human beings. Therefore, we have the right to some respect.' Sure, they'd paid less than those on deck. So what? They were all in the same situation. War, dictatorship, the unstable climate had chased them off their land. They were all fleeing from something. And they were all looking for a life. Never mind the color of their skin, their ethnicity, their social status or their religion. Whether they were unbelievers, believers in one God, or in many gods. If the boat was going to capsize, the Mediterranean wouldn't distinguish between those in the hold and those on deck. The only certainty they had was that there wouldn't be any chance at all of getting out as long as they were locked in below. She would challenge anyone, even the best swimmers, herself included, to find their way to this damned trapdoor, then open it while fighting the Mediterranean, the darkness, and the lack of air. In a word, in the absence of any solidarity, it was their right to at least demand some respect.

'It's not normal they closed the hatch up there. If this continues, we'll all die from heat and asphyxiation. And the sacrifices we've made, the ordeals we've endured—you all know what I'm talking about, even you guys—will have all been for nothing. Pointless, right?'

She revealed her plan to the cargo in the hold, who listened in silence. Not another groan. Just some intermittent whispering from someone translating her words for Francophone friends. It almost seemed as if, in the space of an ebb, even the Mediterranean had rolled back in the face of the strength she conveyed. Inside the hold they no longer heard the waves or the wind. And yet, as Semhar was speaking her heart was pounding as if to break against her rib cage. She was worried that her neighbors would surely hear the noise it made. In fact, she wasn't used to speaking in public. At school she hated reciting a lesson or a poem, standing in the center of the classroom, or worse, up in front of everyone with the eyes of the teacher and her classmates fixed on her frail little person. Even though here she was bolstered by the darkness, she did not feel comfortable. Not legitimate. Her words seemed incoherent to her and she was afraid she wouldn't be understood. But still she went on. She had to make the best of it. And she approached it as only Toughy Semhar would. A true Guevara in skirts, Shoshana praised her later, revived by her speech. From her guts she pulled words she didn't think she knew, played her voice like a musical instrument, seducing, scolding, electrifying her audience. They had to attack the trapdoor, or they would all go down, she concluded.

However, her words didn't have the effect she'd hoped for. A heavy silence followed her discourse. 'You could cut it with a chainsaw, girlfriend,' Meaza would have said to play it down. How much time went by? A minute? Three? A quarter of an hour? It felt very long to her. You could hear the entire hold breathing. In regular intervals but out of step. Like a choir in canon, chopping its phrasing for lack of air before rushing to catch up once it was found. Then a man's voice was raised in the semi-darkness. It said in French that up on deck they were armed. They had knives, baseball bats, steel bars. 'We're empty-handed. If we're patient, if we take it upon ourselves, we'll manage. With patience you can, in the end, even see the navel of an ant. It's just a question of time.' As he was talking voices whispered the simultaneous translation in several languages. He hadn't finished speaking yet when others wanted to be heard. Chaotically. As if that's all they'd been waiting for.

'The gentleman is right,' a woman said in English.

'It would be an unfair contest,' another man said in a mixture of Tigrinya and Arabic.

'Or David against Goliath,' Semhar retorted. 'Little David armed with his slingshot against the Philistine giant with his coat of mail and his enormous spear. But we all know who won in the end. By the grace of the Almighty. By the strength of the ancestors. By his own bravery.'

Having said that, Semhar specified, it wasn't about declaring war to those on deck. Although, if that's what they wanted, they could have it. Their numbers were greater and their opponents were not armed with guns. They could surround them quickly and get the upper hand. Having done almost two years of military service in her country, she knew what she was talking about. But it wasn't what she was suggesting. They just needed to negotiate with them about keeping the hatch open. And maybe to bring the weakest and most vulnerable above deck. Everyone would win that way.

'As for the rest, do you really believe we're going to make it under these conditions?' she answered the first speaker. 'Look around you, my brother. We're all at the end of our tether. There are pregnant women here, children, your children, who are weaker than we are. There's a dead teenager right here next to me. And he's not the only one. Who'll be next? You? Me? Who?'

Semhar's words were still not getting the full approval of the hold. The herd there was diffident, afraid to bet their last chip and lose everything before the end of the game. As long as they were alive there was hope. Why go tempt the devil and precipitate a death that no divinity may have planned? Semhar had run out of arguments. She was frustrated. Her face misted over without knowing whether it was with sweat or tears. All of a sudden, she looked her tender age, her lack of experience. She was ready to give up. Or at least leave it in the hands of the Redeemer. He would find a way to speak to the heart of these people or bring them safe and sound to the other side of the Mediterranean. Hadn't he changed water into wine? Multiplied bread and fishes? Brought Lazarus back from the dead? Christ continued to be her last resort. 'As for me,' she thought, 'I fought the good fight, I finished the race, I've kept my faith. From here on in, the crown of justice will be reserved for me; the Lord, who is a fair judge, will bestow it on me...'

At that moment Shoshana's voice ripped through the silence that had followed her friend's last words. A strong and beautiful head voice. A natural voice she'd never truly trained. As an adolescent, she was her parents' pride. Even more so when she began to sing at weddings, at *B'nai* and *B'not Mitzvahs*. Her reputation had gone beyond the limits of their own small community. In Onitsha, people were prepared to pay for her to come and enliven their ceremonies. But it held no interest for her at all. Her only pleasure was to bring joy to her own. To see their eyes shine in ecstasy, forgetting their small everyday concerns for an hour or two. And also for them to sing to the glory of He who shall not be named, as King David had taught them. That was enough for her. The first powerful gospel notes arose. Swelling, expanding, filling every nook of the hold, penetrating the hearts. As a result the air grew lighter, breathable.

> *Joshua fit the battle of Jericho*
> *Jericho, Jericho*
> *Joshua fit the battle of Jericho*
> *And the walls came tumblin' down*
> *Hallelujah*
>
> *You may talk about the men of Gideon*
> *You may talk about the men of Saul*
> *But there's none like good old Joshua*
> *At the battle of Jericho*
> *Hallelujah*

Suddenly the spirits were awake at the suggestion of the shofars of good old Joshua and his army bringing down the thick walls of Jericho like dominoes. For an instant, the cargo in the hold forgot the foul heap they had become, the heat, the fear. The winds again roaring outside, accomplices of the Mediterranean in manhandling the trawler. The hull groaning over and over again, louder and louder. Galvanized by the song, the passengers, these nobodies, grew into a chorus and responded: *Hallelujah!* And then the entire hold was singing with Shoshana. Sustained by the audience, she pushed her voice to its height, accompanying herself by snapping her fingers and tapping her feet to provide the rhythm. All by herself she was a percussion section at the apex of its harmony. A one-woman orchestra. Inside her head she sang with Mahalia Jackson, whom she admired with all her soul. Since she was a little girl. Since her father had introduced her to the singer. She must have been seven or eight. She was interpreting the version of the woman from New Orleans. 'Go blow them horns, cried Joshua, I'll do the rest.' *Hallelujah!* the cargo replied in chorus.

> *Up to the walls of Jericho*
> *With sword drawn in his hand*
> *Go blow them horns, cried Joshua*
> *The battle is in my hands*
> *Then the lamb ram sheep horns began to blow*
> *The trumpets began to sound*
> *Old Joshua shouted glory*
> *And the walls came tumblin' down*

Unexpectedly, something amazing happened. While some were picking up the refrain with Shoshana, *Joshua fit the battle of Jericho*, others climbed up to attack the hatch. No one knew who was standing on whose shoulders, but it didn't matter. They went at it in good faith. Outside the waves doubled their raging assaults against the hull. Either the people in the hold didn't hear them or they ignored them, wholly immersed in their deliverance. They were two or three hundred, maybe more. But one would have thought thousands, their lungs were disgorging hope that loudly. Determined, their bare fists banging on the trapdoor, banging as they sought air. Sought freedom. The ship started to pitch even more under the double attack from the cattle and the waves. Terror showed in the eyes of those on deck who sensed that beneath their feet something very serious was happening. In a panic, Dima wondered whether the *znuje* had gone mad. It must be the work of those two impertinent women at boarding time. There was no doubt about that. She imagined them all around her. As one man the smugglers stood up. On their guard, bats and knives in hand. 'We've got to shut them up,' the old man said. 'Shut them up, in God's name,' he repeated, as if to convince himself. As if the song carried by these hundreds of lungs were a lethal weapon. Stronger than waves and winds. More dangerous than the Mediterranean itself.

NAVAL BATTLE

WHAT FOLLOWED NEXT came from the realm of the unspeakable. Or a horror film. So many scenes of violence surpassed comprehension. Swept up by Shoshana's voice, the men in the hold saw themselves as Joshua's troops attacking the walls of Jericho. Their repeated efforts smashed the hatch's outside lock to pieces. They wrested mixed cries of bewilderment and terror from the passengers on deck, who were anything but expecting a revolt from the folks that some of them had contemptuously baptized *kelouch*, *zenji*, or *qird*. Especially since they were busy, fighting winds and waves. And then there was the damned steersman who had seemingly lost control of the ship. They really didn't need that, too. 'What did the Negroes have in mind this time,' Dima wondered, unnerved. 'What kind of abomination were they going to inflict on her and her angels now?' In a mother-hen reflex, she drew her two daughters under her arms as if, all by herself, she could have protected them from a horde of assailants.

Armed with their assorted weapons, the old man's assistants stood at the trapdoor, ready and waiting for the mutineers. And they didn't have long to wait. Some would later say they'd committed their atrocities in collaboration with those passengers who were against going back to Sabratha. When interrogated by the Italian *carabinieri*, others argued that those travelers had been mere spectators, if not indifferent at the very least powerless. That the mob, who were able to control all the passengers, was large enough to defend itself. All the same, it was carnage such as the annals of the Mediterranean couldn't have recorded in ages. And in all likelihood, it took more than the gang of eight to carry it out, especially in such a short time.

As they were coming out of their hole, the human cargo were executed. Throats slit. Stabbed in the abdomen if they had the bad luck to come into view. Caught off guard by blows from baseball bats and steel bars to skull, shoulders, chest. Before falling back down to where they'd come from, into the belly of the boat. Or being hoisted up on deck so their executioners could finish the job. Even so, the flow didn't stop. The hatch shattered, causing a stream of light to spill into the hold and, as a witness on deck recounted, the cattle surged towards the opening, destabilizing the trawler even more. It rolled over to one side as if it had collided head on with a pirate galleon under full sail. Those below kept pushing and pushing, one after another teetering on the next one's shoulders. Behind them, their comrades in adversity were champing at the bit, yearning for the light outside. Inadvertently trampling the weakest in the crush.

At first, the ones in back didn't realize what fate lay in store for those ahead of them. They were pushing with all the strength that the wretched of the earth possess. Starving for oxygen and light. Their efforts were accompanied by shouts of anger and anxiety, adding to the confusion. While Shoshana's voice rang behind them: *'Joshua fit the battle of Jericho.'* So dense a surge made it impossible for the old man's cohorts to execute them all. Some who hadn't perished right away refused to be slaughtered like sheep for the feast of Eid. They put up fierce resistance, fueled by the force of despair. Those who managed to come through unscathed grabbed the chance to extend a hand to companions from below and pull them up, both out of solidarity and a need for backup. Ultimately, the numbers of the cargo on deck were great and determined to sell their lives dearly. The terrorized deck passengers crowded near the stern, leaving room for the combatants, who were now in a space all to themselves, as if in an MMA cage, that martial art where everything is permitted.

'Show no mercy,' the old man yelled, like a general sending his troops to attack a fortress. He himself remained in the background, however, content to give the deathblow to already wounded mutineers. 'Show no mercy. Kill 'em all, these sons of bitches.'

The fighting had spread across the deck. The two groups traded blow for blow. The cargo defended themselves furiously, led by a six-foot-two, extremely muscular and feisty young Senegalese, one of the two Muslims who a few hours earlier had recited the *Salat Janaza* for their murdered comrade. Having been sequestered below, the fight was providing them some exercise to stretch their stiff limbs and release some of their pent-up stress. Despite the risks, their lot was less desperate than that of the slaves who'd left Gorée, pulled out of the hold where they were rotting away by slave traders, who then cracked their whips and forced them to dance once a day to get their circulation moving. A little movement would permit their merchandise, which is what they were, to arrive on the other side of the Atlantic in better shape. The Senegalese fought to do them posthumous justice.

Disarmed, dehydrated, blinded by the daylight, exhausted from the oppressive conditions on the ship, the cargo had trouble matching their adversaries after the first surge of their attack. Still, they kept it up. Despite broken arms, entrails hanging from the abdomen, an eyeball out of its socket being held in with one hand while the other arm was swinging around blindly looking to punch one of the killers. No doubt they assumed they wouldn't be shown any mercy, so concluded they might as well go down fighting and die in dignity, as befitted their human condition. They would die, but first they'd make these bastards pay. And so the injured and dead piled up on deck where, not daring to throw their forces into the melee, horrified passengers led by the young scholar wouldn't stop screaming:

'Stop! Stop it! For the love of God!'

The entreaties came in the countless variations and intonations of the Arabic language. In the heat of the moment,
the assailants didn't hear it. Or they didn't give a damn. Some
because they wanted to put down the rebellion to prevent
it growing any further. Others so they wouldn't end up as
victims themselves. The battle raged on, the sound of bones
snapping under the blows of baseball bats, the screams of
men, women, and children attacked in cold blood, when
they'd barely poked their noses outside of the hold.

Semhar and Shoshana managed to thread their way
through the middle of the clash without too much harm,
other than a knife cut on Shoshana's arm, fortunately not very
deep. As soon as they were nestled among other passengers,
Semhar quickly wrapped a bandage around the wound. The
fighting continued a while longer under the equally ferocious
battle of breaking waves and winds. It seemed the trawler
was the prize of victory for whichever element was the first
to crush it to a pulp and send it to the bottom of the sea. The
first to shout victory, mission accomplished, indifferent to
the victims' fate.

At first, the athletically built Senegalese and his group
succeeded in disarming the old man's horde of its knives.
Then the rebel leader got hold of the debris of the hatch,
held it over his head with both hands and tossed it into
the sea. But the victory was short-lived. Identified as the
leader, he became the traffickers' target. One of them, the
smaller blond one, slipped behind his back and grasped
one of his legs, clutching it like a hyena at the back of
an elephant's knee. They managed to knock him down,

kicking him and beating him with steel bars. The baseball bats had all broken in the fight. Although pinned down, the Senegalese didn't surrender. He continued fighting, like an animal refusing to die. With a last wrench of his torso he was able to throw off his aggressor and get up again. Then he ran to the hatch and threw himself headfirst into the hold for protection.

No other fighter came out again. The human cargo had at last taken stock of the massacre when they discovered the number of corpses piled up on deck. Not counting the dozens of wounded who'd fallen back down, breathed their last in the aftermath and whom they gathered up, stunned, like so many testimonials to the failure of their attempt. Added to that, the even more impressive number of the beaten who were bleeding like stuck pigs in the back of the hold. The initial help brought by their companions was of as much use as a bandage on a wooden leg. The Senegalese wrestler had suffered cuts and scratches, bruises and a dislocated shoulder resulting from his headfirst dive into the hold. In their anguish they had been victorious nevertheless, he thought: the hatch stayed open. Which is what he'd subsequently tell the *carabinieri* and the journalists who came to interview him. From then on, depending on the trawler's progress and the angle of the sun, light cut across the recesses of the hold again.

On deck, the old man and company, with blood-spattered clothes and faces, began to clean up. They summoned passengers to help them throw the vanquished into the sea. Were any of them still breathing? The traffickers ignored the groans. Once the bodies were tossed overboard, they washed the deck down with huge buckets of seawater. Without a doubt so they wouldn't leave any trace of their crimes to be noticed upon arrival, in case the ship were to be boarded and inspected by the authorities. With their dirty work done, they changed their soiled clothes for clean and dry ones, kept in waterproof bags. While Dima spent her time trying to turn her daughters' eyes away from the horrifying spectacle, she hadn't noticed that the two *zenji* from when they boarded were now sitting right next to them.

The old man stuck his head through the hatch to let the cattle below know that the hold would stay open for the rest of the trip. As if it were a gesture of gallantry on his part, not a right obtained after a hard-fought struggle by the people below. Now that they had what they wanted, the old man continued, it would be in their interest to stick to the rules, unless they wanted to meet with the same fate as their comrades. Especially if they cared about arriving at their destination. They wouldn't be stupid enough to give it all up so close to their goal. For attacking them was to give up. Give up their plan. Their life. Just so they knew: they would stay vigilant up on deck. He said it in French, English, and Arabic to make sure everyone understood. A well-controlled delivery from beginning to end, his tone deliberately firm. With a satisfied smile on his lips he then turned to the blond boy. Asked him to light a joint so he could relax. They really deserved it, didn't they? Other than a few punches and scratches—nothing new to them—their group hadn't suffered any losses. His eyes closed, he took two drags before passing the joint to

Mickey. During the brawl, short as it was, the man standing by the captain's side had stuck his head out the cabin door. Then, satisfied that the situation was under control, he had resumed his place, not to be seen again.

SOS MEDITERRANEAN

SHOSHANA AND SEMHAR were still recovering from their emotional ordeal while trying not to attract any attention. Without a doubt, Shoshana was the happier of the two. She couldn't believe it. Outside at last! Inhaling deeply, she filled her lungs with fresh air, drunk on liberty and light. The power struggle between wind and water? Nothing but a spat. Trifles passing her by compared to what she'd lived through so far, buried in the dark belly of the boat. Gradually, her heart found its natural rhythm again. But a small worry drifted through her head. What if someone were to snitch on her? In the confusion she'd huddled wherever she could, without paying attention. Well, she shouldn't let it ruin her happiness. And, if worse came to worst, Shoshana reassured herself, the hatch was staying open and would let some light into their dungeon. That way she'd be able to keep her demons at a distance, fight them on almost equal terms until they arrived on Lampedusa. For now, she savored her little personal victory. To the point of forgetting about her flesh wound.

Pragmatic as always, Semhar brought her back to reality. With a confident movement, she ripped the sleeve, already nearly ruined by the knife blade, and prepared to use it as a bandage. It was better that way, even if the wound wasn't bleeding much anymore. Having finally noticed the presence of the two, Dima was watching their every move. She wasn't going to spend the rest of the journey monitoring them. For a moment she considered betraying them to the smugglers, especially the heavyset Negress with the big mouth, and have them sent back to the place from which they should never have emerged. That would make her eat her words, that bitch. But she remembered Allah's command to suppress your anger and forgive. If only to ease her heart, Dima thought. As soon as Semhar had torn the fabric, Dima took a plastic flask with 90% alcohol out of her bag, lifted the cap halfway, and handed it to her:

'This might be useful. You'll give it back to me when you're done,' she said in English.

Semhar thanked the generous benefactor. The alcohol came just in time to disinfect the wound, which urgently needed it. The shirt hadn't been washed in ages, and had collected a multitude of germs between the hangar in Sabratha and the hold of the ship. When Shoshana raised her head to thank her, too, her blood froze. She recognized the lady from the embarkation. The one who'd compared her to a monkey. It gave her such a shock that the pain in her arm came back.

'Ouch! You're hurting me,' she reproached Semhar. 'Sorry, sister.' She came down on her friend only to keep from jumping all over the other one, that bitch. Shoshana and Semhar stared at each other. Dima didn't want to lower her eyes in front of the *zenjiyeh*. Anyway, she'd followed her heart, as any good Muslim would have done in her place. The Prophet— may Allah's peace and blessing be his—had shown them the way. Shoshana, on her end, didn't have time to refuse, to say: 'I'd rather die.' Semhar had already poured some alcohol on a piece of cotton another passenger had given her and started to clean the wound. When she was done, she returned the flask to Dima and thanked her again.

'You're welcome,' she said. 'Don't hesitate to ask if you need more,' she added, continuing to challenge Shoshana with her look. A provocation that compensated for the feeling she'd been too kind, therefore too bloody stupid.

At the time Hakim didn't comment at all. He was content to just take in the scene unobtrusively. Dima wasn't even aware of it. His remark would come later, when the two Black women had their back turned and seemed disconnected from their exchange with Dima. Still, Hakim was careful to speak softly, more to protect their privacy than to avoid being heard by the *zenjiyat*. Anyhow, he thought, they wouldn't understand Arabic.

'I thought that family came before all else. And now there you go, helping those folks. What if the killers had seen you? You want them to come after us, too? The scene you saw before wasn't enough for you?'

'Rest assured; they didn't see anything. They were too busy cleaning up. Unless you're going to betray us, they haven't even noticed that we're here.'

The voice that answered wasn't Dima's. Despite his precautions, Semhar had heard and understood. Hakim didn't know where to hide. He would like to have been a thousand miles away to get away from his small-mindedness. Even in the hold would be better. He hoped the girls hadn't heard him. His words were the exact opposite of what he'd always taught them—compassion, empathy, solidarity. His wife's dark look made him withdraw even further behind his cowardice. A silence followed, then Hana, the older one, asked Shoshana how her injury was. Did it hurt? Was she in a lot of pain? The little girls asked her questions in basic English, the result of private classes she and her younger sister had taken in Aleppo. 'It's important for your future,' Dima had explained to them without consulting her husband. And she was right. As usual. The proof: Hana had been understood by the *zenjiyeh*.

'It'll be alright, sweetie,' Shoshana said. 'It'll be alright.'

Still in her father's arms, it was little Shayma's turn to offer a few words and said, this time in Arabic:

'It's a booboo, it will go away.'

Dima's baby spoke with all her childlike sweetness, wrapped in a tired smile. When Semhar translated it for her, Shoshana replied, all smiles herself: '*Shukran*, sweetheart', one of the few words she knew in Arabic. 'What's your name?' 'Shayma,' the little girl answered, happy that the lady had asked her. 'It means "very beautiful",' she added proudly. Children shouldn't have to pay for their parents' foolishness,

Shoshana thought. Perhaps the little girls had experienced the same from their stupid bitch of a mother, too. Shoshana hung on to that thin bit of hope. But when Shayma asked her in turn: 'And you, what's your name?' an angel unfurled its immaculate wings over the little group. How to say her name without giving herself away? Semhar came to mitigate the discomfort, saying something in Arabic that her friend didn't understand while the boat creaked from all sides and kept moving forward, bloodied by the waves and yet unbowed. At least, that was what Shoshana thought. And the passengers on deck with her, including the man in the command cabin and the captain.

One, maybe two hours went by this way, the trawler yielding, grinding, but not breaking yet. A scattering of seagulls appeared in the distance, whirling around, thereby suggesting dry land was near and bringing hope. The exhausted passengers made the most of the daylight and a slightly calmer sea to doze off. The earlier ordeals had eroded their resistance. Even those like Shoshana, deathly afraid of the immensity of the Mediterranean and its vagaries, allowed themselves to drop off into a light sleep. Dima in fits and starts, the little ones as if they were in their own bed. Alas, the reprieve didn't last very long. A shriek of terror arising from the hold woke them with a start.

'We're taking on water. We're taking on water.'

At first, no one seemed to understand. Maybe they were coming out of a dream, still trying to wake up. Maybe the alert had been given in a language that those above didn't understand. Later, the journalists who'd come to cover the story were told that it was shouted in Swahili. Others swore it was Lingala, a detail that to them seemed of utmost importance. When the cries in Tigrinya reached Semhar's ears, things changed abruptly. With one leap, the young Eritrean tore herself from the mass of bodies around her and screamed the translation to the old man and his cronies. They didn't react right away. No doubt because they were afraid to be tricked by the *khalech* below. But the horrified cries kept on mounting from the hold in languages they didn't understand. Then in English, soon after in Arabic. Two or three from the Maghreb and a few Libyans were the last to cry out at the top of their lungs. Surrounded by his cronies, the old man finally grasped the situation.

He reacted with unbelievable calm and asked the blond boy and the man with the crewcut to get a flashlight and go down to verify. 'You never know with that sort.' Then he called Mickey and told him to alert the man who'd been next to the captain ever since the departure but who never left the cabin. No one could tell whether he was the second in command or a trafficker of an even higher rank than the old man. A taciturn type. Nobody had heard a word come out of his mouth during the entire trip. The news had moved like a trail of mad ants, sowing panic among the passengers on deck, while wailing arose from every corner. The quickest to react made sure that they and their loved ones had their lifejackets around their necks.

Dima clasped her daughters under her arms, her eyes signaling her anxiety. It didn't cross her mind that, in case of a shipwreck, she wouldn't be able to save them. She who didn't even know which limbs, arms or legs, needed to move first to do the breaststroke. Shoshana nestled close against Semhar, seeking physical reassurance. They didn't speak. The tension around them was already quite acute. Showing in the looks, the rigidity of their bodies, the prayers that instinctively came from lips. Softly, Shoshana chanted: 'I lift up my eyes to the hills—where does my help come from? My help comes from the Lord, the Maker of heaven and earth.' Semhar uttered more or less the same words: 'The Lord is your keeper. [...] The Lord will guard your going out and your coming in. From this time forth and forever.' At the peak of the shrieks and the panic Dima, too, turned her eyes toward heaven: 'Your Lord is He who makes the ship wander at sea, for you, so that you will go in quest of His blessings.'

Only the innumerable children on deck hadn't noticed the impending danger. In their mind this couldn't be anything worse than what they'd experienced until now. Despite the looks of fear that came and went in their eyes, they seemed to have accepted nature's fury as part of this adventure. An adventure they would tell their friends about on arrival via Instagram. Including the moments of anxiety, but also the delight when the sea was smooth and flying fish would surface under their eyes before disappearing into the water a few meters farther on. Shayma assured her older sister she'd seen a dolphin racing the boat while she was sleeping. Hana told her she was making it up, which made her cross, so she went into a sulk. Meanwhile, the old man tried to calm the passengers down.

'There's nothing to worry about,' he shouted. 'Everything's under control. Quite the contrary, it would be better for you to remain calm so as not to make things worse.'

He had to intervene to prevent the situation from getting away from him, he'd decide on a course of action when his cohorts came back with more reliable information. But it was tough going since the terror around him was escalating. He ordered his companions who were still among the passengers to keep down the noise of the screams coming from the hold. The catchphrase: 'There's no reason to panic.' They were already in the Sicilian Strait, somewhere between Lampedusa and Malta. Even if they couldn't see dry land yet. If ever something were to go awry, which it would not, the coastguard would have time to intercede. International law obligated them to come to the rescue. When the two representatives finally came back up, what the old man read in their looks was more telling than any words could be. The trawler was taking in water: at the bow, on portside, they briefed him seriously in their slender nautical vocabulary.

'Something must be done, boss,' the blond said, alarmed.

'Calm down,' the old man responded, without dropping his cool, 'Give me the specifics. How fast is it coming in?'

'It's serious, boss,' the man with the crewcut said. 'Very serious.'

'Shit,' the old man came back. 'That's not what I asked.'

'We can't tell, boss. But it's coming in fast. It's coming hard, it's pouring in. If we don't do anything, the hold will be completely flooded in two or three hours.'

'OK,' the old man said. 'Come with me. There are three buckets of tar in the captain's cabin. We'll get those. You,' he said pointing to Mickey and the two others, 'go down and plug the holes. Above all, keep your mouth shut. If the people on deck ask, it's nothing. Try to make those below hold their tongues. Even if you have to use force. Take a steel bar with you, you never know. Me, I'm going to talk to the two in the cabin.'

In the hold, the water was entering in a steady flow through a crack about thirty centimeters long by twenty wide. It was bound to get bigger as the trawler endured the attacks of the waves, unless something was done to plug it up. The two crooks used a piece of wood, a mixture of tar and oakum to stop the flow, under the worried stares of the cargo in the hold. They did the best they could, but the water kept seeping in. Clearly the caulking wouldn't hold for hours and, besides, there wasn't any more tar. The two men had used the rest to caulk other crevices found here and there in the front of the hull. They left the empty buckets for those in the hold to bail out the water already there. One of them would stay near the trapdoor to give them a leg up and help with emptying the buckets. Thereafter their fate was bound to the captain's expertise. He'd have to go full speed ahead to bring them to their destination, as they explained in detail to the old man when they came back up.

Shaking his head, he listened to their report. Vertical creases showed on his forehead, a sign that he was thinking. He asked very specific questions to get the most exact information about the state of the hull before he went back to the cabin where he negotiated for a while with the man next to the captain. They seemed to be on the same wavelength. The conversation over, the taciturn one pulled a satellite phone from the pocket of his fluorescent yellow jacket. He dialed the number of the general command of the port authorities in Rome. When they picked up, he reported the situation in a rush of broken English and Italian.

'We're about to be shipwrecked. Our boat is sixty-five miles south of Lampedusa. Help us. Be quick. We're about to die. There are more than seven hundred of us. Many women and children. Some already dead.'

Despite a reception that kept breaking up, the official got the basic information, which he transmitted to his superior. Often overloaded lately, the port authorities only handled the most urgent cases and sometimes, for lack of a budget and adequate means, wouldn't intervene at all. The Mediterranean had turned into a veritable highway, one of the deadliest for migrants being transported by amateur sailors. Even with the best will in the world, they couldn't rescue them all. At other times, they would simply not react to avoid having to deal with all the trouble that would result. Voices had been raised, especially those of the Lega Nord and the Five Star Movement parties in Italy, which accused them, if not of conniving with the traffickers, at least of encouraging the country to be invaded by hordes of migrants from outside the EU and Muslims. The opinions of these political parties were relayed by an alarmist television, ready to highlight and exaggerate the slightest lapse on the part of any refugee. From the other side, NGOs of every persuasion, which offered a modicum of work to the countless unemployed, human rights organizations, charities and religious groups condemned their inertia in the face of the greatest humanitarian catastrophe of the early twenty-first century.

Caught in the crossfire between the different groups, the port authorities often had nothing on their side but their conscience as men and women. The many summit meetings between the various leaders of the European Union had given rise to declarations of intent. As always. In the end, between the Eastern European countries, the majority of which had tipped over to the extreme right, and the eternal sermonizers like the Vatican and France, no one lifted a finger. Other than a few tens of millions of Euros paid to create agencies that served no purpose, like Frontex, Mare Nostrum, or Triton, to buy themselves a good conscience at a small fee. From time to time, Pope Francis would preach from his palace balcony to deaf ears, would declare *urbi et orbi* that 'no human being is garbage'. That the problem wouldn't be resolved by 'raising barriers' and 'fomenting fear of others.' After Spain and Greece, Italy found itself, very much in spite of itself, at the forefront of the struggle to drive back or welcome the migrants, who continued to die en masse. As they had on 3 October 2013, eight months earlier, when three-hundred-sixty-six of them found their death at Lampedusa's doors, traumatizing the island's entire population, as the commander recalled.

It didn't take him long to deal with this umpteenth call of distress. The man had provided him with quite precise and alarming details to make them spring into action. As luck would have it, that day there was a young non-commissioned officer present who spoke English fairly well. The commander summoned her, had her listen to the message he'd received and asked her to send another one with as many details as possible to the ships cruising in the area. Three minutes later the radio spat out the call from the general command.

THE RESCUE

ON FRIDAY, 18 JULY 2014, at twelve-forty-five in the afternoon, Peter Sams, the captain of the Danish oil tanker Torm Lotte, picked up an SOS sent by the Italian port authorities. A trawler with almost seven-hundred-and-fifty migrants on board–among whom were more than a hundred children— was in grave distress in the waters between Malta and Libya. Dozens of dead had already been reported among the passengers. Once the communication was completed, Captain Sams turned the tanker away from its original destination—the port of La Skhira in Tunisia—and headed for the indicated position. Without taking too many risks, he drove the engines a little harder. He had a full cargo of oil on board and there was no way he was going to have his engines explode and find himself stuck at high sea, possibly with a fire on his hands. It would be a godsend for the vegan environmentalists who wouldn't fail to accuse him of polluting the entire planet. Of compromising the future of their kids and their kids' kids. At the same time, he needed to think about saving those wretched Africans, so desperate that they'd taken to the sea without evaluating its dangers.

It would take Captain Sams four hours and fifteen minutes before he had visual contact with the ship in distress. He then started to move in closer toward it to decide how to approach the situation. But the captain of the trawler wasn't going to make his task any easier, to say the least. Either he wasn't a professional or he was doing everything he could to avoid being helped. Why had he sent out the SOS call then? The closer Torm Lotte came the more the man engaged in maneuvers that defied all navigational logic. Admittedly, the sea was rough and when the Mediterranean was up to its usual tricks one had to be cautious. The boat, truly an old tub, was collapsing under its passengers. Poor folks, who knew how many days they'd been wandering at sea. At the sight of the tanker, the bravest among the passengers had straddled the guardrail and were grasping the edge, either to be among the first to be rescued or to celebrate the arrival of their saviors. It was obvious that the captain himself was a danger to his own vessel. More than once the Torm Lotte and her crew were forced to make a U-turn to avoid colliding with the trawler.

Captain Sams had to use a megaphone—the ship in distress wasn't equipped with any communications devices—to explain what he was preparing to do. That was no easy task either. Not only did the captain and his assistants have a rather poor command of English, they also struggled to understand the Dane's technical jargon. The panic-stricken passengers were yelling in every language of the globe. Children were weeping uncontrollably, without a doubt frightened by the screaming of the adults. Everything combined to complicate the exchange between the two ships. Around seven-thirty in the evening the Torm Lotte managed to maintain a secure distance, whereupon the commander gave his crew the order to launch a first lifeboat. And then something happened that the Dane would never have imagined even in his worst nightmares. Panic broke out. Two young men had the disastrous idea to jump in the water to try to reach the dinghy already coming toward them. Dozens of other migrants followed in their wake. As if only a limited number of passengers would be rescued, on a 'first come, first served' basis. Later, when the Italian authorities and the journalists approached him, Captain Sams would say that the majority of them didn't know how to swim. They must have thought they could improvise it without having learned how. If they had, it would have saved so many lives.

On his end, the trawler's captain had no control whatsoever over his people. Nor over his crew if he had one. The passengers who'd remained on board had all, or almost all, moved over to the side facing the tanker, so that the boat began to tilt dangerously. This unleashed a new uproar of screams and lamentations, causing other terrified unfortunates to throw themselves into the water, complicating the task of the Torm Lotte rescuers even more. At the time, the latter tried to identify those who were struggling the most to toss them life buoys, for which even those who could swim felt no reluctance to compete. It was hard for the rescuers to deal with these conflicts from the lifeboats. To make those who'd seized them—sometime two or three of them—understand that the buoys weren't meant for them. Instead they rushed to get them on board the tanker so they could return to the others as quickly as possible, hoping the waves hadn't swallowed them up by then.

On the trawler, Semhar, Shoshana, Dima and her family moved behind the cabin in the middle, on the opposite side from the oil tanker. It was Semhar's idea. In the heat of the action, she'd rediscovered the instincts she'd acquired during her military training. She conducted herself like a true commando leader, spoke in a voice so purposeful that the others followed her without posing any questions. Dima and Hakim were each holding one of their daughters by the hand. Everyone in the little group hung on to the rough edges and the open door of the cabin, which the occupants had judged it wise to abandon. Semhar's reasoning was lucid: if ever the trawler were to capsize, they would be on the upper side and, in the time it would take the vessel to sink completely, the tanker's crew would save them. That's what she explained to the others clustered around her, all too happy in their distress to have found a shoulder to lean on. Even if it belonged to a mere slip of a woman no taller than Hana, Dima's eldest.

While their colleagues in the lifeboats were fighting to save as many lives as possible, the sailors of the Torm Lotte had lowered an accommodation ladder for the shipwrecked already in the water, swimming but running out of steam.

This provoked another ruthless stampede. The survivors tore at each other to be the first to reach the ladder. Even though, when one of them caught it he wouldn't necessarily reach safety. He might be pulled off by someone more desperate than he. Piranhas devouring each other just to catch the pieces of meat thrown at them from a canoe.

The sea was rumbling like an immense geyser. Swallowing bodies whose futile life vests it rejected, like a snake regurgitating the shell of the egg it had just gobbled up. The wind had started to blow again, whipping up the surface of the Mediterranean, closing and widening the gap between the two ships in a rhythmic dance. With each separating movement the passengers of the trawler would shout in desperation, seeing their dreams go up in smoke. 'Like Moses seeing the Promised Land without being able to enter it', Shoshana thought, clinging to her piece of the cabin.

As the rescue operation continued, three patrol boats, two from the island of Lampedusa and one from Valetta, the capital of Malta, had joined the rescue. Far from reassuring them, the presence of the launches upset the shipwrecked even more. They all wanted to leave the trawler as fast as possible, as if the boat on which they'd been traveling until now had suddenly been destroyed by an all-consuming fire and the flames were licking at their heels. More than once, the ship was about to capsize before it miraculously righted itself once again. However, this didn't stop a large number of survivors from throwing themselves into the water, ignoring the calls for calm from a member of the Italian coastguard, who was also using a megaphone:

'*Calmatevi! Keep quiet. We're here to save you.*'

'*Cazzo! Non possono rimanere tranquilli, 'sti stronzi?*' one *carabiniere* muttered to a colleague. 'Fuck! Can't they stay calm, these assholes?'

All of a sudden, a huge gust of wind from port side shoved the trawler up against the oil tanker, whose captain, as if driving a car, immediately changed tack to avoid an accident. The jolt threw the passengers on deck off balance, causing more than one to let go. Little Shayma, Dima's younger one, was propelled into the water. Her father who was holding her hand, was unable to prevent it. As a paralyzed Hakim stood wondering what to do, Semhar dove into the choppy waves without a second thought. There she was, fighting the waves, trying to grab the little girl who'd seen her and was holding out her arm. Shayma struggled as best she could but wasn't able to stay above the surface. Like her mother, she didn't know how to swim. The Mediterranean swallowed her, spat her back out, swallowed her again. Rushing toward her, Semhar kept her eyes riveted on her only reference point, the orange jacket. Luckily, it was summer and still light, despite the late hour. But she had to move fast since the visibility was dwindling. Every time the sea brought her back up, Semhar could see the terror in the little girl's eyes, her frail limbs struggling as she fought not to go under and drown.

Up on deck, Dima's guts were in knots. One arm gripping the cabin door and the other held tightly around her older child's chest. Helpless. Hakim, too, was watching the scene, incapacitated. His heart hammering with guilt. His head in one hand, the other clutching the cabin. He didn't have the strength to react. Or to scream. In any case, who would hear him above the mayhem? Praying out loud, he placed his faith in the Prophet and Allah the Merciful. Dima soon followed his example. Husband and wife now praying as one.

Next to them, a distraught Shoshana was scanning each falling wave. Her blood had run cold. She was incapable of moving even a finger. When she finally became aware of a tingling in her extremities, she held out her hand to Dima and grabbed the hand she kept fixed to the cabin door. Without knowing the bliss of motherhood, Shoshana was discovering its sorrow. Dima didn't resist or perhaps didn't notice. Shoshana feared as much for the little one as for her friend. For the millionth time she recited the traveler's prayer. Beseeched, in her deepest self, the One who shall not be named to spare the two lives that still had their whole future before them. Especially Semhar, whose dreams she knew. Her woman's goodness and courage. The proof, Hashem, is that she didn't hesitate to confront the Mediterranean fury to try to save a life. As You have taught us. Nevertheless, if for some reason that wasn't in her power as a mere mortal to judge, He decided to keep only one, let it be the little girl, Shoshana heard herself say. Shayma was much too innocent to die. And what would her older sister do later, facing the world that would open before her?

All the prayers sent up to heaven must have been heard. In a last effort, Semhar managed to snatch the jacket, then the little girl's arm, which she secured under one armpit before swimming to the nearest patrol boat. An Italian policeman threw them a buoy that with her free hand Semhar caught. Drained from her battle with the Mediterranean, she let herself be pulled the few meters they still had to go. Once they were hoisted aboard, Semhar's legs were shaking. Relief and fear came simultaneously. Followed by the satisfying feeling of having taken revenge on destiny. Having brought back to life her little five-year old cousin whom the Red Sea had carried off from under her watchful gaze one autumn afternoon. She made the sign of the cross and thanked the members of the coastguard with the few Italian words she knew: 'Grazie. Grazie di cuore. Dio vi benedica.' The carabinieri were touched to hear the Eritrean woman thank them in their own language. Up on the trawler's deck, Dima embraced her husband, her older daughter, and Shoshana. That's when her nerves surrendered, and she burst into tears. Tears that combined with those of Hakim and Hana, who cried because she saw her parents cry. As she distanced herself from the family embrace, Shoshana, on the other hand, let out a sigh of relief. In the aftermath her body began to relax. And as she gave thanks to Hashem, she felt electric jolts in her arm: her wound was reminding her of its existence.

The Mediterranean was now wrapped in complete darkness, with an occasional light projected from the patrol boats searching for survivors who might have escaped from the rescuers' vigilance and self-sacrifice. It was impossible to continue the search under these conditions, all the more because the sea hadn't completely calmed down. Captain Sams ordered the crew to shut off the engines. The launches did the same. The Danish commander still hoped to hear some calls for help in the darkness. Due to his intuition and determination, another handful of lives was saved from the immense cemetery that the Mediterranean had become over the past fifteen years or so. Other travelers weren't so lucky. A two-year old toddler fell into the water, his mother jumping after him in a vain attempt to save him, even though she herself couldn't swim either. After trying for several minutes, the divers brought the mother back up with the lifeless body of little Momo, and then about twenty more bodies that were stuck beneath the trawler. In agreement with the commanders of the other vessels, the Danish captain finally decided to stop the search.

Until then, the transfer from one ship to another had been done in one direction, the passengers from the boat in distress to the tanker, picked up by the crew of the Torm Lotte or of one of the three patrol boats. When the sailors set foot on board the trawler, looking for more potential survivors perhaps injured in the general chaos or too weak to move on their own, they discovered a far more sinister reality. Corpses lay strewn across the hold. At first sight, some were obvious victims of a brawl, their bodies bearing the traces of the blows their killers had delivered. Others had been asphyxiated by the exhaust and lack of air. So grisly was the scene that some of these burly men, having crossed many seas and seen plenty of atrocities in their life, couldn't keep from retching. The Maltese coastguard took charge of the corpses. The authorities in their country refused to receive any refugees, officially because of a lack of space in their detention centers, but they did allow dead bodies to be brought ashore for burial. Except for little Momo who with his mother would make the journey to Italy on the Danish tanker.

All the trawler's survivors were now on board the Torm Lotte. Altogether, the crew of the oil tanker had rescued five-hundred-sixty-nine migrants from sub-Saharan Africa, the Maghreb, the Middle East, and the Arabian Peninsula. In spite of their extreme state of exhaustion, the survivors improvised a song of gratitude both to their rescuers and their deities. The song rang through the Mediterranean night, reducing winds and waves to silence. Even the sea went quiet, as if pacified by the melody. Others didn't have any strength left, except to weep. With exhaustion, with fear. With joy as well, no doubt. Their dreams were within their grasp.

Shoshana, Dima, Hakim, and Hana were reunited with Semhar and little Shayma, whom the Italian coastguard had delivered to the tanker's crew. Dima couldn't stop thanking Semhar—may Allah bless you and keep you from all evil!—while Hakim and Hana took Shayma into their arms. The oil tanker headed for the south of Italy, escorted by the two vessels from Lampedusa. The Maltese ship, on the other hand, went to Valetta, with dozens of body bags on board. The trawler was to stay in place. The hold was filling with water furiously gushing in. The caulking had given way long before the rescuers arrived, the hull had opened up in several places. In a matter of hours, it would end up on the bottom of the Mediterranean. Like hundreds of others that didn't reach their destination. On the Torm Lotte, Semhar and Shoshana found a spot away from the other survivors. As she hugged her tightly, Shoshana gently scolded her friend. 'Don't do anything like this to me again. Or else, even if you die, I'll kill you all over again. I don't want to lose another friend, you hear me?' Later, when all these people were back on dry land, during the interrogations and the cross-checking of information, it turned out that one-hundred-and-eighty-one hopeful travelers were missing.

TERRA FIRMA

SPRAWLED ON Paradiso Beach, vacationers watch in disbelief as the immense oil tanker, Torm Lotte, arrives in the Bay of Messina. As large as a cruise ship, if not larger, the witnesses would later exaggerate when they told their friends. For security reasons, the port authority asked the Danish tanker with its strange group of passengers to cast anchor a few miles off the coast. Pilot and tugboats, better able to enter the narrow canal that led to the port, would take over to transfer them to land. At the sight of the tanker, summer tourists open their cell phones, from which they cannot be separated, even when they go in the water. Some want to immortalize the event; others are looking for information about the disembarkation of migrants in their town.

As if attracted by a gigantic magnetic force, migrants ordinarily end up on Lampedusa, when they're not taken by the navy, NGO ships, or fishermen who saved them from a disaster. Sometimes, too, they dock in Palermo after being boarded and inspected at high sea by the military vessels of Frontex. Rarely do they arrive directly in Messina. Hence the incredulity of the vacationing yachtsmen when they watch them disembark that day in ragged groups, mostly in flip-flops and covered in the traditional, gold-colored insulated blankets, faces sallow and gloomy. As if setting foot on Italian soil wasn't quite what they were hoping for. Smiling, skipping around all over the place, only the children show a semblance of enthusiasm despite their exhaustion.

Before the Danish tanker even presents itself in the harbor, social networks, NGO's, support and solidarity associations, political parties, each according to its sympathy and its own interests, assault the Web and, with the help of indulgent media or those desperate for a scoop, relay news items, one more unreliable than the next. Truth be told, few know what really happened between the rescue of the migrants and the arrival of Torm Lotte in the waters of Paradise Beach.

For the survivors who were finally aboard the tanker, the crossing to Messina wasn't a pleasure trip, however. Very quickly, the tone on board had grown harsher. Pushed to the limit, three clans were accusing each other of instigating the carnage found in the hold. It took the intervention of no less than twenty crew members to prevent them from coming to blows and causing a bloodbath. Obviously there were griev-ances among the refugees that the sailors of the Torm Lotte couldn't unravel. Impossible to sort out true from false in that

Babel of shouts and verbiage. 'It's not our job,' Captain Sams cut in. 'The Italian authorities will deal with it once they're on land.' Until then he wanted peace on his ship. So, everybody quiet. He ordered his second in command to dispatch the rival groups to separate zones under the vigilant eye of a dozen or so sailors, ready to play at being blue berets, in case of trouble. The survivors understood, even without an interpreter, that it would be in their interest to hold their tongue. The commander's stern tone was sufficient. But for the entire journey the situation remained tense.

Upon arrival, the accusations started up again, unabated. Some—led by Shoshana, Semhar, and the Senegalese wrestler, his shoulder in a scarf, demanded immediate justice for the victims of the massacre. The killers had cold-bloodedly stabbed men, women, and children before throwing their bodies into the water. Some among them still alive. Sheer butchery. As if by coincidence, the victims were black and their executioners Arab, added Shoshana, who had recovered the fastest. Others refused to see it as racism. For them it was a simple affair: at the height of the storm a fight had broken out between partisans of returning to Sabratha, on the one hand, and on the other, those who wanted to continue the trip at all costs. They'd invested all their savings and had no intention of going back. Each group had defended itself to the last breath, and those who advocated going back had lost. That was all, they claimed during the early interrogations, made possible thanks to some volunteer interpreters. More to calm people down than to set a real judicial process in motion. 'This is not the place,' the police officer stated.

According to those on the side of the old man and his team, seeing racism everywhere risked rendering the word meaningless. It could even turn out to be counterproductive with regard to the real battle for equality among human beings. By crying wolf, you know… 'The proof that it wasn't racist,' one of them said, 'is that one of my neighbors, a Syrian woman, vanished.' 'And an Iraqi traveling companion of mine,' said another.

A third group reported to the *carabinieri* that the *khalech* had been fighting among themselves. 'Among *negri* as you Italians say'. The Arabs had nothing to do with it. Those people wanted to demonize them in the eyes of the Europeans, already prepared to see every Muslim as a follower of Daesh. But that's not what Islam is. It's a religion of harmony and love. That's why its followers greet each other saying 'May peace be upon you!' Hakim was one of the most ardent supporters of this thesis. 'Some *znuje*,' he argued, 'had never seen the sea. They panicked. Understandable. They were afraid. But so were we. The wind never stopped blowing. Then there was that crack in the hull, adding to the general mayhem. Anyway, it would have been impossible to find room for everyone on deck. We were already crammed together like sardines. Later they went nuts and killed each other. That's the whole story.'

Dima couldn't believe she was hearing her husband spout such untruths. And what was worse, in front of the girls, whose attention she tried to divert, and of the *zenjiyeh* who could have lost her life while trying to save Shayma's. The lie wasn't part of the values she wanted to instill in them. Yet, it

didn't stop her from being one of the first at the wharf leading the revolt with a group of Syrian women who, stubborn
as mules, refused to get on the same bus as the Africans to
be transferred to the reception center. They'd already traveled together under conditions you wouldn't transport pigs
in. Nothing forced them to prolong their cohabitation any
longer on dry land. They held firm to their position despite
the conciliatory words of the interpreter, a young Italian
woman who'd lived in Iraq and had been assigned to them.
'She's wasting her time, that little one,' a buxom middle-aged
woman from Normandy said. She was married—her second
marriage—to a Syrian-Sicilian who'd been settled in Messina
for fifteen years and was an activist for the rapprochement
between peoples. 'Syrian women are as hardheaded as
Bretons.' Voices rose up among the migrant support groups
to deplore their arrogance.

'*Ma chi si credono di essere, 'ste donne?*' 'Really, who do
they think they are, these women?'

At the end of their rope, the port authority agents gave in
to their request and put a special bus at their disposal for the
sole purpose of accelerating the disembarkation process. This
could go on forever and they had to finish up before nightfall. Other than this miscalculation, the rest of the process
continued without any notable incident. The presence of the
eighty children among the survivors touched the hearts of
many inhabitants of Messina and beyond. Some were accompanied by their parents. Others had lost them along the way,
before or after boarding the trawler of death, nobody knew.
Still others had traveled without anyone identified as family.

The most sorrowful moment came when two sailors arrived with the coffin of little Momo, the boy who had drowned after falling in the water. His inconsolable mother followed closely, supported by a female *carabiniere* and a Red Cross volunteer. Always on the look-out for scenes that would appeal to the sentimental, the image made cameramen and journalists happy. It was played over and over again for three days running on Italian television, contributing to family arguments at the dinner table.

'What responsible parents,' some preached, 'would send their children off on such a dangerous adventure?'

'You wonder where the father went,' one old man said.

'They're desperate,' others replied. 'Don't you understand? We, too, were scattered around the world for decades, in search of a better life. Why would we have more rights than they?'

'It's because of people like you and your fine sentiments that they continue to invade us. I hope you all have a rock-solid life insurance. When they've plundered your house and raped your daughters, you might have a change of heart.'

'You'll have to get used to it, it's not going to stop anytime soon,' the most cynical ones insisted.

As soon as the arrival of the refugees was announced, the prefect of Messina had summoned to his offices the officials of City Hall, Port Authority, the Navy, the Emergency Services, the Association of Security and Prevention, and the Red Cross. It was the objective of this summit meeting to identify a suitable structure to accommodate the migrants.

'We have very little time,' the prefect stated right off the bat. His pragmatic language signified that political divergencies and the tendency of some to take advantage of any meeting to tackle issues not on the agenda, were to be set aside. The assembled participants understood the urgency of the situation although, as a matter of principle, not without grumbling. Very quickly it was decided that the new arrivals would be put up on the premises of the Pascoli-Crispi elementary school, adjacent to police headquarters. Right after that, around three o'clock, volunteers arrived at the school to help turn it into a welcoming center. They spent the afternoon going up and down the three floors, moving mattresses, sleeping cots, blankets, bottled water, food, toiletries, and more. All of it with easy-going banter and an unwavering faith in humanity.

'Not too long from now they'll be good little Italians,' an older gentleman declared.

'And they'll finance our pension,' joked a woman in her sixties.

While it was only July, the prefect emphasized the temporary nature of the undertaking. They would have to find an alternate solution as soon as possible before the opening of school in September. It was out of the question for the situation to become permanent, as happened so often in Italy. This didn't prevent a coalition of opponents from alerting the population the next day to the sanitary hazards for its children when they returned to school, alleging that the school risked being turned into a petri dish for infectious diseases. They were supported by *Generazione identitaria* and the Lega Nord, which whipped up a demonstration to denounce 'Italy's being taken over by non-EU migrants with the complicity of their local collaborators.'

For a week, the Institute Pascoli-Crispi sheltered the five hundred and sixty-six refugees. Shoshana and Semhar never stopped rejoicing. 'Dry land, at last,' Shoshana said, whose loose gait seemed to carry within it the memory of the storm. She was slowly but surely regaining a sensuality that lit sparks in the eyes of a number of male volunteers. As soon as she had a chance, she locked herself in the shower for a long time, so that other refugees had to raise their voice until she agreed to get out and leave some for the rest of them, too. But Shoshana was all too eager to get rid of the misery and hardship clinging to her skin, to recover from all the negative emotions accumulated since she'd left her native village, already nine months ago.

In English, Paolo, an activist from the association 'Mare nostrum. Terra nostra', explained to the two of them that they weren't required to leave their fingerprints when they registered their case. The Dublin III Regulation obliged migrants to file their asylum application in the first country they landed in when entering Europe. Thus, if their request were rejected by the Italian authorities, no other Schengen State would agree to receive them. 'Everyone passes the buck. Other than the Northern European countries and Germany. With all the others it's just words. Empty words,' the young man complained., In view of the ill wind blowing across the peninsula, a refusal from Italy was likely. Then they would have the choice of going back home, this time by plane, and enter clandestinely. And that left the door open to all kinds of exploitation. Especially for women. The two of them had to try everything they could to slow down the administrative process and give the aid associations time to put together an alternative strategy.

After two days at the reception center, the two still didn't know where to go. They considered the fact they'd arrived safe and sound to be a blessing from heaven. Tens of thousands of their peers didn't have that luck, had met with death on the Mediterranean and on other paths toward survival. They were grateful, one thanking God, the other thanking the One who shall not be named. Thereafter, Italy or another European country. It wasn't that they didn't care, but all things considered, they remained convinced that fate was finally smiling on them. That they would find a place where they wouldn't be seen as pariahs. Where they could make a new life. 'Have fun in a club to goy music,' Shoshana said, swaying her hips as her friend laughed.

Dima was without a doubt the luckiest of the three. Her situation in Syria and the two children she had with her almost assured her of getting war refugee status. Especially since Europe, with the complicity of the United States, would already have taken out Bashar al-Assad, whom it held partly responsible for the flood of migrants landing on its shores, if Putin hadn't been protecting him. The family could even settle in Italy if she so desired. But Dima was dreaming of England for her daughters or, in the worst case, of a northern

European country, despite the cold, which they said was brutal. There they would have a better future. It seemed that those societies were more tolerant of Muslims. In any event, it was already great that Allah had allowed them to arrive at their destination—blessed be his Holy Name; that they could receive refugee status, as their referent had promised her. During the interview, the man also assured her that Caritas would facilitate settling families like hers in hotels that were refurbished into welcome centers. That's where she would think things over, once they had regained a little privacy.

Semhar had a very good chance of obtaining political refugee status as well. The international community was aware of the situation in her country, of the unenviable fate of tens of thousands of young Eritreans under the military dictatorship of Isaias Afwerki. Ideally, Paolo said, she would have someone elsewhere in Europe who could answer for her. The Italian administration looked favorably upon that, as a sign that the asylum applicant wasn't planning to stay in the country. Semhar quickly counted her potential sources of support. Amanuel would be prepared to vouch for her: 'That goes without saying, cousin.' She also remembered that Dawit, her friend Meaza's fiancé, had a friend who'd told her she could call him once she arrived and that he would help her as much as he'd be able to. Meaza had insisted she memorize Solomon's—the man in question—telephone number. You never know. And so she had. In her eagerness to marry her off, Meaza had lauded his qualities: 'A fine guy. And he's single too.'

For Shoshana, on the other hand, it was more complicated.

Unless she could provide proof of political persecutions in her country, which she couldn't. Italy considered Nigerians primarily as economic refugees. People fleeing poverty who ended up, women especially, falling prey to pimps and the Italo-Nigerian mafia. Therefore they were not very likely to have their asylum application accepted. Hadn't she been threatened by Boko Haram, Paolo questioned Shoshana, that small group of radical Islamists who claimed to represent Al Qaeda? Hadn't she been raped and become pregnant? That could play in her favor. Otherwise all she could do was leave it up to the magnanimity of the officials vis-à-vis women, who were fewer in number among the Mediterranean risk-takers. They were aware of the hell that the majority of them had endured on their path of exile. Just for that alone they deserved to stay, as the most sensitive souls among them justified it to themselves.

As he was giving her this information, Shoshana could only think about one thing: calling her parents to let them know she'd finally arrived. She was still hesitating, even while holding a Nokia phone and a prepaid SIM card in her hand. Volunteers had handed out some of them to those refugees without a phone. Others were offered an old Samsung. For two days she kept turning the matter over in her head. How to tell them that her little brother had been left behind? That she had no news from him since Sabratha. Right now, he must be doing slave labor for his jailers, suffering the worst physical abuse. To dispel these dark thoughts, she told herself that Rachel and her expert eye would have appreciated the handsome Italian.

'Cute little ass,' her friend would have commented. 'I'd really like to get my hands on him.'

From time to time the three women—Nigerian, Eritrean, and Syrian—would see each other in the school courtyard without the courage to speak. As if they'd never met before. Or as if, remaining aloof, each of them was waiting for the other to take the first step, say the first hello. 'How are things since we came ashore? Do you know where you'll be going yet when you leave here?' But nothing happened. Until the day, half a week later, when Hana recognized the woman who'd saved her little sister from the raging Mediterranean. The little girl ran over to Semhar and threw herself into her arms. As she would have done with a family member. It wasn't hard for her since they were almost the same height. When Dima, too, approached, she looked like she was scolding her older child:

'Stop annoying the lady.' 'She's not bothering me at all. On the contrary,' Semhar said. Then the three women exchanged a few words and over the next few days made it their habit to greet each other when their paths crossed by chance in the playground.

The Sunday after the Torm Lotte arrived in the Bay of Messina, on the evidence of several witnesses, the Italian police succeeded in getting their hands on the old man with the crewcut, on the one with the beard, and on Mickey Mouse, all of whom had slipped in among the hundreds of survivors. Identified as the perpetrators of the carnage committed on the trawler, they were taken into custody where they awaited justice. All three were of Tunisian nationality, as Dima had inferred from their accent. Five more accomplices: two Moroccans, one Palestinian, one Syrian, and one Saudi were arrested the next day. Thanks to their Italian network they'd managed to leave the Institute Pascoli-Crispi without being photographed or registered among the asylum seekers. They were caught by the *carabinieri* the very moment they were about to board a bus for Milan. No one knew what happened to the captain, whose face had never been seen by any passenger. The man standing next to him during the crossing was never found. Vanished into thin air.

On Friday, July 25th, a week after the refugees getting off the Danish tanker were taken care of, the Messina Prefecture published the following press release:

> *In accordance with the specific agreements with the Department of Civil Liberties and of Immigration of the Ministry of the Interior, places available for the transfer of the refugees who disembarked in the port of Messina on this past July 20th, and were temporarily housed in the school made available by the municipality, have been identified by the welcome center of SPRAR (The Protection System for Asylum Seekers and Refugees).*
>
> *After direct contact with the SPRAR central service, the refugee transfers [...] were arranged and this evening the school, concerning which serious criticism was raised from the point of view of hygiene and good health, has been completely evacuated.*

According to the most recent news, Dima and her family obtained war refugee status as anticipated and were part of the quota authorized to settle in England, as she'd wished. Semhar also secured the precious open Sesame and left to join her cousin Amanuel in Sweden. Before she went, she had a long heart-to-heart talk with Shoshana. Since she was spending more and more time on the phone with Solomon, who apparently couldn't let a day pass by without hearing her voice, it was quite probable... 'Well, you know what I mean.' 'I don't know what you mean,' Shoshana teased. She'd even spoken about it to her parents via Amanuel's family; they'd given her their blessing. 'God will provide,' her mother had commented. In Meaza's absence, she would like Shoshana to be her bridesmaid: 'Please, don't say no.'

As both of them knew, all of it depended on the administrative decision concerning Shoshana's status. They hadn't given her a straight-out no that she might appeal. The bureaucratic vagueness in all its splendor would drag her from one center to another for some time to come. From one town to another. She could have used it as an opportunity to disappear but Paolo, the Italian interpreter, advised her against it. He'd kept in touch and put her in contact with a group of women who were very active in the reception of migrants and promised to do everything to get her out of SPRAR. The association's attorney made it her personal business, she had good arguments and high hopes. 'You'll see, we'll be together again,' Semhar told her before disappearing into her arms for the hundredth embrace. 'It's Toughy Semhar who tells you so.'

REFERENCES

Some bibliographic references pertaining to the tragedy of the trawler and the rescue of its passengers by the Danish oil tanker Torm Lotte that are mentioned in the novel.

Marco Aime, *L'isola del non arrivo : Voci da Lampedusa,* Bollati Borin- ghieri, 2018

Jean-Paul Mari, *Les Bateaux ivres. L'Odyssée des migrants en Méditerranée,* Lattès, 2015

Laura Bellomi, « In preghiera per il bimbo siriano. Musulmani e cristiani uniti per il piccolo Ahmed », https://www.credere.it/n-32-2014/ahmed-in-preghiera-per-il-bimbo-siriano.html

Frédéric Bobin, « Libye : Sabratha, la capitale des passeurs de migrants », https ://www.cercledesvoisins.org/blog/index.php/rubriques/actualite/776-libye-sabratha-la-capitale-des-passeurs-de-migrants-2-3

Frédéric Bobin et Jérôme Cautheret, « Entre la Libye et l'Italie, un accord en eaux troubles contre les migrants », https ://www.letemps.ch/monde/entre-libye-litalie-un-accord-eaux-troubles-contre-migrants

Ilaria Calabrò, « Messina, gli agghiaccianti racconti degli immigrati : 5 arresti, avrebbero ucciso decine di africani », "http://www.stretto- web.com/ 2014/07/messina-gli-agghiaccianti-racconti-degli-immigrati-5-arresti-avrebbero-ucciso-decine-africani-nomi-foto/163142/

« Shipping companies warn of migrant rescue risks », https://www.ft. com/content/d8d0f67a-9bfe-11e4-b6cc-00144feabdc0

Stefano Liberti, « Le grand business des centres d'accueil en Italie », https://asile.ch/chronique/chronique-italie-stefano-liberti-le-grand-business-des-centres-daccueil-en-italie/

Luca Misculin, « I dati su i migranti in Italia, una volta per tutte », https://www.ilpost.it/2018/06/12/dati-italia-immigrazione/

Alessandro Puglia, Francesco Viviano, «I naufraghi superstiti : "Barcone strapieno, ne sono annegati180"»,https://www.repubblica.it/cronaca/2014/07/22/news/i_naufraghi_superstiti_barcone_strapieno_ne_sono_ annegati_180-92107078/

Alessandra Serio, « Sbarco Torn Lotte, gli scafisti sconteranno 25 anni di carcere », https ://www.tempostretto.it/news/migranti-sbarco-torn-lotte-scafisti-sconteranno-25-anni-carcere.html

« Product tanker Torm Lotte helps to save up to 300 lives », https://mari- timecyprus.com/ 2014 / 07 /28/product-tanker-torm-lotte-helps-to-save- up-to-300-lives/

« Il viaggio della morte "Uccisi a coltellate e gettati in mare" », http://ricerca.gelocal.it/iltirreno/archivio/iltirreno/ 2014/ 07/ 23/LM_ 06_A.html

« "Ho visto sessanta miei compagni pugnalati e dati in pasto ai pesci". I racconti dei sopravvissuti del barcone soccorso il 19 luglio dalla petroliera Torm Lotte », https ://

www.iltempo.it/politica/2014/07/23/gallery/ho-visto-sessanta-miei-compagni-pugnalati-e-dati-in-pasto-ai-pesci-948732/

« Si erano nascosti tra i migranti della petroliera Torm Lotte. Presi tre sospetti scafisti », http://www.messinaora.it/notizia/2014/07/21/si-erano-nascosti-tra-i-migranti-della-petroliera-torm-lotte-presi-tre-sos-petti-sca-fisti/37293

St.-John Perse. Denis Devlin, translator, Exile and Other Poems, Published by Pantheon Books, New York, NY, 1962

Derek Walcott. "The Sea Is History" from *Selected Poems* by Derek Walcott. Copyright © 2007 by Derek Walcott. Reprinted by permission of Farrar, Straus and Giroux, LLC.

ACKNOWLEDGMENTS

For the writing of this novel the author was the beneficiary of the *Prix Résidence d'auteur* awarded by the Fondation des Treilles,* of a writing residence from the multimedia library Les Silos (city of Chaumont), and of the Program "Hors Les Murs Stendhal" of the Institut Français for a month's stay on Lampedusa.

For the writing of this book, the author also received a residence at the Villa Départementale Marguerite Yourcenar and a grant from the Département du Nord.

For their availability and their generosity, the author would like to thank Anne Bourjade, former Director General of the Fondation des Treilles; Sandrine Bresolin, Director of the multimedia library Les Silos; Laurence Diebold, Valérie Dubec-Monoyez, Anne du Parquet; the Syrian poet and film director Hala Mohammad; and the Italian novelist and essayist Marco Aime.

★

---

*   Created by Anne Gruner Schlumberger, The Fondation des Treilles has as its goal the nurturing of the dialogue between sciences and art in order to stimulate the advancement of creativity and research. It welcomes and accommodates researchers and creative artists at its estate of Treilles (Var) www.les-treilles.com.

As the translator of this book, I would like to express my sincere gratitude to Timothy Schaffner for his unceasing encouragement and true devotion to the art of literary translation. In addition, my great thanks to David Vita, my husband, who with his fine-tuned ear and sensitive insights as my first reader never fails to help me improve my work.

—MdJ

AVAILABLE AND COMING SOON
FROM PUSHKIN PRESS

Pushkin Press was founded in 1997, and publishes novels, essays, memoirs, children's books—everything from timeless classics to the urgent and contemporary.

Our books represent exciting, high-quality writing from around the world: we publish some of the twentieth century's most widely acclaimed, brilliant authors such as Stefan Zweig, Yasushi Inoue, Teffi, Antal Szerb, Gerard Reve and Elsa Morante, as well as compelling and award-winning contemporary writers, including Dorthe Nors, Edith Pearlman, Perumal Murugan, Ayelet Gundar-Goshen and Chigozie Obioma.

Pushkin Press publishes the world's best stories, to be read and read again. To discover more, visit www.pushkinpress.com.

TENDER IS THE FLESH
AGUSTINA BAZTERRICA

WHEN WE CEASE TO UNDERSTAND THE WORLD
BENJAMÍN LABATUT

LIAR
AYELET GUNDAR-GOSHEN

MISS ICELAND
AUDUR AVA ÓLAFSDÓTTIR

WILD SWIMS
DORTHE NORS

MS ICE SANDWICH
MIEKO KAWAKAMI